IN HIS BONES

MYRANDA RAE

Publisher: MyrandaRae.com

Publication date: July 2025

Author: Myranda Rae

Email: connect@myrandarae.com

Website: myrandarae.com

Cover by: Efellana

Character Art: Messyartani

Please direct all inquiries to the author.

A WORD OF WARNING...

Noah is a bad guy; he does bad guy shit.

For a list of triggers, visit my website myrandarae.com

ONE

CLOSING MY EYES, I push down the wave of dizzying nausea making my head spin. His jerky, brake-heavy driving isn't helping.

I should have eaten something earlier.

"Our reservation isn't for another forty-five minutes, but I thought we could sit at the bar and grab drinks."

"Great!" I try to sound enthusiastic, forcing my lips into a smile. I don't want to argue tonight. Not over something small. He really lacks the ability to read a room, though. My stomach is practically eating itself, and his solution is alcohol. Not great.

I won't let my irritation show. I never do.

Maybe the bar will have food.

As he pulls the car into the valet, a wave of warmth crawls up my neck. The kind that isn't from the late summer heat.

My stomach clenches. I swallow hard.

I might actually vomit.

"Can you grab a menu? I'm going to run to the ladies'." I force another smile, even though my legs feel wobbly and there's a fine sheen of sweat above my lip.

Weaving through the Friday night crowd, I find the bathroom tucked at the back of the dining room. The lighting is soft and golden. Romantic. This is nice. He planned this for me.

Gripping the sink, I steady myself. My reflection stares back—pale skin and glassy eyes.

I exhale slowly.

"Power through," I murmur through gritted teeth.

This is my first, first anniversary. The longest relationship I've ever had. That has to mean something. Stability. A normal life. I'm finally on the right path, aren't I?

We are celebrating.

This is a big deal. One year is a feat.

Lifting my chin, I smooth my dress and walk out of the bathroom, letting the delicious scent of food guide me back to the packed bar.

"There you are!" His voice is too bright, too loud. "I ordered you a mojito."

"Thanks," I cringe.

Not only do I hate mint, but one sip of this thing would put me on my ass. The smell of alcohol wafting through the air is making me tipsy.

I stir the drink idly, not drinking, not arguing.

"Work was brutal today." He runs a hand through his thick blond hair. "The market took a beating, with heavy sell-offs across key sectors. Investors panicked, and our phones were ringing off the hook. Volatility spiked, and with the S&P dipping below a key support level, we could be looking at more downside pressure unless we see a shift in sentiment."

I nod and smile like I understand. Like this all means something to me.

A good boyfriend. A steady job. Stability.

That's what matters, right?

"I had a rough day too—"

"Oh yeah, that case started today, right?" he cuts in, already half-distracted by the notifications lighting up his phone.

The tightness in my chest comes back, hard.

Right. Of course. My day doesn't compare. "Yeah, it did."

"Did Connors find a way to fuck it up already?" He chuckles.

"No." Heat and defensiveness creep up my neck. "He did great."

"Whoa," he slides his phone back into his pocket. "I was only kidding. I'm sure that nerd will do great."

"He's not a nerd, Colson! Why do you always have to insult him?"

"Because he thinks he's something special. He's not even the District Attorney; he's the Assistant. I'm just kidding." He knocks back a shot and flags down the bartender.

"He's the assistant district attorney. I'm just an assistant." I point out.

"Oh, come on, Candace." He rolls his eyes. "Here we go. Don't make it about you. I was kidding." There is a bite of irritation in his voice that makes me cower back.

"You're right. I'm sorry. I just think he's a good guy and people treat him badly." I try to smooth things over quickly. I don't want him to be angry with me.

"Because he's a pushover. It's a dog-eat-dog world. You can't be a pussy and expect people to respect you." He shrugs, downing another shot. "Are you not going to drink that?"

"I was thinking that maybe I shouldn't, so that I can drive us home."

His head falls back, and he laughs. "I love you, but you're not driving the Lotus, babe. We'll take an Uber home. Drink up!"

He takes a few more shots while rambling about the stock

market. The bartender is apparently enthralled with the topic. The two of them happily chat, leaving me out of it.

When the hostess finally comes to bring us to our table, my stomach aches, and my eyes feel heavy. I'm equal parts hungry and tired.

"So," he leans toward me slightly. "Have you seen any of the pictures that the superintendent allegedly took?" His eyes light up.

"Colson." I sigh. Not this again. "You know I can't talk about cases."

"Oh, come on. You must have seen them! Just tell me what they look like."

"Honestly, I haven't seen them." I wouldn't look even if I did have access to case evidence. Those poor girls have enough people looking at their naked bodies; I don't want to add myself to the list.

"I feel bad for him." He flips through the menu absent-mindedly.

"What? How could you?"

"It seems like he's being railroaded. How do we know that they didn't send him those pictures just to fuck up his life? Women are conniving." He shrugs lightly.

"Those girls are absolutely distraught by this. They didn't send those pictures because they wanted to! The superintendent of the school district threatened that they wouldn't graduate if they didn't send them! He took advantage of their vulnerability and his position of power!"

"Ha!" He claps. "So you have seen the pictures! I knew it."

"I didn't look at the pictures. I'm a secretary, not an investigator. There is no reason for me to look at evidence."

"Don't you handle the files, though? I would have to sneak a peek!" He leans back.

My mouth falls open, unsure of how to respond when our server comes to the table.

"Good evening! I'm Caroline, and I'll be your server tonight. I heard this was a special occasion! Happy anniversary!" She gives us a wide, cheerful smile.

"Thank you." I blush.

"Have you had a chance to look over the menu? Can I get you started with an appetizer?"

"We'll start with the charcuterie board."

"Right away." Her smile falters at his tone.

She barely had time to step away from the table before he rolls his eyes. "The service here has really gone downhill since McMillan sold. We used to come here all the time. It was so much better."

"The service has been fine." I flinch.

"You're not used to luxury, baby. This ain't it."

My shoulders slump.

"Oh, come on," he laughs. "You're so fucking sensitive."

"I just wish you wouldn't be like this tonight. We're here to have a nice dinner to celebrate." I whisper.

"Well, as the customer and the one about to drop a few hundred on this meal, I expect better. Maybe when you can afford things like this, you'll understand."

"Yeah, maybe."

I'm not going to complain about the service, but a few slices of cheese and meat are not enough to satisfy the gnawing hunger in my stomach. I wish she would hurry back to take the orders.

"I'm going to get the strip." He closes his menu.

"I was thinking—"

"They have a wedge salad here that my mom loves. You should get that."

"A salad?"

"Yeah, so you can stay in shape and all that." He carelessly points to my body as he takes another gulp of his drink.

My face falls. I can feel it happening, and I can't stop it.

"It's good for you." The stern expression on his face has me nodding along in agreement. "You need to take care of yourself."

"Have you decided what you would like?" Caroline interrupts my frantic thoughts. Her eyes are less sparkly than before. She heard him.

"I'm going to have the six-ounce strip, rare. With the Béarnaise on the side. Mixed vegetables and rice pilaf." There is something so forceful about the way he orders. It's like a challenge.

"And for you." She looks uncomfortable as she turns to me.

My mind is blank. I don't remember anything from the menu.

"She'll have the wedge. Dressing on the side." He cuts in when I don't immediately respond. He never even looks at me while he orders for me, no quick check-in to make sure his suggestion is actually something I want.

The next several minutes feel like they happen in a vacuum. He talks about this and that. Work. The upcoming boys' trips to Vegas and Cancún. More stocks. His family's cabin in Aspen. The words wash over me, a stream of importance that I'm supposed to nod along to, supposed to be interested in.

I hardly hear any of it.

When our food comes, I eat my salad slowly, trying to force my stomach to feel satisfied with lettuce and bacon bits. It hardly tastes like anything. Across the table, he's cutting into his steak—the scent of charred meat and buttered vegetables teasing my stomach.

It looks so much better than this.

I know if I asked for something else, he'd give me that look. The one that says I should be grateful, that says I should take care of myself, that says he's just helping me make better choices.

So I don't ask.

I just eat quietly until the half head of lettuce set on my plate is gone.

"We have something special from the chef." Caroline sets a plate in front of me, something decadent and sweet. But it's not the dessert that stops my breath short.

It's the word written in chocolate script on the plate.

Wife.

My eyes snap onto Colson, who is smirking with a ring box sitting in his open hand.

"Want to make this thing official?" He opens the box to reveal a huge, single-stone ring. He's too casual. This is the biggest moment in our lives. Anyone watching with no context would think he was asking me if I wanted to see a movie.

"Oh my god." I clap my hand over my mouth—stunned.

His brow furrows. "Give me your hand, Candace."

Reaching across the table, I let him slide the ring onto my trembling fingers.

The people at the surrounding tables break into light applause.

"Congratulations!" Caroline sets two flutes of champagne on the table.

I should feel happy. This is good. This is stability. Safety.

I should be grateful.

Staring at the ring on my finger, the diamond catches the light in a way that should feel magical.

"You have no idea how much this helps my image at work," he hums, leaning back in his chair like he just sealed a business deal. "Married men are taken more seriously. Shows I'm stable, committed. Leadership material."

I blink, my stomach twisting. "That's... great?"

"And my grandma will be thrilled. She's been on me for a while about settling down. This guarantees I stay in her good graces, which means—" He laughs, shaking his head. "Well, let's just say the married grandkids get a bigger cut of the inheritance. Not that I need it, but, you know, it's nice."

I can't even force a smile. I swallow, my throat dry. "So, you proposed because it's good for business and family politics?"

He frowns like I've said something weird. "What? No. I proposed because I want to spend my life with you."

But there's no warmth or love behind it. It's a line. Something he heard in a movie once that he thinks he should repeat because it sounds like the right thing to say.

He reaches for his drink again. "Of course, we'll need a prenup. Just to protect my assets—nothing personal."

I pull my hand back, the weight of the ring suddenly suffocating. "Nothing personal," I echo, my voice flat.

He finally notices my expression, his brows drawing together. "Candace, this is just how things are done. It's practical. Don't get all weird. It will protect you, too! I'll make sure it's fair to you."

It seems we're both doing this for the wrong reasons...

TWO

DRAGGING MY FEET, I walk up the little gravel path to our door.

I don't want to do this. But I have to.

Stella's going to take one look at me and know. She always knows.

Even before I unlock the door, I can hear music inside—her cleaning playlist. The same one she's been blasting since we were thirteen.

My stomach tightens. That means she's in one of her moods —scrubbing the floors like they personally offended her. Guilt flares up in my chest. I hope it's not because of me. I should have come home last night. She probably stayed up most of the night worrying.

When I open the door, she immediately turns off the vacuum. Her brows lift, eyes wide and searching. "So, you stayed the night." She looks nervous, but her voice sounds hopeful.

"Yeah, I did." My voice cracks, and my eyes well up with tears.

"Oh God, Candace." In a second flat, she's got me in her arms, squeezing the life out of me in a bear hug. "What happened?"

I don't have the words, so I just hold out my hand.

She gasps, her fingers flying to her mouth as she stares at the ring. "Holy shit."

I let out a shaky breath. "I felt like I had to go back to his place after."

Her brows pull together in deep concern as she tries to put the pieces together. "And what happened?"

I swallow hard. "Well... we had sex." I force out a humorless laugh. "But luckily, he was pretty drunk, so it only lasted a few minutes. He passed out right after, so he didn't know that I cried again."

Her eyes well up instantly. "Candace..."

I shake my head, fighting back the lump in my throat. "How am I going to marry him if I can't have sex without crying? What is wrong with me?"

"There is nothing wrong with you." She takes my shoulders in her hands and gives me a little shake. "If you're not ready, you're not ready."

"But we've been together a year. You'd think after three or four times, I'd start to feel comfortable. I'm just... not."

"There's nothing wrong with that."

"Well, it's definitely not normal."

"Fuck normal," she scoffs. "Who wants to be normal, anyway?"

"Right." I chuckle.

"Listen." She gets serious again. "You know, I'll never ask you to tell me, but have you reconsidered therapy? I'm telling you, it is incredible, and maybe you can get to the bottom of what's going on."

"I just don't want to talk about it with anyone." The thought of anyone knowing makes me sick to my stomach.

She holds her hands up. "Ok. I'm not going to push."

"I brought you breakfast." I hold up the greasy fast food bag.

"I was really hoping that you had something in that bag for me, but I didn't want to assume." She flashes me a cheesy grin before we tear into our breakfasts.

I devour my cheesy, fatty sausage and egg sandwich. When I woke up this morning, I was still hungry from last night.

Then, as I finish the last bite of my sandwich, she clears her throat. "So... Are we going to talk about this? Are congratulations in order?"

I stare down at the ring, turning it on my finger. "Yeah... I'm happy about it."

The words feel hollow, and I know she hears it too. I can feel her physically holding herself back from telling me how much she hates his guts.

"How did he do it?" She sounds cautiously optimistic.

"At the restaurant."

"Oh, no." She cringes. "Did everyone stare?"

"Yup."

She groans. "I would've died."

I roll my eyes, but a small smile tugs at my lips. "Trust me, I wanted to."

I'm not going to mention our post-proposal conversation. Her parents are still together after almost forty years, and they both love her. She doesn't understand how important finding someone stable is.

She studies me again, but instead of pressing, she suddenly straightens, eyes glinting with excitement. "Okay, well, I have news too."

I raise an eyebrow. "Yeah?"

Her grin spreads wide, and I can tell this is big. "Noah is getting out."

It takes me a second to process. "Wait—now?"

She nods, bouncing in place. "Eight months early. Good behavior!"

A rush of shock—and something else I can't quite name—shoots through me.

"Holy shit," I breathe.

"Who knew he could behave himself, right?" She leans back, blinking the tears from her eyes.

The rest of the afternoon is spent cleaning. This is her stress reliever, and I'm not about to let her clean the whole apartment by herself.

Normally, I don't understand this form of stress release. A jog, a nap, a long bath— those are my usual go tos. But today I feel some comfort in scrubbing the shit out of our bathtub and doing some long overdue reorganization at my desk.

"Can you help me pull the fridge forward? I want to clean behind it!" She yells down the hallway.

"Stella, seriously? I was just starting to understand this whole stress cleaning thing, but that is too far."

"Yes, I'm serious! I'm going to pull the washer and dryer out, too. Everything gets dust behind it, Candace." She wipes her brow before putting her hand on her hip.

"Fine." I help her slide the refrigerator forward. "Do you want to talk about this? Why are you stress cleaning?"

She climbs onto the counter and jumps down into the hidden place. "Wow, it's disgusting back here! Hand me the vacuum hose!" She pokes her head out. "We'll talk after I get all this dust!"

I've never met a person in my life who gets so excited by dust removal.

The loud whirring of the vacuum stops, and she sighs. "I'm

afraid that he's going to get out and struggle. He's only been in for nineteen months, but things change so fast. And what if he has a hard time because he has a record?"

Jumping up to sit on the counter, I look down at her—hunched over on the floor, scrubbing. "You're not wrong to be worried, but he went to prison for negligence; he didn't brutally murder someone. He got distracted and hit him with a car." I bite back the nauseous feeling I get whenever I talk about him.

"Right, but Parker's family still lives here. They hate him. They don't care that it was an accident or the circumstances. He killed their loved one. Nothing else matters. What if they try to hurt him?"

"I hadn't even thought of that." My personal feelings about Parker Moreland clouded my judgment. I guess it makes sense that his family would want the person who killed him, accidentally or otherwise, to be punished for longer than nineteen months.

"He's already got a job lined up. At least there's that."

"Already? Where?"

"Remember his friend from high school, Jace Klein?"

His face pops into my head. "Of course, I haven't seen him since the trial!"

"Well, I guess he opened a club up in Columbia. Noah is going to live there and work as a bouncer or a bartender or something."

"Good for him."

"That's probably the hardest step, and he's already set. I shouldn't be freaking out like this." She sits on the floor, stress still etched into her face.

"I'll help you clean behind the washer and dryer if you want." I offer just to see that sad, anxious look drop from her face.

"I know that's just pity, but I'll take it!"

THREE

THE BANNER WON'T STAY STRAIGHT.

I smooth my hands over the wrinkled fabric, trying to press the letters into place as if that will somehow settle the tremor in my chest.

WELCOME HOME, NOAH.

The words feel too small for what this moment is, for what it means.

Two years. I can't imagine being away from home that long.

Two years of silence and unwritten letters, I never had the courage to write. Two years of trying to forget the sound of my own screams or to live with the nightmares. Two years of carrying this secret alone while he sat in a cell.

He never even knew what he did for me.

I should've told him. I should've written the damn letter.

It eats at me that he feels guilt. He accidentally killed someone. That's got to weigh on his soul. I hope it doesn't. But if I could just find the courage to tell him that the man he killed was a monster—a wolf in preppy clothing—maybe he would feel less guilt.

I press my palms against the banner again, exhaling slowly. The house is quiet, just the soft creak of the walls settling around me. Everyone else is at the prison, picking him up. He'll be home soon. I shouldn't be this nervous.

But my hands shake anyway.

It's just Noah.

I wonder what he'll look like or if prison has changed him. If I'll see it in his eyes the way it's settled into my bones—this thing between us, the truth he doesn't even know.

Part of me is worried. He was always quiet and kind. I practically lived here, especially in high school, but we never really talked much. When we did, he was nicer than the boys in my grade. He was older, more mature.

He drove Stella and me to homecoming junior year.

His laid-back nature meant that he could teach us how to drive when Mrs. Gaines was too panicked to get in the car with either of us behind the wheel. He was a good teacher. Soft—patient.

The sound of a car pulling up outside makes my breath catch.

They're here. He's here.

My heart beats so loud I can hear it in my ears as the door swings open. And then—

Noah.

He steps inside, and the entire room tilts like the air shifts just to make space for him. He looks the same, but different.

Bigger, broader. He's always been serious, but it's sharper now. He's a little harder around the edges. His eyes sweep the room, landing on me.

The breath leaves my lungs. He still looks like him, but he's a man now. He was already a man when he went in, twenty-six. But now...

I don't think. I just move.

My body reacts, and I lunge at him, my arms locking around his neck, my chest pressed tight to his. He's solid. A steady rock to anchor myself to.

He doesn't hesitate. His arms come around me, holding me just as tight. For a second, I swear I feel the breath leave his chest in a shaky rush, like maybe—somehow—he needed this too.

Then I remember where we are.

Heat rushes to my face as I pull back too fast, almost stumbling. I glance around, hoping no one noticed, but my skin prickles with embarrassment anyway.

Noah doesn't look upset. He just watches me like he's trying to figure something out.

"Hey, Ace," his voice is the same. Low and raspy.

My throat feels tight. "Hey."

Ace. It's a perfectly reasonable nickname for Candace, but no one else calls me that. Only Noah. When I was younger, it made me feel special. Maybe it still does.

He glances around. There is a softness in his expression. I've been here hundreds, maybe thousands of times in the last two years. His childhood home. But he hasn't been here. It must be overwhelming. His eyes land on the banner. "Did you do this?"

I nod, not trusting my voice.

A slow smile tugs at his mouth, something soft hidden beneath it. "Looks good."

His dad claps him on the shoulder, pulling him into what I suspect is one of many hugs he's received today. "It's good to have you back, son."

"Glad to be back."

"I've got all your favorites made!" His mom chimes in, her eyes glassy. "Dad's smoking ribs in the back!"

"Oh, I can't wait." He runs his tattooed hand over his stomach. The thin t-shirt he's wearing leaves little to the imagination. He got ripped.

I shouldn't be thinking about him like that. It's weird.

It's strange how easy it feels–how normal.

He's home now, back where he belongs.

"We've got at least another hour until the food will be ready. Go ahead and take a shower, son. Take a nap if you want to. You don't have to entertain us." He gets another hug from his mom. She whispers something to him. I can't hear it, but by the way her hand grips his shirt, I'm sure it's more emotional than welcoming sentiments.

When he walks down the hallway and disappears, I feel my chest deflate.

"Oh, my god." Stella lets out a breath, too. "It's fucking weird."

"Yeah." I look up at the spinning ceiling fan.

"Why? This is his house, too. Why does it feel so foreign having him here? He wasn't gone for twenty years or something. I need to call my therapist." She digs through her purse, frantically looking for her phone.

"Stella, it's on the couch." I point.

"Oh! Thanks. I'm so frazzled. I'll be in the backyard if you need me!"

Walking down the dark hallway, I pause as I pass the bathroom. The sound of the water running comes through the door.

An indescribable peace settles in my chest, knowing that he's in there.

I slip into Stella's old bedroom to wait. Sinking onto the edge of her bed, I stare at the walls. The air still smells like her vanilla perfume. It must be soaked into the paint at this point.

This bedroom felt more like mine than my actual room at home. I was more loved and welcomed here. Falling back onto the mattress, I let my eyes flutter closed and let my mind go blank.

Then the door opens.

Noah steps inside, fresh from the shower, his damp hair curling slightly at the ends, wearing nothing but gray sweatpants that hang too low on his hips.

Jesus Christ.

"Stella told me you two live together now." He says casually, like he isn't standing there like a carved statue.

"Um, yeah. In the little apartments on Grover Ave." I try to sound unaffected, but my face is on fire. "We've been there for almost two years now..." My voice trails off, catching on the weight of my own words. Guilt presses on my chest, making it hard to take a breath. "Sorry."

His expression doesn't change, but something flickers in his eyes—something sharp, something wounded. "It's alright. You were allowed to have a life while I was away."

The words feel like an accusation, even though they shouldn't. I don't think he meant them that way. My projections are clouding my mind.

"Right." I stare at the carpet.

A heavy silence stretches between us before his voice cuts through it, lower now—angry. "What is that?"

I blink at him. "What?"

His jaw tightens. He lifts a finger, pointing at my hand. "On your finger."

I glance down at my rings, and my stomach twists into a knot.

"Oh." I freeze.

He takes a step closer, his shadow engulfing me. I feel like a deer in the headlights–small and helpless against the oncoming danger.

I flinch, and he freezes. "Ace." His tone softens. "What is that?"

"I'm engaged." The words taste like acid. They sizzle on my tongue and make me nauseous. This should be exciting news to share, but I feel more panic than joy.

"To who?"

I swallow hard; my throat is so dry suddenly. "Um. His name is Colson Barrington."

His expression sharpens. "Barrington?" He sneers and doesn't even attempt to hide his disgust. "As in, Barrington Luxury Car Dealers?"

"Yes." Of course, he'd put that together. Barrington isn't exactly a common name in this town, and Colson's family practically owns half of it. I brace myself for whatever comes next, but nothing could have prepared me for the way his jaw clenches, the flicker of something unreadable in his eyes.

He exhales sharply. "Jesus Christ."

Then he sits beside me, the mattress dipping under his weight. Anger wafts from him like heat that I can feel. "How long?"

"How long, what?"

"Have you been with him?"

"A year."

A low hum vibrates from his chest. His eyes drop to my hand, laser-focused on the very large diamond sparkling on my finger. His lips part, but he doesn't say anything. Silence stretches between us before he exhales through his nose, slow and measured.

"I guess congratulations are in order."

It doesn't sound like congratulations. It sounds like something else — like disappointment.

I feel like I let him down somehow, but I don't understand why.

Before I can say anything, he stands up and walks out of the room. The door doesn't exactly slam, but he closed it with force.

Left sitting there stunned, I stare at my hand.

Why is he mad at me?

Colson never mentioned knowing him. But they were in the same grade in school, and Noah Gaines was the talk of the town for years—first because of the accident, then the trial. How could Colson have never told me they knew each other? It seems like something that should have come up when he met Stella.

Pulling my phone out of my pocket, checking for a message that I know isn't there. He never just sends a message to check in during the day.

Peeking out the window, I see Stella lying like a starfish in the center of the old trampoline in the backyard. In elementary school, that was the coolest thing in the world. In high school, we would use it as a place to lie out and tan.

She looks relaxed, with her phone beside her as she talks.

Maybe she's right. I should see a therapist.

I just can't stomach it. I don't want to tell anyone about what happened. I know I'm not the only one. It happens every day. But I feel alone. I feel used and disgusting.

Tears burn in my eyes. I'm overwhelmed today. There are too many emotions coursing through me to think about that again. Pushing it down, I wipe the tears from my eyes.

"Food's ready!" Mrs. Gaines yells from the kitchen.

Stella sits up, smiling at her phone as she ends her session.

When I open the door, the familiar scent of meat fills the air. I bet she made macaroni and cheese and buttermilk biscuits, too. And there is probably peach cobbler for dessert.

Rounding the corner into the kitchen, I'm met with their warm, smiling faces. "Get a plate, girlie!" She hands me a paper plate tucked inside a plastic plate holder.

Walking around the island in the center of the kitchen, I take some meat and a biscuit. I don't need all the carbs.

Sliding the back door open, I sit at the long bench table that they only use for special occasions.

Climbing onto the bench, the first one out here, I pick at my food.

The door creaks open again, and he steps out.

I don't look up right away, but I feel him. Is he still mad? I don't want to find out.

A plate drops in front of me, heavier than my own. More food—meat, macaroni, potato salad.

"You need to eat." His voice is soft but firm.

I glance up at him. "I have food."

"You need more protein."

I swallow, unsure if this is an olive branch. But I don't argue. I pick up my fork and take a bite.

FOUR

NOAH

SHE'S SO FUCKING THIN.

The engagement issue can wait; it's less pressing than the bones sticking out at her collar. When was the last time she had a good meal?

Stella said she was doing well. That's obviously a lie. Or maybe Stella is just too blind to see the truth—she's too close to it. She looks exhausted. Her body is smaller than I remember, and I don't fucking like it.

My hands clench beneath the table as I watch her eat from the plate I made. Good girl. Every last bite. I imagine prying her mouth open, pressing my fingers against her tongue to make sure she swallowed. My restraint is paper-thin.

I wasn't sure how I would react after not seeing her for so long. Five hundred and eighty-four days. I wondered if things might have changed. But when she hugged me, the scent of her hair filling my lungs, my body reacting instantly—I knew. Nothing had changed. If anything, the hunger has grown sharper. The need is even more pressing.

I wanted to drag her straight to my bedroom, lock the door, and make up for lost time.

Patience.

I can't swoop in like a fucking psycho after all this time. I have to be slow and steady.

She's never been this forward before–never just ran up and threw her arms around me. I want to ask why—to hear her stumble through an answer and watch that pink blush creep up her cheeks. I'll spare her. For now.

She slips the fork between her lips, taking a bite and letting her eyes flutter closed. It's like a jolt of electricity straight to my cock. It punches the air right out of my lungs.

God, I ache for her.

I've always watched her. At first, it was innocent—she needed someone to look out for her, to protect her from the trash-people she calls family. I don't know when it turned into something else. Watching became wanting. Wanting became needing. Then, the need became possession.

Two years in prison should've broken the compulsion. That isolation should have severed the sickness. But it didn't. If anything, it cemented it.

I am not broken.

I do not need to be fixed.

And she's already mine. She just doesn't know it yet.

"How's the food, son?" Dad draws my attention away from her.

"Delicious." I turn my attention back to her.

"When do you start work?" Stella pulls me away again.

"I meet with my parole officer next week. After that, I'll head up to Columbia."

She looks at me, her big, honey-colored eyes peeking through her bangs. I want to bite that bottom lip. To suck her tongue into my mouth. To taste every inch of her.

"Are you sure you have to go all the way to Columbia? An hour is pretty far away." Mom repeats the same sentiment she's expressed twenty times since hearing the plan.

"I'm sure." Don't worry. I'll be here a lot more than you realize. My muscles tighten, eager to get started.

The thought of watching her sleep again after so long...

Rolling my neck, I force those urges into the deep recesses of my mind.

Patience.

She takes the last bite from her plate.

"What exactly are you going to be doing at that club?" Stella talks with her mouth full, the same way she did when we were kids.

Taking a rib from my plate, I set it on hers. A silent command. Eat.

She doesn't even realize that ribs aren't my favorite meal, not even close. But it is hers. So that's what I choose. Every time.

"I'll do whatever Jace needs. I know he's short a bartender, but he also needs a bouncer."

"Do you even know how to mix drinks?"

"I can pour a shot."

They keep talking. About people and things that don't fucking matter. I don't care about the club. I don't care about parole.

I care about her.

And she's right here, close enough to touch.

Close enough to take.

Patience.

FIVE

HER HACKING COUGH greets me at the door.

"Candy, is that you?" From the distance of her voice, I know she's on the back porch.

"It's me."

"I'm almost done!" I hear her scrambling around her plastic chair, scraping against the concrete. Then she coughs again, so loud and forceful it seems like she's going to split in half.

After a few seconds, the screen creaks loudly, and she rushes inside.

The stale, sour smell of smoke clings to everything. It makes my stomach roll.

"I wasn't expecting you today!" She plops down on the sagging couch with a grunt.

"Um, yeah. Sorry for dropping in. I wanted to tell you something."

"I'm not doing anything but watching my soaps." She unpauses the ancient TV. The screen flickers, static lines rolling down over the paused tape in her boxy VCR. "It doesn't matter how many times I watch this one; I can't tear myself away. I cry every time Tony finds out about the baby."

The theme song starts, the volume is always set much too loudly, and I sit uncomfortably on the couch.

"Mom, I wanted to tell you something."

"Go ahead." She doesn't look away from the screen. She's watched this series in its entirety at least twice.

"Can you pause that, please?"

Her lips purse, and she clicks the button, openly annoyed. "What is it, Candy? This is my one day off this week. I just want to—"

"Colson asked me to marry him." I blurt out.

"Holy shit!" She gasps. "Oh, baby, that's wonderful!"

I nod, forcing a smile.

Of course, she doesn't notice.

"You're going to be a Barrington. My daughter. I'll be damned." She shakes her head and laughs, a raspy, wheezing chuckle. "Do you even realize what this means? We're set for life!"

"Mom, I—"

"They've got more money than god, Candace." I can see the wheels turning in her mind. "You could buy me a car that doesn't break down every hundred miles."

"Yeah, right." I smile and nod. I'm not going to argue right now.

Now she seems to notice.

"What?" She looks at me with a deep, annoyed frown. "What is that face?"

I swallow hard. "Um, I don't know. It doesn't feel how I thought it would. I'm unsure."

"Did he knock someone up or something?"

"What? No! Nothing like that!" I groan. "I don't think he loves me. He doesn't care about how I feel—"

She leans back, pulling a cigarette out of the pack in her pocket. "Does he hit you?" She lights it between her lips.

"No." I blink.

"Then who cares if he's nice, Candy?" She exhales a cloud of smoke. "Men aren't nice. But with that much money? It makes up for it. If you want love, get a dog."

I open my mouth, but no sound comes out.

"You marry him, and you won't ever have to worry about anything ever again. Even with a prenup, you'll be set for life. You could go to Hawaii. Or buy one of those damn expensive stationary bikes. People like us don't get handed chances like this. I married three fucking losers that weren't worth shit." She points her cigarette at me. "You would be a damn fool to walk away from him."

Her words sink into my stomach like hot rocks.

I don't know what I was expecting. This is exactly what I knew she would say.

"I'll tell you something. None of the useless men I married ever did a damn thing for me. Every man is going to disappoint you, baby. You might as well be disappointed in a mansion." She taps her cigarette ash into a piece of tinfoil she fashioned into an ashtray.

"Right."

"He's not hitting you or cheating. You're being too picky." She takes another long drag. "My own daughter, a Barrington." She smiles to herself and turns her show on.

"I'm going to head out. I have work." I lie. It's Saturday. But she's so wrapped up in the lives of the characters that she won't question it.

"Alright, baby. See you later." She pulls another cigarette out of the pack.

I leave quickly before she lights it.

Pulling the big sweatshirt off, I wrap it up tight and put it in my trunk so the smell doesn't linger in my car.

I knew she would say that. Her life has only shown her that.

But I've seen different.

Mr. Gaines loves his wife. He talks to her. They share a life, not just a house. It's more than a marriage of convenience and benefit. They are best friends.

Is it too much to ask for that?

Leaning back in my seat, I close my eyes. I can't even picture my life in ten years.

Of course, Noah's face pops into my head right now. He is the last person I should be thinking about.

He just got out of prison.

I'm getting married. And he needs to figure out his life.

SIX

I HAVEN'T SLEPT WELL in years. Sometimes, I think the dreams are worse than the real thing. It only lasted a few agonizing minutes. The dreams suck me in and hold on tight for hours.

I can feel them coming. There's a very specific kind of discomfort—a cold chill even on the warmest day.

I've tried to convince myself that it's a self-fulfilling prophecy. I feel that way, and then it's my own fear and over-thinking that make the dreams come.

If I could just gain control— if I could have the strength of mind over matter. But I never do.

I feel it again tonight. It's hanging over my head like a weight, waiting for the opportunity to drop down on top of me.

My stomach is turning and queasy, and I have an itch at the base of my skull. The kind you can't scratch. The kind that doesn't go away. It's just there, irritating incessantly, until it's the only thing I can focus on.

I don't want to go to bed. If I sleep, I will relive it. It's like a slow-moving train; it's coming, I see it–but I'm tied to the track.

No matter how hard I try to get away, it's coming—it's inevitable.

I know as soon as I close my eyes, I'll be back there.

I fight against it for as long as I can by reading, watching movies, cleaning, listening to music, and doing anything I can think of to keep my eyes open.

But my body can't stay awake forever.

When my eyes burn, desperate to close, and my neck can't hold up the heavy weight of my head anymore, I slump over my desk.

I try to cling to something. Noah. For some reason, since yesterday, I can't stop thinking about him. The way he watched me...

I thought it was all in my head, but every time I would pluck up the courage to look at him, he was already looking at me.

I know I'm drifting as it happens. His broad shoulders— a silhouette that blocks out the sun.

Everything is hazy. It feels like waking up, but I don't remember falling asleep.

The room is dark–suffocating. Each breath feels like a victory. My body won't move. I'm only barely conscious, but there is a disconnect somewhere. When I try to lift my head, it doesn't rise. Neither do my arms. My eyelids are heavy and hard to open.

When I open my mouth, no sounds come out, so I groan instead.

"Shhh." His breath is hot against my ear. He's on top of me.

The stale, wheaty smell of beer forces its way into my nose. It makes me gag.

I try to speak again. Everything is fading in and out. Sounds are distorted—the distant thump of a bass vibrates in the distance.

When my eyes open this time, I feel like I've been sprayed with ice water.

"Oh, my god!" I scream, and frantic energy courses through me. "What are you doing?"

He pins me down roughly. "Be quiet."

"Help!" I scream before his hand claps over my mouth hard. My cheeks press into my teeth, splitting open and filling my mouth with the taste of blood.

Pressing my eyes closed, I try to think, but I can't. My mind is racing in a million different directions.

It hurts.

My hips hurt, pressed open into the hard ground.

My thighs hurt.

"You're so pretty, Candy." He grunts, thrusting his hips, forcing himself further into me. It ripples and aches.

"P-Parker?" It's taken this long to understand who this is. He sat in front of me in chemistry junior year. I haven't seen him since graduation. "W-Wha—"

"Shh," he moans.

Tears spill past my lashes, sliding down my face and pooling in my ears.

"Please stop," I beg, my voice muffled against his hand.

His weight crushes me, grinding me into the ground.

Somewhere deep inside, I hope for a savior. Someone— anyone to come rescue me. But no one does.

When I open my eyes, my vision is blurry. A dim string of yellow lights dangles above us, twinkling every few seconds.

Where am I? I don't know how I got here.

He falls down on top of me, grunting and moaning– disgusting sounds that echo in my mind.

I'm vaguely aware of him standing and zipping his pants.

And he leaves me there on the ground, in the dark.

Just as a cracked sob tears through me, I gasp, jolting awake.

My shirt is soaked through and clinging to my skin. Covering my face with my hands, I curl into myself, bring my knees up to my chest.

I feel it all over again.

I can smell the beer and feel his hands on me.

He's dead.

He's dead.

Parker Moreland is dead.

He died in the street like roadkill.

The thought flashes in my mind and takes root, sinking in the way it always does.

I saw the pictures in court. The prosecution was trying to use Parker's mangled body to play to the jury's emotions. I looked at their faces. All twelve of them, I went from juror to juror, studying their reactions.

Horror, pity, disgust.

All I felt was calm.

He deserved that. His bloody, broken body and wide-open eyes should haunt my nightmares, but it is soothing.

He's dead.

He can't ever hurt me again.

Everyone came out of the woodworks, people crying and talking about what a wonderful–son, brother, nephew, friend– he was.

He was an animal.

It's been six years now. Six years since my assault. Six years since he was run over.

The trial took almost four years to make it to court.

I had to think about him every day during that time. I had to hear people talking about it. Blue ribbons were hung up around town in his honor. The special light that was lost tragically. The only thing tragic about it was that he didn't die more slowly and painfully.

For months, I had to swallow down vomit every time someone started to talk about the 'promising young man' we lost too soon.

People treated the Gaines' like pariahs.

Noah is my hero, and he doesn't even know it. He killed him. It doesn't matter that it was an accident.

He's dead. And he can never hurt me again.

But the past didn't die just because he did. The nightmares didn't go away.

Wiping the sweat and tears from my face, I start to change my clothes. As I pull a dry shirt over my head, I hear something. It sounded like the scrape of gravel.

My spine stiffens, and I freeze.

When my fight-or-flight response kicks in, I turn and run. Sprinting in the dark, I rush out into the hallway.

"Ace?" His voice stops me in my tracks.

"Noah?"

"What's wrong?" He steps out of the living room, his silhouette blocking the end of the hallway.

"What are you doing here?" I feel the cold leaving my body, starting in my toes—warmth spreads through me.

"I was asleep on the couch." He takes a step forward. "What were you dreaming about?"

"You could hear me?" I'm horrified.

"Ace, what were you dreaming about?"

"Monsters." I bite back the urge to cry.

"Come here." He takes my hand, leading me back into my bedroom.

"There was a sound. I heard something." I look toward the window.

"No one is going to get you. Get in bed." There is no room

for argument in his tone. He pulls my blanket back, holding it open for me to crawl under.

I gasp as he lies down beside me—just a small, sharp inhale, but he hears it.

He pulls me into his shoulder, nestled in safe—next to his heart.

"Go to sleep, Ace. You look exhausted." His big hand presses down on my shoulder like a weighted blanket. I'm engulfed in warmth and safety.

"Noah," I whisper.

"Yeah?" His voice is low and soothing.

"Thank you."

"For what?"

"Everything," my voice wobbles. All the things I can't say but wish he knew. Thank you for all of it.

He hums and tightens his grip around me. I couldn't stay awake if I wanted to. As I feel myself drifting, floating away, knowing that I'm tethered to him and can't drift aimlessly, my last coherent thought is to wonder when the last time I felt like this was.

Six years ago?

Further back than that?

Maybe never.

There's something so real and sure about this.

His heart beats beneath my head, a calm, steady rhythm.

There's no end or beginning to it. When my eyes flutter open, sunlight is streaming in through my window, and I'm alone.

I don't know when he left. I was in such a deep sleep that I didn't notice that he had untangled himself from me.

Reaching for my phone, I click the single message notification.

I'll see you around, Ace.

He put his number in my phone?

I linger on the message, wondering if I should text him back. Should I thank him for last night?

Feeling awake and rested in a way that I haven't felt in years, I climb out of bed and creep quietly to the kitchen.

I'm going to make Stella breakfast.

Putting on a cheerful playlist, I start pulling ingredients out of the refrigerator.

"Whoa," her laughter behind me makes me jump. "What are you doing?"

"Making breakfast!" I adjust her to all the ingredients on the counter. "Pancakes, eggs, sausage, and anything else you want."

"Someone woke up on the sunny side of the bed this morning." She starts making a cup of coffee. Her hair is wild, and her bangs are sticking straight up. I can tell by the sound of her voice that she hasn't taken her retainer out yet.

My heart always feels warm when I look at her.

There is exactly one secret in my life that I've kept from Stella. Just one.

I don't know if I should tell her that Noah came into my room. I don't think she would be upset. I wouldn't be if I had an older brother, anyway.

My throat feels dry as I forcefully swallow down the confession. Two secrets. That is where I draw the line.

Or at least that's what I'm telling myself.

"I'm using the last of the eggs. I'll stop at the store and get more." I ignore the guilt and push past it.

"I'm working nine to nine today. This breakfast is going to be the only thing that gets me through it." She cringes.

"I'm off today." I feel like I'm rubbing salt in the wound.

"Lucky bitch." She chuckles and drops her head down on the counter.

I cook as she grumbles.

"Oh, hey! My mom wants to drive up to Columbia and bring a bunch of *housewarming* things to Noah." She exaggerates 'housewarming' because we both know she is doing it to calm her worries about his new living situation. "Want to come? We're going to go shopping and get him towels and plates and shit."

"Yeah, sure."

Noah.

Why am I blushing?

SEVEN

Eggs
Bodywash
Toothpaste
Strawberries
Butter

DRIFTING THROUGH THE AISLES, I toss things into the cart. We don't need ice cream, frozen pizzas, or cookies, but I'm getting them anyway.

I haven't had pizza in months.

My hair is tied up in a rushed, messy bun, and a coffee stain is dribbled down the front of my favorite shirt. I didn't even notice until I got out of the car, and by then, it was too late to turn back. Whatever.

I'm alone in the snack foods aisle, trying to decide which chips to buy when goosebumps spread over my skin.

That unsettling tickle at the base of my skull. The unmistakable weight of eyes on me.

Spinning around, I don't see anyone.

It's broad daylight in the middle of the grocery store. Chill out.

I grip the handle of the cart tighter, pushing it forward, turning the corner into another aisle—

And he's there.

Right in front of me. Like he was waiting for me.

For a split second, my brain scrambles—glitching as a memory floats through my head. Because I've seen him like this before—years ago.

I was a freshman in high school. He was a junior. I walked out of the bathroom in the middle of the night, and he was standing there. Leaning against the wall, arms crossed, eyes already on me. Just like now.

I remember the way my breath caught and my skin flushed. He didn't say anything. Just watched me, with an unreadable expression on his face.

When he stepped around me into the bathroom, I tried to tell myself he was just waiting, but it felt weird. He wasn't waiting for the bathroom; it was like he was waiting for me.

Just like now.

"Ace." His voice is deep. Steady. The same. He never was one to say much, but when he speaks, it's steady. He only says what he needs to and no more.

"Noah." I shift on my feet, suddenly all too aware of the way I look—completely gross. "Hey."

A smirk tugs at his lips, and my stomach twists.

"Hey."

He has a handbasket with a few things in it—toothpaste.

Oh, yeah. That's why I came to this aisle. I step around my cart to look at the toothpaste, but he's distracting me, so I just grab a random one. It's all the same, anyway.

"Did you sleep all right?"

Heat flashes up my chest, neck, and cheeks. "Oh, yeah. Thanks."

His free hand flexes and then clenches into a tight fist. He steps closer, so close that the toes of our shoes touch.

"Are those the same boots from before?" I don't know why I asked that. I'm too warm and he's too close.

"Yes." He reaches out, plucking the frozen pizza from my cart. "What is this?"

"I haven't had pizza in a while. It just sounded good." Doubt creeps in. He's right; I shouldn't get that, it's bad for me. I should go back to the produce section and get more fruit and vegetables.

"Come get real pizza with me."

"What?"

"I haven't had pizza in a while either." A lopsided grin tugs at one side of his lips.

"But... right now?" I looked down at my clothes.

"Right now."

"Noah, I look—"

"Gorgeous. Let's go," he interrupts smoothly, taking the cart from me and steering it toward the checkout like I've already agreed.

I hesitate, but he's already moving. I jog after him, my protest swallowed by his certainty. He tosses his handbasket onto a random shelf without a second thought, pushing the cart straight to self-checkout.

"Noah, wait, I..."

He pulls the box of tampons out and scans them while holding eye contact.

"Can I run in and change my shirt, at least?"

"Yes." He scans the last item and reaches for his wallet.

"Hey, wait! What are you doing?" I rush forward as he slides his card into the reader.

"Noah!" I whisper-shout, stomping my foot. "I'm paying for lunch."

"Why?"

"Because you aren't buying my tampons and my lunch."

He gathers all the bags in one hand. "I want to buy your tampons." His eyes darken.

"W-Why?" A wheezing sound that hopefully only I hear comes from deep in my throat.

Instead of answering, he starts walking to the door, leaving me standing there with my mouth hanging open.

Running out after him, I follow him straight to my car. "Look at that. We're parked beside each other."

He puts the groceries in the back of his truck. "I'll follow you home, then we'll take my car."

"Ok." I slide into my car.

He isn't demanding. His tone isn't harsh or commanding, but he isn't asking.

I'm nervous and jittery driving back to our apartment. I keep checking the rearview mirror. He's right there every time. He taught me how to drive. I don't want to fuck this up.

Pulling into our complex, I try to ignore the sweat on the back of my neck.

We slept in the same bed together last night. Why am I freaking out about being in the apartment alone with him?

I know I'm safe with Noah. I've known him my whole life. He would never hurt me. But it's deeper than that. It's something unspoken and tangible. He really wouldn't hurt me.

He parks beside me and hops out of his truck, his boots scraping against the asphalt.

"I'll be quick," I promise as I fumble with my key ring.

"I'm in no hurry." He follows me into the apartment.

Running down the hallway, I closed the door. My fingers hover over the lock.

Turning, I pull off my stained, sloppy shirt, rifling through my closet. My fingers brush over fabric—dresses. Cute, soft, pretty things. Dresses that Colson likes me to wear.

I don't want to wear those.

As I reach for a simple shirt, I realize that I'm not wearing my ring.

"Shit." Scrambling around, I try to fix my hair enough to make the messiness look intentional.

I left my ring by the sink. What is wrong with me?

When I come down the hallway, he's finishing with the groceries. There is a bag on the floor at the opening of the hall-way. My toiletries.

"Thank you for doing that, you didn't have–" My voice fades as he tilts his head to one side, studying me with an intense expression.

Without a word, he takes purposeful steps toward me. I step back but hit the wall behind me.

He's so close that his foot is nudged in between mine now— our chests are touching. "Take it off."

"What?" As soon as the word leaves my mouth, I know what he's talking about.

"Noah, I–"

"Take it off, Ace." His voice is quieter this time, but there's no mistaking the demand. "I'm not taking you out with another man's ring on your finger." A chill runs up my spine. His fingers take my chin, not hard, but with enough pressure to make my breath hitch. "Give it to me."

My hands tremble as I pull off the ring and place it in his open palm. "I'm sorry."

He walks back into my bedroom, disappearing for a moment before returning. "Let's go."

"Did you throw it away?"

He chuckles, opening the door for me. "No. It's in your bathroom."

"Oh. Right."

As we step out to his truck, his hand moves to the back of my neck, his fingers curling just enough to make goosebumps prickle down my arms. He guides me toward his truck, not with force, but with something else...

He opens the door for me.

"Is Pasco's still your favorite?"

I barely register the question as he reaches inside, pulling the seat belt over me. His arm brushes my chest, and instinct kicks in—I stop breathing.

"Um." He said something. I didn't hear it.

His voice drops, smoother this time. "Pasco's, baby. Is it still your favorite pizza?"

Baby.

"Y-Yeah." I clear my throat.

He nods and closes the door. I let out a harsh breath. Baby?

When he climbs inside and the engine roars to life, he leans back slightly, adjusting the steering wheel in his left hand. His right hand grabs my thigh—he grips and tugs, sliding me across the bench seat until I'm pressed right up against him.

Somewhere deep in my mind, all the way in the back with the dust and cobwebs, a little voice is quietly whispering. I'm engaged. This isn't right.

"How's work? You're still with the DA's office, right?"

"Yeah. It's good. I'm the assistant DA's assistant." I cringe.

"Mathew Connors is a good guy."

"You know him?" I whip around to look at his face.

"Yes," he chuckles. "He runs a prison outreach program. He does these seminars—"

"About finances and the stock market!"

"Yeah." He smiles, one of the rare ones that shows his teeth. "I went to all of them."

"Really?" My chest swells. "I'm so happy to hear that. Everyone at the office gives him a hard time about that. They think he's wasting time and resources–" I stop. "I mean, I don't think he is–"

"It's alright, Ace. It doesn't surprise or offend me that people aren't excited about spending resources on criminals."

The tension in my shoulder releases. "I'm glad you went to them. He's been the best boss I've ever had."

"Good." He squeezes my thigh.

He pulls into the parking lot with ease. There is something so calm and collected about him.

The pizza place is small, dimly lit, and smells like garlic. It's the kind of smell that has nostalgia attached to it.

I slide into the booth, expecting him to sit across from me. He doesn't.

He slides in beside me.

Too close.

Without looking at the menu, he flags down a server.

"Bring her a lemonade. I'll have water."

She smiles at him. "And to eat?"

"An order of the cheesy bread and two medium pepperoni pizzas. Ranch on the side. A lot of it–borderline too much. Bring what you would usually bring for five people."

My cheeks burn bright red. I don't know why it surprises me that he remembers this. It seems he remembers everything.

His hand finds my thigh, and I freeze.

"You look so familiar. Do you come here a lot?" She bats her lashes.

"You probably remember me from the news a few years ago. I killed someone."

I choke, and her face pales.

"I'll be right back with your food."

"Noah!"

"What?" His thumb brushes over the fabric of my leggings, a slow, lazy stroke that makes my breath catch.

I turn my head, looking at him, searching his face for— something. An explanation. A warning.

"Why did you put your number in my phone last night?" I ask.

He doesn't blink.

"Because I wanted to have it." His fingers tighten, just for a second, enough to make me aware of them. "And I wanted you to have mine."

EIGHT

NOAH

THE BLUSH on her cheeks when the server dropped off enough ranch dressing for a dozen people was worth at least two years in prison. Maybe more.

"Eat, Ace." I slide her pizza closer, watching the hesitation in her delicate features. She should be devouring this—pizza is one of her favorites. "Why haven't you had pizza lately?"

"Oh, well..." Her voice is too soft—uncertain. She's afraid to answer me.

Her fingers knot together in her lap. I want to smooth them out, take her hands in mine, and press my lips to each knuckle until she stops thinking about it..

I give her thigh a little squeeze under the table, not just to stop her fidgeting but because I need to touch her. A single point of contact to keep myself from doing something reckless—like laying her on the table and eating her instead of the pizza.

"Answer the question. Even if you think I won't like it."

She swallows. "Colson doesn't really like pizza. He's more of a fine dining guy. Plus, I'm trying to stay in shape."

My jaw ticks. I'm going to clench so hard my fucking teeth are going to crack. "Your bones are sticking out, Ace."

Colson. I should have known it had something to do with her dumbfuck fiancé.

She sucks in a breath, her shoulders slumping.

"I know, but—"

"Look at me."

Her eyes come up, but not enough to make eye contact. Uh-huh, baby. All the way up.

"Look at me, baby." I tuck a strand of hair behind her ear, using the position to slide my hand around the side of her neck and force her head up. Her pulse pounds against my fingers. "I never want to hear that shit come out of your mouth again. Do you understand? It makes me want to do violent things." I give her neck a light squeeze before moving my hand back down to her thigh, higher up this time.

Just a few inches up from my pinky, her cunt is waiting for me. If I just stretched my finger out—just moved it up—I could feel her, own her.

A violent shudder racks through me. My cock strains against my zipper, pulsing with the need to claim—to mark. She's fucking oblivious. Sitting here—innocent and nervous—while I unravel piece by piece.

"Eat." The word is guttural, almost a growl. I don't mean to sound so feral, but I am one second away from losing my fucking mind.

She lifts the pizza to her lips, takes a bite, and my cock twitches. Goddamnit. Fuck.

"That's right, baby. Just like that." I'm practically panting. She's such a good girl for me.

Her eyes flick up to mine—wide, obedient. She takes another bite. Slowly. Deliberately.

Is she doing this shit on purpose?

"Keep looking at me like that, angel," I warn, my fingers twitching against the table. It's a promise. A threat. If she keeps pushing me, I won't be responsible for what happens next.

I'll ruin her. And she'll thank me for it.

Focusing on my pizza, I take a bite. I hardly taste it.

Last night, I sat up while she slept. Imagining the taste of it kept me awake.

"Can I ask you something?" Her soft, sweet voice asks from beside me.

"Anything. Always."

"What was prison like?"

"It actually wasn't bad. Jace's cousin is on the inside, doing life, so he looked out for me in the beginning."

"Really?" She perks up. "I didn't know that."

"Once people know that they can't fuck with you, they pretty much leave you alone as long as you keep your head down."

"Stella told me you were taking a bunch of classes. Mechanics courses and stuff like that."

"Were you keeping tabs on me, baby?" I always wondered if Stella mentioning that she asked about me or sent her best was just talk.

"I just wanted to make sure you were alright in there."

I hum, watching her pick up another slice and dip it into that fucking ranch dressing.

"This is so good." She smiles, and the thin chord holding my restraint back snaps. I thought I was doing well. Being normal. Talking. But that fucking smile? That's all it took to unravel me.

Venom courses through my veins. The need is so sharp, so fucking visceral, it hurts.

"Goddamn it, Ace." I let my head fall forward.

Her little fingers touch my wrist. "What? What's wrong?"

"This pizza is fine, but it's not what I want to be eating."
I'm coming unglued.

"What do you want?"

"You." I turn toward her, pushing myself forward so that
she's trapped–stuck between me and the wall.

"If you let me, I'd lay you open on this table and devour you
until you scream." My voice is a low growl, thick with restraint
and something darker, something primal. "I want to taste you so
bad I can't fucking sleep. Years, Ace. Do you hear me? Years."
My breath is ragged and burns in my lungs. "I have fought
myself for so long, trying to wait until you're ready. But if you
keep looking at me like that..." I exhale sharply, my forehead
almost touching hers. "I will lose control."

"I-I-" She stammers, her lips parted to let out short, quick
breaths. She panicking.

God, the big doe-eyed thing makes my blood burn.

Her panic only fuels the fire inside me. I reach for her neck,
wrapping my fingers around the delicate throat—not tight, just
enough to feel the frantic pulse beneath her skin. I drag my
nose along her cheek, inhaling her scent, letting it fill my lungs
—my mind.

"Tell me to stop." My voice is barely human—a rasp of
need. "Because if you don't, I won't. I need you, baby."

"Noah," she whimpers, and my hips rut forward like a
horny fucking teenager.

"You have no idea, baby." It takes all the self-control I have
not to lick her fucking face just to get a little taste of her skin.

I'll kill her fucking fiancé if I have to. He needs to move out
of my way.

"Stop, Noah," she whispers, and I pull away like someone
shoved me. It's violent and painful, but she has to want it.

"When you're ready. I'm waiting." I place my hand back on
her thigh, and she squeezes them together. "Finish your pizza."

NINE

IT'S BEEN THREE DAYS, and I still haven't been able to catch my breath. I can feel his hand on my throat.

I'm sitting here, next to the man I've promised to marry, and I'm thinking about Noah. What is wrong with me?

My hands tremble as I smooth out the skirt of my dress beneath the table.

Colson picked this outfit, but I feel out of place. His family is dressed like they're going to Easter service.

Everything about me feels big and clumsy under their watchful eyes.

I always feel like they're waiting for me to spill my wine or use the wrong fork.

We've been here for forty-five minutes, and the staff has only brought out two of what I'm told will be five courses.

The dining table seats twenty-six. There are six of us here.

Everything is oak, delicate crystal, and polished silver. The art hanging from the walls is original. A Monet and a Degas.

There is wealth and luxury in every minor detail. Everything in this room, from the furniture to the drapes to the salt and pepper shakers, costs more than my salary.

His father has taken three business calls since we got here. His mother is so elegant and poised. Her hair is perfect, and there isn't a single wrinkle in her cream-colored silk blouse. When we got here, she gave me a thin, tight-lipped smile and then went to the drink cart to make a martini.

Today, we have the pleasure of dining with his aunt and his grandmother. I can never tell which one hates me more.

His aunt has sharp eyes with pointed features and a face that doesn't really move or express emotion when she talks.

His grandma, who didn't bother to acknowledge me at all, is wealth personified. She just looks like money. The simple, understated pearl earrings she's wearing probably cost more than my car. She's the most put-together woman I've ever seen in a room full of other put-together women.

Colson's beside me with his hand on my knee under the table.

I think he's trying to comfort me. It's not working.

At least his older brother and his girlfriend aren't here today. Watching them smile warmly at Brittany only makes their icy disinterest in me that much more noticeable.

It's not outright rudeness. No one is cruel to my face. They nod, they smile—curt, distant. They ask polite, surface-level questions about my job and my interests. I could tell they weren't pleased when they found out that I was neither an accomplished equestrian or even remotely interested in archery, golf, or tennis.

Staring at my salad, I try to keep my lips from tugging too noticeably downward.

A tomato salad. A whole salad of just tomatoes. I hate tomatoes.

Colson clears his throat, and I freeze. Oh, god, not yet.

"We wanted to share some news." He turns to me with a small smile before facing his family again. "Candace and I are engaged."

Silence.

No one moves or makes a sound for several seconds.

It feels like it stretches on for eternity.

His mother blinks, and his aunt sets down her fork. His grandmother exhales through her nose. I think his dad might be using his phone to read emails below the table.

"Well," his mom clears her throat, "that's unexpected."

No congratulations are given. No one asks to see the ring.

This must be really bad because even Colson looks uncomfortable, and he's usually oblivious to how much they don't like me.

"I'm finally settling down." He looks toward his moneybags grandma—the dollar signs practically glowing in his eyes.

"I suppose we should start planning, then." She looks like she's holding back a sigh. "And, of course, we'll need to speak with the lawyers."

Of course.

His mother and aunt begin planning the wedding right there. The best dates, venues, and people they need to invite—I'm not included or considered at any point. His grandmother just stares, almost blankly, sometimes her eyes finding me, then her lips spread flat, and she looks away.

Colson and his dad talk cars and stocks.

I'm excluded from both conversations, so I just sit and sip my water, waiting for this course to be over.

By the time lunch is finally over, I feel like we've been sitting here for five days. They've decided on an outdoor wedding in the spring.

Apparently, Brittany wants a winter wedding, so they want to keep it open just in case.

How kind of them to consider her thoughts for a hypothetical wedding when planning my real one?

After the world's longest lunch, I excuse myself.

Staring at my baby pink dress in the mirror, I feel ridiculous. I don't look chic; I look like a child. The little flowers all over the fabric are mocking me.

The diamond on my finger feels like a boulder pulling me down and drowning me.

The house is massive, artwork strategically lining the walls, statues in niches—rooms just for sitting and even stranger rooms just for looking at.

Walking as slowly as I can, I look at the paintings—planning my escape.

Colson has to be at the airport in three hours. That means we have to leave in two or he won't have time to drop me at home.

I can make two more hours. That's just one hundred and twenty minutes. Sixty minutes twice. It's just four half hours.

They make me feel so small and worthless. I can learn to fit in. It might not happen overnight, but I will make myself the kind of woman who doesn't embarrass their family.

Stopping in the middle of the hallway, I turn, looking behind me. I think I made a wrong turn somewhere.

Walking toward the back of the house, I listen for voices.

The open French doors that lead out to the terrace seem like a logical place to look.

I hear the faint clinking of glass and hushed voices, so I stop short.

Pausing just out of sight, I listen.

His mother, his aunt, and his grandmother huddled together under a large, white deck umbrella. One or all of them are smoking. I can smell the acrid scent that permeated every surface of my childhood home. Their voices are low but sharp. I shouldn't listen.

"She's classless," his mom sighs. "A state school girl? We sent him to Harvard! He couldn't meet a respectable young lady there?"

"Cheap," his grandmother adds. "It's embarrassing. The Barrington name deserves better. Candy." She sighs. "Of course, her name is Candy." This is more words than I've ever heard her speak.

"And a gold digger, obviously." His aunt tuts. "This is exactly why we need that prenup finalized. Quickly."

Then, someone gasps. "Oh, god! I hope she's not pregnant!" His mom sounds like she might sob at any second.

"That would at least make this make sense!" His aunt laughs bitterly. "Honestly, what is he thinking?"

"He isn't." His grandmother sounds angry now. "Well, at least not with his head. If he did get her pregnant, maybe we can use that to our advantage. I'm sure a trashy girl like that would take money. We could pay her off. Abort and leave him alone. She would probably jump for half a million, but we can make it even just to be safe."

"I'll call him tonight. If she is pregnant, we have to act fast."

"Call Trent. He listens to him. Isn't he going on this 'boys' trip?' Maybe he can pull him aside, have a heart-to-heart." His aunt sounds hopeful.

"I'll call him right now!"

My heart hurts.

I knew they didn't like me. They never tried to hide it. But this is worse than I thought.

Stepping back, careful not to make a sound, I rush back down the hallway. My vision blurs, but I won't cry. Not because of them.

Squaring my shoulders and raising my chin, I search for the kitchen. I'll ask anyone I can find to bring me to Colson.

He chose me.

He wants to marry me.

They can hate me if they want to.

For the next hour and twenty-six minutes, I count in my head. Minute after minute in silence. No one speaks to me, so I don't even attempt to add anything to the conversation.

They talk about cousin Claudia and her upcoming baby shower. I've never met Claudia. Then, they talk about the current state of the luxury car market. It's riveting stuff.

"The luxury car market is at a crossroads." His dad shakes his head. "We're caught between heritage and the future."

"People are trying to be conscious of their carbon footprints now." Colson looks equally saddened by this.

"Brands I never thought would give in to that kind of pressure are scrambling to stay relevant in this new era. Status symbols are shifting from raw horsepower to eco-conscious innovation. Fucking woke bullshit." His dad grinds his teeth.

My mind drifts far away from here. Back to a greasy little pizza parlor with Noah.

I don't want to think about it. About him. But the memory sneaks, slipping into my mind at the worst possible times.

Noah.

The way he touched me... the things he said.

My stomach churns, all of that fancy, expensive food rolling around.

I shift in my chair, trying to shake the feeling, but it lingers —heavy, sticky, impossible to ignore.

He made me feel things I don't understand. A squirming, fluttering, warm feeling in my stomach that thumped in time with my pulse.

Days later, I still feel flushed.

"Candy, we should head out. I have to catch my flight." Colson finally squeezes my knee.

I have to fight the urge to jump for joy.

After a short, cold goodbye, we're finally out. I can finally breathe.

Colson drives down the long driveway and through the wrought-iron gates onto the street inside their gated community.

He hums along with the radio, happy as a clam.

For a few moments, I try to keep quiet, but the weight of this afternoon is sitting heavily on my chest.

"I overheard your mom, aunt, and grandmother talking about me after lunch."

Colson glances at me, his eyebrows pulling in. "What are you talking about?"

I take a shaky breath. "I overheard them on the terrace. They called me classless and cheap. They're afraid that I'm pregnant, and that's why we're getting married."

His hands tighten on the steering wheel, his jaw shifting. "Candace...you must have misheard them."

"I didn't."

He exhales sharply, shaking his head. "They wouldn't say things like that."

"I'm telling you I heard them. Clear as day. There was no room for interpretation. They're planning to call your brother to get him to talk to you on your trip!"

He angrily turns off the radio. "They're just...protective. We're wealthy, Candace. People are always trying to take advantage of that. They have to be cautious. Don't take it personally."

My chest tightens. "So you're defending them? They called me trash, Colson. I'm going to take that personally!"

He glances at me again, something unreadable flickering in

his eyes. "I'm saying they're looking out for me. For our family. If you had a single decent person in your family, you would understand."

"Maybe my family is trash, but they would never treat you like that!"

"Of course they wouldn't! I'm rich! They wouldn't want to run off their meal ticket!" He presses his foot down on the accelerator, and the car lurches forward as he speeds around other cars—weaving through traffic.

"Meal ticket?" I scoff. "First of all, you have never given a cent to anyone in my family! I pay all of my own bills and bought everything I own!"

He rolls his eyes. "Right, but when we get married, you don't think we're moving into your shitty apartment, do you? You obviously can't afford to live where I do. I'll be paying for that."

My shitty apartment. I'm proud of that apartment and my independence.

I sit back in my seat and close my eyes.

"What do you want me to do, Candy? They're my family."

"And I'm going to be your wife!"

He turns hard left, pulling into my apartment complex.

"I'll see you next week. Fix this attitude before I get back."

Yanking my seatbelt off, I climb out of the car and slam the door. Without looking back, I jog into the apartment and slam that door closed, too.

"Fuck!"

"Whoa!" Stella steps out of the kitchen. "What happened?"

"Nothing. I don't want to talk about it."

She nods. "Want to drink about it instead?"

"Yes!" I have a lot to drink about.

TEN

"I'M GOING to put on pantyhose." I run back into my room. I won't enjoy myself in a skirt this short without a barrier of protection against unwanted contact.

"There's a live band, apparently." She yells across the house from her room.

I rush out into the hallway, almost tripping over my half-pulled-on tights. Her bucket list! "Wait—"

"I'm trying it! Fuck it!" She squeals. "Tonight is the night! I'm doing it!"

I manage to stumble out into the hallway, hopping on one foot to adjust the other leg. "Wait, don't you at least want to see if they're any good first?"

She stops. "Yeah, you're right. If I'm going to fuck a lead singer, I want him to at least be a good singer." She laughs.

I roll my eyes, but can't help the smile tugging at my lips. Tonight is going to be interesting.

"You can drink, though. I'll drive." She snatches my keys from my hand and throws them across the living room.

"I'll drive. I don't mind." I won't drink unless someone I trust is going to be sober. Never again.

"No way, girl." She shakes her head. "I'm driving. I have absolutely no shame. I don't need to be drunk to fuck a stranger!" She laughs. "You look smoking hot. You go ahead and drink. Have fun, and I'll have your back."

"Thanks." I almost choke on the word. She doesn't know. But she does. We've never talked about it. Not about the specifics. But sometimes she says things like that, and it almost knocks me off my feet.

She gives me a knowing smile and throws her arm around my shoulders. "Let's roll, baby!"

It's not until I'm securely trapped by my seatbelt and she has already started to drive that she tells me the more important details of this trip.

"So, this club is in Columbia..." She grits her teeth and stares straight ahead.

"Columbia? We're driving an hour to go to a club?" Then it hits me. Of course. She has ulterior motives!

"Be honest with me." I turn in my seat to face her. "Are you going to this club because you want to scope it out before your brother starts working there?"

"What?" She sounds offended by the accusation, but her refusal to make eye contact with me tells me what I need to know.

"Stella Marie Gaines!"

"Alright!" She hangs her head. "I'm worried about him! I just want to make sure it's not some sleezy place!"

"What if it is a sleezy place? And we're there alone, dressed like this!" I gesture down to the skirt that feels like it's shrinking by the second. "He's almost thirty!"

"I know!" She cringes. "But he just got out of jail. I'm worried about him. He's always been a loner. Jace was his only friend. I'm just checking it out. If it's awful, we'll leave! I promise! And I'll buy you ice cream on the way home."

Narrowing my eyes, I can't help but think that she doesn't know her brother very well. Something tells me he's much more capable than she thinks he is...

"A double scoop. Triple!"

"Fine," I grumble.

"Thank you. I love you!"

"Yeah, yeah."

"It's called The Violet House." She hums. "That's a good sign, right?"

"Definitely! Any place named after the prettiest color can't be bad."

"Well, we'll just double-check."

"Noah is so lucky he has his two guard dogs!" I tease her.

"He's only twenty-nine! And barely breaking six feet four! Practically a baby!" Her voice cracks, her laughter slipping through.

"Yeah, a helpless baby, alright."

"I'm sorry!" She pretends to cry. "My mom is putting all these stupid ideas in my head. She's convinced he's going to be a drug dealer or something."

"It's fine. Maybe it's a nice club. Just tell me the truth. If I had known this was a scouting mission, I wouldn't have worn this skirt." I tug at the hem, willing it to grow another inch.

"The skirt is amazing. It makes your ass look great."

"Right." I swallow the knot in my throat.

"You're not showing any skin." She must sense my nervousness. "You look gorgeous, but very classy."

If she's trying to make me feel better, she's having the opposite effect. I didn't tell her about Colson's family. I know she would be furious. It's too embarrassing. I don't feel classy.

"In case this place sucks, we should have fun in the car." She hands me her phone. "You can be DJ Jams tonight."

"Alright, alright, it's Friday night, and you know what that means—time to turn it up and let loose! I'm DJ Jams, and I've got a lineup of the hottest throwbacks to kickstart your weekend. First up, we've got a banger that'll have you sweating—let's go!" I yell out in my best radio host voice before starting an early 2000s boy band classic.

We spend the rest of the drive singing obnoxiously loud and dancing.

Even if the club is terrible, this part made it worth it.

"It doesn't look like we're in a dangerous ghost town." I look out the window at the streets as we get close to the club. "The GPS says we're arriving in two minutes."

"Is that it?" I point across the street to a corner with a line wrapped around the side of a building.

"Oh, my god, it is!" She lets out a loud sigh of relief. "It actually looks nice!"

"I think we can pay to park in this lot."

"I was so nervous, Candy!" She squeals. "This looks like a legit club. I'm so relieved."

There is a buzz in the air as we walk toward the crowd.

A man in a suit is standing on the corner, scanning the line. "You two, come inside."

"Us?" I look behind to see if he's talking to someone else.

"Yes. We let the pretty girls cut the line here."

"Hell yeah!" Stella cheers as my cheeks burn.

Inside, the whole place hums with energy, a pulsing, electric charge that rumbles in my chest the moment we step inside. It's the kind of place that makes you feel alive, whether you want to or not.

The walls are sleek black, polished and smooth like glass that absorbs the flashes of bright neon light. Lights pulse in time with the music—it's like standing in the middle of a lightning storm. There is a modern, funky feeling—a mix of old and new. I like it.

Two long bars stretch across opposite ends of the club, and rows of glass shelves are backlit in violet light, making the bottles look like amethyst crystals.

The dance floor in the center of the room is a writhing mass of people. There is something distinctly sexual about the music. The live band onstage isn't just playing—they're performing. The lead singer— a woman— with a voice like honey and smoke, sings the seductive lyrics.

I swallow hard, already feeling the burn in my stomach, that nervous twisting that never really goes away, no matter what I do.

"Drink?" Stella yells over the noise, leaning in close so I can hear.

I hesitate, then nod. Just one. Just enough to loosen the knot in my chest.

We slip through the crowd to the nearest bar, where a bartender with silver rings on every finger and a lip piercing raises an eyebrow at me. "What's your poison?"

"Tequila, please."

Stella orders a club soda and spins around to lean against the bar while she watches the club.

"The singer is a woman." She frowns.

"She's pretty." I shrug.

"Gorgeous, but not my type."

I know her type. Tall, blonde, and preferably pierced in unmentionable places. The bartender might be a good fit.

"Here you go, ladies." He sets our drinks down, and his eyes linger on Stella.

Shaking my head, I take the glass. It's cool against my fingers. Taking a breath, I toss it back and pinch my eyes closed. A trail of heat blazes down my throat and into my stomach.

"I'm going to hold off on ordering another." I find Stella already watching me.

"No pressure. Have another, or don't. It's up to you." She smiles, and I genuinely feel no pressure.

"Come on," she yells, taking my hand. "Dance with me."

I let her pull me onto the dance floor. The heavy bass of this song rattles my bones. We move with the music, holding hands to stay together.

The tightly packed bodies are overwhelming–too many people touching me– but I close my eyes and listen to the lyrics.

"Give it to me again. Pull my hair. Bring me over to the mirror so I can see it go in..."

My eyes fly open. Holy shit.

Suddenly, it feels like someone is standing too close. We're packed in here, but this person is all up in our space.

Turning, I recognize him immediately, even with his new look.

"Jace!" Stella screams, grabbing him by the neck to hug him.

He looks very different from the last time I saw him. He has always been a tall, lanky guy with buzzed hair. At Noah's trial, he had a few tattoos on his arms. Now he has them up his neck and on his head. Plus, he grew a full beard.

"Are you having a good time?" He looks between us.

"Yes! This place is amazing!"

"I love the decorations." I lean in.

He smirks at me but quickly turns to Stella. "Can I buy you a drink?"

"Oh, not me. I'm driving tonight! But you can dance with me!" She takes his hand.

He doesn't hesitate. He pulls her into him, and just like that —he's putty in her hands.

They look good together.

I step back, giving them space to move. The second I do, something shifts. A wave of unease rolls down my spine.

I spin around just as a hand clamps around my wrist.

He's holding me too tightly.

And he's standing too close—tall and cocky, with the kind of smirk that makes my skin crawl. "Come dance." He's already pulling me in before I can answer.

"No, thanks." I yank my arm back, but his fingers tighten, dragging me a few steps closer.

"Don't be like that. Just one dance. I promise you'll have fun!"

"P-Please, I don't want to." I feel panic—my heart pounds against my ribs. I need to get away. I grab his hand and try to pull his hand off.

His grip tightens, but only for a second.

And then it vanishes—releasing me completely.

A hand comes out of nowhere, grabbing the guy's wrist and yanking him backward with enough force to nearly knock him off balance.

Noah.

I don't even have to see his face to know it's him. His hands.

The guy stumbles, blinking up at the man who now towers over him. "What the fu—"

Noah leans in, his voice so low I can't hear what he says, but whatever it is, it drains the blood from the guy's face. His smirk vanishes, and his body goes rigid.

Without a word or another glance, he's gone—disappearing into the crowd.

Noah straightens, his gaze snapping to mine. His expression is unreadable, but his grip on my wrist is firm. Possessive.

He doesn't say a word. He just pulls me off the dance floor, and I let him.

Through the club and into a back hallway, he doesn't say a word. In the dimly lit hall, he punches a code into a keypad, and a large metal door opens.

It's an office.

"Noah, wha—"

He grabs me, pulling me up into his arms—slamming my back against the wall.

"Don't let people touch you, Ace." He rubs his nose against my neck.

"I didn't want him to. I was trying to stop him."

He hums, "Wrap your legs around me."

"Wait...I—"

"Do it."

When my legs lock around his waist, he groans. "Good girl."

Behind him, on the opposite wall, is a window; the mirrored glass is the shelves full of alcohol behind the bar.

"Where are we?"

"My office."

"You have an office here?" Why would a bouncer and possible bartender have an office?

"I'm going to go find that motherfucker and break his fucking hands."

"Wait. No! Noah, you're on probation!"

He laughs, his head falling back.

On the column of his throat, the skull tattooed on his skin is staring right at me.

"What are you doing here?" He brings his face level with mine.

"Um..." I don't want to rat Stella out.

He hums, a lopsided smile pulling at his lips. "I see. Don't come here again unless I'm with you."

I feel myself nodding.

"Good." His eyes move around my face. "You look so pretty tonight, baby."

"Thank you," I whisper.

Something about the way he says it makes me believe it.

"I want to go out there and pluck the eyes from everyone who saw you. They don't deserve it."

A horrified chuckle bubbles up in my throat. "You're so violent!"

"It's my nature."

"No, it's not." An ache settles in behind my heart.

"Oh, no?" His eyebrows quirk up. "What's my nature then, baby?"

"I've never seen you do a single violent thing. And I've known you a long time."

He hums. "I hide it well, but trust me, deep down, it's pitch black. I only care about one thing."

"Only one?"

"Just one." He shifts his hips slightly, and I feel him between my legs.

"N-Noah—"

"Tell me you're ready for it. Give it to me." He leans in, his lips ghostly over mine.

"Noah, I'm engaged." I stutter.

"Fuck him."

"I—" Bile rises in my throat.

"Fuck." He roars and sets me down on my feet. "Come on."

Taking my hand again, he stalks out of the office, letting the door slam behind us. He seems angry, but his grip on me is soft.

We walk down the long hallway, away from the dance floor and out a back door.

"I just need air." He sucks in a breath.

A group of young-looking men, probably very early twenties, are gathered around smoking.

"Put those out." He tells them calmly but with a heavy authority.

"What?" One of them scoffs.

"Put the fucking cigarettes out. Now." He steps in front of me. I'm not sure if it's his height, the circumference of his arms, or the tattoos—maybe a combination—but they quickly obey.

After they leave, he steps off the curb, spinning me like a ballerina before sitting down and bringing me into his lap. Our noses touch—we're always too close. He wraps his arms around me, resting his hands on my ass.

"Noah," I whisper. He makes me feel so confused. I should run away, but I can't ever make my legs move.

ELEVEN

NOAH

"DO YOU WANT ANOTHER DRINK?"

"Another?" Her brows knit together. "How do you know I had one?"

I smile. Slow. Easy. Let her wonder. "I was watching you."

It's cute that she hasn't figured that out yet.

Having her sit like this is dangerous. The warmth of her body is so fucking close, the way she shifts without realizing the effect she has. It makes every depraved thought I've ever had about her throb like an open wound. I could touch her. I could wreck her. She wouldn't stop me.

She has no idea.

I bet her pussy is just as perfect as the rest of her—soft, tight, trembling under my hands.

I should've stopped this before it started. When I realized they were coming here, I almost called Stella to make plans just to stop them. This was fucking dangerous. She can't be out like this.

What the fuck were they thinking? If I hadn't called Manny, they would still be standing outside in line.

Fucking reckless.

She shifts, eyes darting to my mouth, then back up. Her lips part. She's nervous. Good.

"Why are you looking at me like that?" She whispers.

I tip my head, dragging my gaze over her, slow and deliberate. Letting her feel it. "Because I want to punish you for putting yourself in danger tonight."

Her breath hitches. "Punish me?"

"Yes, baby."

"How?"

Those fucking doe eyes. Goddamn it.

"Do you feel how hard I am for you?" I rock my hips up. She squeezes her thighs around my hips. "I would make you come until you couldn't take another one. You wouldn't be able to move the next day without feeling me everywhere."

"That's how you would punish me?" Her breathless voice and the slight rasp in it make my cock leak.

"Yes. You would have to beg me to stop eating your pussy. And then I would make you come again before I actually stopped."

Her breath catches.

"You didn't wear the ring tonight." I move on quickly, jerking her away from the fire before she gets burned.

"No." She looks down.

"Good girl."

Her eyes flash up to meet mine. "Did you get this tattoo in prison?"

"Which one?"

Her fingers come up, nervous and hesitant to touch my throat.

More pre-cum.

"Yes. My cellmate was very talented."

She hums.

"You need to go home, Ace."

"But—"

"No buts. Right now." The look in her eyes almost makes me reconsider. I could drive her home myself. But if I did that, I'm fucking her. There's no way around that.

"I want you to do something for me."

"What?" She picks her nails.

"Tonight, when you get into your bed, after you've taken off this little tiny skirt and washed off your makeup, I want you to make yourself come."

She gasps and her body jerks, just enough to give my cock enough friction to make me groan. Dropping my head back, I stare up at the cloudy night sky.

"Noah, I can't—" she whispers. "I can't do that."

"Yes, you can." My body is screaming.

"I don't do that."

"Ever?"

Oh, fuck. It's going to be better than I thought.

She shakes her head, nervousness rippling in her eyes.

"Stand up."

She looks confused, but does it anyway.

Spinning her around, I bring her back down into my lap with her back to my chest. With one arm wrapped around her chest, holding her still, I let the other hand rest on her stomach.

"You're going to take off your panties and slip your hand down between your legs."

Her breaths come out in shallow pants as I slide my fingers under her skirt and the sheer black tights she's wearing.

"Then you're going to rub your fingers in circles on your clit just like this." I touch her, and her body jerks.

"Noah!" Her voice and body tremble.

"Can you do that for me, baby? Just like that."

She relaxes as I pull my hand out.

"Ok." Her whisper is so quiet. I almost don't hear it.

"Come on." I help her stand and then lead her back inside. She's wobbly. Good.

Wading through the crowd, I keep a tight grip on her little hand, holding her close.

Stella and Jace are grinding on each other in the center of the dance floor.

"Take her home." I grab her shoulder. "Now."

She opens her mouth to protest, but Jace leans in, whispering something that has her face lighting up.

"Alright." She smiles sweetly. I watch them walk out, hand in hand.

I'll give them a few minutes' head start. If I don't take care of my cock, I'm not going to make it home.

Jace lifts his chin, and I do the same. I don't have time for small talk and bullshit.

Fuck. It hurts. The pressure has moved up into my stomach, a crippling, desperate ache. I've got my belt open before I even manage to slam the door to my truck.

Yanking it out, I spit on it and immediately start a fast rhythm with my fist.

Leaning back in my seat, I don't try to keep quiet. I've been hard for so long. This has to be fast and loud.

I was so close. If I had just slid my fingers down, I would have been able to feel her soft skin. She was wet. I know she was. The fear didn't outweigh the arousal.

Pressing my heels into the floorboard, I rock my hips forward to meet each stroke.

"Ace, holy fuck!" I imagine her tongue giving little kitten licks to the head of my cock. I make a mess, coming all over my chest with a groan.

I'm barely satisfied.
But it will do for now.
Maybe I'll go again while watching her.

TWELVE

I'M SO NERVOUS.

This is stupid. I pace around my room.

Stella excitedly talked about Jace all the way home. She didn't even notice my panic, which was good. But now I'm home with this horrible task in front of me.

How am I going to do this?

My pussy is broken. It can't feel pleasure. I think he stole that from that night. It's not that I haven't tried. I just can't find anything that feels right.

Staring up at the ceiling, I consider crawling into bed and sleeping. He'll never know I didn't do it.

Turning out the light, I bury myself in my blankets.

I did everything else he said. My face is clean, and I'm not wearing panties under my pajama bottoms.

That's good enough. I tried.

My phone dings. I scramble to grab it. Colson hasn't responded to any of my texts all day.

> Did you get home ok?

I don't reply right away. My thumb hovers over the keyboard before I force myself to type something neutral.

Yeah. You?

His response comes quicker than I expected. It's immediate.

Good.

Good? That doesn't answer my question.

Taking a deep breath, I push my hand past the waistband of my pajamas, my fingers hesitating against my skin. I can do this.

I don't want to—but I should try. At least, I think I don't want to. Maybe I do. Maybe this will quiet my thoughts, ease the restless energy curling through my veins.

"I'll just touch exactly where he did." I roll my shoulders back. My phone dings.

Little circles, baby.

I gasp, sitting up and throwing my covers off my head. I listen in the dark, but there isn't any sound.

"I think it was just an instruction. A reminder." I lie back and cover my face again.

Sliding my hand down again, I place my fingers exactly where his had been, my skin still thrumming with phantom heat. My breathing deepens, and I try—really try—to focus on the sensation, to chase the pleasure I should be feeling.

But my mind won't stay quiet. It refuses to settle into the moment.

Instead, I see him. The way he looked at me—like he

owned me, like he would rip apart the world if it so much as touched me wrong. The protective set of his jaw, the dark suit clinging to his frame, the weight of his gaze.

It's too much.

Frustration knots in my stomach, replacing any flicker of pleasure I felt before. I rip my hand away and roll onto my side, squeezing my eyes shut.

This isn't working.

Shoving my phone under my pillow, I refuse to check it again.

As I start to drift, a nervous feeling creeps up my spine. Oh, god, not tonight.

But it's too late, I'm already gone.

It starts the same. I'm waking up in a fog–with pain all around me and pressure on my chest.

But then something different happens. Something that hasn't ever happened before.

He stops.

When I open my eyes and they adjust to the light, I'm still in the gazebo with the string of dangling lights twinkling about me, but I'm alone.

Sitting up, I look around.

At first, I can't see him, but I feel him. He's nearby.

Noah.

Then he's there.

I don't know how, but he steps into the dream like he belongs there, cutting through the shadows and scattering them.

His hand finds mine—not grabbing, not forcing, just there. A choice.

And I take it.

He makes the dark feel less dark–like there is still light around us.

Sitting here together in the gazebo, we're quiet but not uncomfortable. His presence is enough. We don't have to talk.

It's so nice. I never noticed the cool breeze and the bushes covered in little white flowers growing all around the little wicker hut.

When everything doesn't seem like a shadow ready to pounce, this place is kind of beautiful.

"Thanks, Noah." I rest my head on his shoulder. I don't have to explain it here. He just knows.

Tears prick my eyes, leaving a trail of stinging skin behind when they fall. Bitter and acidic, they burn.

"I wish this were real."

"I know, Ace."

This time when I wake up, I'm not sweating or crying or gasping for air.

Lying in bed, staring up at my ceiling, I imagine what life would be like if that night never happened.

This is a downward spiral I should stay away from.

I know that.

But it's hard not to imagine the possibilities. Maybe I would have continued on to law school. Or maybe some other completely unrelated things would have derailed those plans.

Maybe I would know what it's like to have a healthy, meaningful sex life.

Or maybe I wouldn't.

That night might not have changed anything about the trajectory of my future. It could have never happened, and I still would be exactly where I am today.

Colson never called or texted me.

Good morning! Have fun today!

I'm sure he won't reply.

Rolling out of bed, I make my way to my closet. Moving the clothes around, I find the violet-colored skirt suit that Colson said looked unprofessional.

I'm in a violet mood.

THIRTEEN

SLOWLY, I stand from my desk, gathering my purse and phone to take a much-needed lunch. Today has been a long day, and it's only noon.

Then, I see him.

My body freezes, my muscles locking up. At first, I think I must be imagining it. He shouldn't be here. He has no reason to be here.

Yet there he is.

He's leaning against the front desk like he belongs—his dark eyes scanning the room until they land on me. My fingers tighten around the strap of my bag.

I'm a mouse in a trap.

He's dressed in all black—worn jeans, a fitted t-shirt that clings to his broad chest, the sleeves just barely tight around the muscle in his arms. Ink covers most of his visible skin. And his hair is just a little tousled, like he ran his hands through it too many times.

"Ace." His voice is easy. He has all the time in the world—no rush, no irritation, nothing but time.

I clear my throat. "What are you doing here?"

His lips twitch, but he doesn't quite smile. "Had to meet my parole officer."

"Oh, right." I start to stammer through a response when the door opens behind me.

"Mr. Gaines! I thought that was you!" My boss steps out of his office with a warm smile.

"Mr. Connors." Noah shakes his hand. "Good to see you."

"How's life treating you on the outside? I heard you go out early on good behavior. Keep it up, man." Mr. Connors has a genuine smile on his face and no judgment in his eyes. I hope Noah feels that, too. Like he's accepted and not scrutinized.

"Keeping my nose clean." Noah lifts his hands.

"Glad to hear it. I'm actually trying to roll out a post-parole program that introduces recently released people to local business owners! If you leave your information with Miss. Kennedy, I'll make sure to reach out."

"Oh, absolutely. Do you have a pen, Miss Kennedy?" He turns to me. His eyes pierce into my skin, burning me from the inside out.

"Um, here." I knock several pens out of my cup.

"Are you taking lunch now, Candace?" Mr. Connors is oblivious to what is happening right in front of him.

"Yes." My throat is so dry.

"Great. See you in an hour!" He turns back to Noah. "It was good to see you."

"You too." Noah drops the pen on my desk before sliding a paper with his information toward me.

"Lunch?" He tilts his head, like we do this all the time, like it's not completely absurd that a man like him is standing in the ADA's office, inviting me out.

I should say no. I should make an excuse.

But my mouth betrays me. "Yeah. Alright."

He nods once, satisfied, and holds the door open for me.

My shoes click against the marble floor as we walk through the courthouse lobby.

I step out into the midday sun, suddenly hyper-aware of him walking beside me. He draws attention. People look at him. Maybe it's the slight familiarity of his face from the news all those years ago. Or his height and tattoos. Maybe it's the undeniable attractiveness of his face. Whatever the reason, I feel like we're being watched.

"There are food trucks about a block that way." I point up the street.

"We can go wherever you want."

"Oh," I pick at my cuticles. "Ok."

"You look beautiful." He reaches down and takes my hand, forcing me to stop shredding my skin.

I know my cheeks are bright red.

"This is a good color on you."

"It's my favorite color."

"I know." His lips twitch.

The smell of grilled meat and spices fills the air as we get closer to the little courtyard where they park.

"We don't have to go to the same truck." My palm feels sweaty in his. "If you—"

"Which one do you want, Ace?"

"Tacos." I point.

"I like tacos." He places his hand on my neck—in that way that he always seems to—and leads me to the line.

We step up to order, and as soon as the girl at the window sees him, her entire face lights up.

"Hey there," she purrs, leaning forward just enough to emphasize the low-cut shirt she's wearing. "What can I get for you?"

I don't know why my stomach clenches, why my jaw tightens. I glance up at him, expecting to see him respond. But he doesn't even look at her.

Not once.

His eyes stay on me, unwavering, unreadable. It's unsettling. It's intense.

"What do you want, baby?" He asks, ignoring the girl completely.

I fumble with my purse, rattling off my order before he can rush me. When he orders his own, he reaches for his wallet before I can even attempt to pay. I pull out my card. "I got it."

He doesn't even acknowledge my words. Handing over cash like the idea of me paying is absurd. I frown, crossing my arms.

"You didn't have to do that."

"I know."

The way he says it—calm, matter-of-fact—makes my stomach do that weird flipping thing again. I don't understand it. I don't like it.

We take our food to a little group of picnic tables. The warm sun beats down on my skin, but all I can focus on is him. He's right beside me again. Too close.

The way he moves—quiet but purposeful—like he's always calculating something.

He doesn't speak right away, just unwraps his food and starts eating. Every few seconds, I feel his eyes on me. Not in a way that makes me uncomfortable. If anything, it's the opposite.

It's distracting.

I pick at my food, trying to ignore it, trying to ignore the way my heart is pounding for no reason. The silence stretches between us, thick and heavy. I should say something. Anything.

"So..." I hesitate. "You can't keep paying every time."

He arches a brow. "Yes, I can."

"But," I lean in, whispering. "You just got out. Money must be tight, Noah. You're about to move to Columbia and—"

There's a flicker of amusement in his eyes, but it's gone just as quickly. "I own part of the club."

I blink. "What club?"

"The Violet House."

"What?"

He nods, taking a slow sip of his drink. "I paid for half of the opening costs. I own half of it."

My brain short-circuits. "What?"

His mouth quirks. "I'm a silent partner until I'm off probation."

I stare at him.

My mouth opens, but the only thing I can think to say is 'what' again, so I close it instead.

"How did you pay for half of it?"

"I had a job since the summer I turned sixteen. That was ten years of savings. I transferred it over to him right before I went inside. He opened the club last year, and I've been getting paid since."

"So you're not a bouncer?"

"No." His lips twitch again. "But they don't need to know anything about that."

"Your family?" I don't understand.

"I'm very private. They wouldn't understand if I told them."

"Told them what?"

"What I do."

"For work?" I'm more confused now.

He licks his lips, his hand coming down on my thigh. I press my legs together.

A low hum rumbles in his chest. "I really like this skirt."

My fingers tremble as I pick at the paper my tacos are wrapped in.

"Did you do it?" He leans in. I don't have to ask what he's talking about.

"I—I tried." Oh god. I wish the ground would open up and swallow me whole.

"What happened?"

"It just doesn't feel good." I shrug, my eyes laser-focused on the to-go containers of salsa verde.

He inches closer, our legs pressed together with no more space between us. "You should have called me."

"But—"

His hand comes up to my neck, just a gentle squeeze. And the tip of his nose grazes my cheek. "I want you to try again tonight. And this time, if you're struggling, call."

"Noah," I hate the way my voice sounds so shaky.

"Finish your lunch, baby." He gives my neck one last squeeze before turning back to his food.

I can't eat now.

"Candace." He sets his food down again. "You need to eat your lunch. You'll be hungry later."

My stomach is clenched in a knot.

When I don't move, he lets out a sound that makes my blood pump faster. Kind of a growl. "Open."

"What?" I jerk my head to his.

"Open your fucking mouth." He reaches across and takes one of my tacos.

My eyes are about to fall out of my head as he brings it to my lips.

Slowly, I open my mouth and accept the bite.

"Good girl. Another."

He feeds me bite after bite until the whole thing is gone.

"Do I need to feed you the other one, or can you manage?"

"I'll do it."

He picks up his taco and begins to eat again.

I watch him chew. He even eats attractive...

Time swirls in every direction. The rest of my lunch hour is agonizingly slow but somehow much too fast. When it's time to leave, I don't want to go. But I need to get away from him.

The walk back to my office is so tense I hardly realize I'm walking—his palm firm and possessive against the small of my back. Every step feels slow and deliberate, like he's dragging this out just to make me squirm.

When we step inside, I move toward my desk, but he beats me there, pulling out my chair for me. I hesitate, watching him. The chair isn't an invitation—it's a trap.

I sit anyway.

And he leans down, caging me in, one hand braced on my desk, the other curling around the back of my chair. His breath fans over my cheek. I recognize the desperation in his voice. I heard it outside of the club, too.

"You know what I've been thinking about all fucking day?"

I swallow hard. "No."

His lips brush against my ear. My body is short-circuiting—shutting down.

"How badly I want to bend you over this desk. Push that little skirt up. Spread you open with my fingers and make a mess of you right here."

My stomach flips violently, heat blazing up my spine.

"Noah."

He ignores me, his grip on the chair tightening.

"You'd take it, wouldn't you? Hands splayed out, cheek pressed to the desk, waiting for me to fuck you so deep you'd feel me for days."

My breath stutters.

"I wouldn't be nice about it." His teeth graze my

earlobe. "I'd wreck you. Get you so cock-drunk you'd forget your name."

Oh god.

Sweat gathers on my forehead, and I'm panting like I ran a marathon.

"I bet you'd like that." His hand slides up the back of my chair, tangling in my hair, tugging just enough to make my scalp prickle. "I bet you'd beg for it."

"I—" I can't even get any words out.

He tsks, shaking his head. "I'm trying to be patient." His grip tightens. "Fuck, I'm trying not to rush you, but I can't wait forever. You're killing me. You belong to me, Ace. You always have." He groans. "I know you, baby. And I know you'd let me do whatever I want to you."

I squeeze my thighs together, my entire body burning.

"You're thinking about it now, aren't you?" He presses a kiss to my temple, so soft and gentle it doesn't belong anywhere near this man. "Thinking about me ruining you on this desk."

"No," I whisper, but it's a lie.

He laughs—dark and cold. "That's ok, baby. You don't have to admit it. I'll show you soon."

And then, just as easily as he pulled me under, he straightens up, smoothing his hands down his shirt like he didn't just drag me through the filthiest fantasy of my life.

"Have a good afternoon, Ace." He winks, turning for the door. "I'll see you soon."

I stare after him, chest heaving, body trembling.

What the fuck just happened?

FOURTEEN

"I THINK this is a bad idea, Stel."

"Oh, come on!" She tugs my hand. "Please! You don't have to get a reading. Just come in with me."

"Yeah, right." I know how these people are. Once I'm inside, she'll trap me into paying for a reading, too.

This place looks...shady.

The neon sign outside is flickering, half-dead. The first "R" is burnt out completely, and the "S" is barely hanging on.

"_EADINGS BY MRS. BISJOU"

FADED POSTERS of palmistry charts and zodiac wheels hang, peeling, against the glass with dusty candles on cande-labras decorating a table behind it.

A cardboard sign is taped to the door, written in fat Sharpie. "Cash only. NO refunds."

A curtain of beads and shells hanging on strings clicks as

we walk inside. The smell of incense is overwhelming in the air. My throat is tight and my eyes burn.

"Welcome, ladies!" A low, raspy voice calls from behind a glass counter.

Mrs. Bisjou.

The suspicion in my mind immediately changes to concern.

She is so old and frail. A tiny woman who looks like the weight of her wig and head scarf is going to topple her over. Her moth-eaten lace shawl covers her thin body. She smiles, her overdrawn lips disappearing. "Please come in!"

"Hi!" Stella bounces up to the counter. "I want to have a tarot reading."

"Of course," she gestures to a thick velvet curtain covering a doorway in the back of the shop. "Head on back." Her long, yellowing nails are barely covered in chipped red polish.

"Where is the crystal ball?" I whisper as we walk into the dimly lit back room.

"Shh. That's not tarot!" Stella plops down on the frayed cushions on the floor.

I curl up beside her, looking around at the peeling wallpaper and sunbleached pictures.

"Your aura is so open. It will be easy to get a read. Your energy is electric." She looks at Stella as she slowly eases herself onto her cushion across from us. The low table sitting between us has green felt on it, like it might have been a poker table that she dragged out of a casino dumpster and sawed the legs off of.

She turns her gaze to me, her watery eyes, ringed with smudged eyeliner, make me shift uncomfortably the longer she stares. "Your aura is closed off. You are very dark, darling. Your reading will be very interesting."

"Oh, I'm not–" The words die in my throat. "Ok." I cringe.

It will be a waste of twenty bucks and a few minutes of my time.

As I sit through Stella's reading, my reservations and suspicions fade away.

The Sun card, joy, success.

The Star card, hope and healing.

The Ten of Cups, emotional fulfillment and lasting happiness.

Maybe this isn't going to be so bad.

By the end of her reading, she's glowing.

"And now, you darling. Let's see what the cards want to reveal..." She rasps.

The first card hits the table with an unusually loud thud.

She shakes her head sadly. "The Tower." She purses her lips. "This shows upheaval and the collapse of old structures. Something in your life is crumbling, dear."

Great. Off to a wonderful start.

The second card. "This is the Five of Pentacles. This card brings hardship or feelings of abandonment."

"I'm sensing a trend here." I try to laugh, but it doesn't really come out that way. It's more of a cough.

My palms start to sweat as she flips the third card. "The Ten of Swords."

Stella gasps beside me.

"What? Is that one bad?" I panic.

"The Ten of Swords is a heavy one indeed. Betrayal. Ending. The final blow in a difficult cycle. Are you carrying old wounds, dear? This card signifies a low point but also a turning point. Things will begin to turn around for you."

"Ok." My voice wobbles. This is hitting harder than I thought it would.

She holds the final card in her hand, pausing to take a dramatic breath before flipping it over.

The Lovers.

I exhale, relieved. That can't be bad, right?

"And here is where you begin to see the changes. There are challenges all around you. Upheaval and challenges, but love will guide you through the dark. The Lover's card isn't just the promise of love but of the courage to rebuild, hand in hand, with your partner."

I feel better, and worse.

The negative cards ring true. But the Lovers card feels like a lie.

The only positive card seems out of reach.

We pay and step outside just as the sun is setting in the distance.

"At least yours was good." I lean into Stella as she wraps her arm around my shoulder.

"You had a good one at the end." Her attempt at light and happy falls flat. She feels bad.

"This isn't your fault, you know. I'm just a–" Whatever I was about to say is forgotten. "Is that Noah?" I blurt out, staring at his unmistakable face.

"What the hell is he doing here?" She stops walking mid-step.

He crosses the street, almost leisurely, like he's not surprised to see us at all.

"What are you doing down here?" Stella pulls him into a hug.

"I was meeting a friend."

"Here?" I don't mean to say it out loud.

"What are you doing here?" His eyes burn into mine.

"Tarot readings." Stella smiles.

"I know you're into that, but you, Ace?" He looks shocked.

"Um, no." I shake my head. "Not really. I just–"

"She had a bad reading. Be nice to her." Stella swats at him.

"You did?" His eyes soften.

"It was fine." I lie, pretending it didn't crush my spirit slightly.

"We should go eat!" She grabs my hand. "That will cheer you up!"

Sitting with Noah won't cheer me up; it will only confuse me more.

"Come on, Ace." He almost whispers.

And any reservations I had fly out the window. "Ok."

"What was wrong with your reading?" He takes my elbow, gently tugging me toward the inside of the sidewalk. His warm fingers guiding me, shielding me from the world.

"My cards were ominous." I try to smile, but for some reason, my chin trembles.

Maybe it's the soft way he's watching me. Or how his hand is still holding my elbow.

"You had one good card." Stella is still glowing from the wonderful fate that was just read to her.

"What card?" He stares at me like I'm the only thing in the world.

It's uncomfortable, and it makes me nervous. But... at the same time...

"I got the Lovers card," I whisper.

He doesn't say anything else, but something flickers in his eyes. I can't place it; it's dangerous and soft somehow. He reaches for the door to a restaurant, placing his hand on my back.

FIFTEEN

DIGGING AROUND IN MY CLOSET, I find the smallest pair of shorts I own. So small that the pockets hang out in the front, and my cheeks hang out in the back.

I'm setting a trap.

Maybe everything is a coincidence. But if I've learned one thing working for the DA's office–one coincidence is fine–more than one isn't a coincidence.

And now I'm going to test my theory.

He's watching me. Or at the very least, he's asking Stella about our plans, but I think it's more than that.

The other night, when he texted me, it was too perfectly timed. He knew I was hesitating right then. Then he showed up right as I was about to take lunch.

If he had been one minute later, we would have missed each other. But he was right on time.

Then he just so happens to be outside of a shady psychic's shop downtown? Right. I don't think so.

We're going to grab lunch, then get pedicures. Just a simple errand. If I'm right, he will come out of nowhere. If I'm wrong, I wore a pair of ridiculously short-shorts.

"Hey!" Stella whistles. "You look cute!"

"Ready?" We need to leave now before I lose my nerve. I feel like I'm poking the bear.

"Ready!" She bounces out the door, completely oblivious to what is happening.

The restaurant is busy, filled with the low hum of conversation and the clatter of silverware against plates. Everyone seems relaxed. There is no rush, just easy conversation. I shuffle on my feet, anxious to be seated.

"I'm starving," Stella whispers.

"Me too." A delicious, greasy burger is waiting for me.

But then he walks in.

He moves like a storm cloud, barely leashed rage coiled tight beneath his skin.

His shoulders are stiff, his jaw locked, his hands clenched into fists at his sides. His usual slow, self-assured gait is replaced with something sharper, each step edged with restrained violence. He's heading right for us.

Oh, shit.

My spine stiffens.

"Hey! Noah!" Stella smiles before it quickly morphs into a frown.

"Right this way, ladies." The hostess steps up right in time.

"Table for three." Noah never takes his eyes off me.

"Oh, sure." She quickly grabs another menu, and instead of silverware.

Stella follows her into the restaurant. I attempt to do the same, but his hand comes up to grip the back of my neck.

"You are in so much fucking trouble." He whispers calmly in my ear as he leads me to our table.

Oh, shit.

He doesn't say anything, just pulls out the chair beside me and drops into it, exhaling sharply through his nose.

I glance at him, unsure. His expression is unreadable, but the heat rolling off him is undeniable.

"Um, so you wanted a burger?" Stella tries to cut through the tension.

I nod.

I try to ignore it, focusing on the menu in front of me, but the tension between us is suffocating. He's fuming.

The words ripple on the page, so I can't even read them.

I'm guessing he doesn't like the shorts...

After a beat, I clear my throat, forcing a small, casual smile. "Hey," I say lightly, like I don't feel the weight of his rage vibrating against my skin. "How's work?"

He doesn't look at me. "Fine."

I blink. "That's it?"

His fingers drum against the tabletop, his only response.

Yikes.

I shift, adjusting the napkin in my lap, then try again. "How's the new apartment?"

A muscle clenches in his jaw. "Fine."

Jesus.

The tension is unbearable. I'm about to melt into my seat. I'm a puddle of sweat and nerves.

Stella's phone rings, and for a moment, it's like she forgets where she is.

"Oh, um." She curls her big smile into her mouth. "I have to take this. If they come while I'm gone, will you get me a mushroom bacon burger with fries?"

No! Please don't leave me here alone!

"Sure," I hope the thing happening on my face right now is a smile.

"What the fuck are you wearing?" He turns to face me.

"Well," I look down at my shorts. "I..."

Do I go with the truth here?

"Are you following me?"

"What?" His expression changes. The rage is still there, but his lips twitch, just a little bit, but I notice it.

"Are you following me?"

"Is that what this is? A little trap."

"Yes." I clear my throat. "I thought if you were following me and you saw me dressed like this, it would force you to come out. Did it work?"

He reaches over, taking my hand, and gently sets it down on his pants.

Gasping, I look down at the long, hard bulge in his jeans.

"It worked."

He sets his hand down on top of mine, keeping it there. "So you are following me?"

"Yes."

"Why?"

"I always have."

"What?" I jerk, looking up at him.

"I told you. You belong to me. You're mine, Ace. Always. If you're ever worried about being alone—don't. I'm there."

I want to ask more questions, but Stella comes back to the table like she's floating on cloud nine.

He not only admitted to me that he is watching me, but he always has. Always. What does that even mean?

"Hi, I'm Tracy. I'll be at your server today. Have you had a chance to look over the menu?"

"Go ahead, Stella." I scramble to pick something.

"And for you?"

"I'll just take this." I point to a picture of a burger on the menu.

"The bacon cheeseburger, nice. Fries with that?"

"Yes, please." My voice sounds squeaky. High-pitched and nervous.

"Anything for you?" She turns her attention to Noah.

"No."

"O-Ok. Well, if you change your mind." Her voice fades out. I think she had more to say, but she couldn't bring herself to finish it.

"They have really good shakes here. We should get one after!" Stella looks between us.

"We're going to Finnagan's after," Noah says.

"We are?" Stella and I both ask at the same time.

"Yes."

"I haven't been there in forever!" She smiles. "We never went without you." That soft, loving look takes over her face.

Noah seems completely unaffected by this.

"We'll go get our nails done after ice cream." She turns her attention to me.

"Great."

"You're getting your nails done?" He seems to care about this more than the fact that his family never went to his favorite ice cream place in the two years that he was in prison.

"Yeah, just pedicures." I can't look at him.

The minutes that pass as we wait for our food feel like a slow, torturous death.

Stella tries to make small talk with her brother, and it's not going well. He's only giving short, one-word answers.

"Have you set a wedding date?" She turns to me, apparently giving up on him.

Why would she choose the worst possible subject?

"Um, no. He's in Vegas until tomorrow night. His family has a lot of ideas about the wedding and how it should go. So..." I'm rambling.

"Is he going to stop going on so many boys' trips when you get married?" She frowns.

"Um, yeah, maybe." Not likely.

The server comes toward our table with a tray. Thank god. The food will give me something else to think about.

She sets our plates on the table impressively fast while managing to avoid looking at Noah once. She scurries away as fast as her legs will take her.

"Oh, my god! This looks amazing!"

"It does!" I picked up my burger almost before the plate was on the table. If I don't start eating immediately, he will feed me again. I doubt he cares if Stella is here to see it.

His hand comes down to rest on my thigh. He doesn't squeeze, just places it there gently. I think he's happy.

"Want some fries?" I hope he'll take my peace offering.

He takes one, eats it, and returns his hand to my leg.

His thumb rubs little circles on my skin. It's very distracting.

"Hi! I'm Karen, the manager! Are you enjoying your meals? How's everything?" A woman with long gray hair and shimmery green eyeshadow stops at the table.

I open my mouth, and so does Stella, but his low voice growls before we can get a word out.

"Her water has been empty for six minutes." He gestures to my empty glass.

"Oh! I'm so sorry about that! I'll take care of that right away!" She rushes off.

"Noah!" I gasp.

The look on his face silences any scolding I might have given him.

Karen rushes back with a fresh glass in her hands. "Here you go!"

Noah pulls out a few folded bills from his wallet. "This should cover it."

"Thank you!" Stella calls after her. "Jesus Christ, Noah! Why are you so grumpy?"

"Let's go. You can do your nails. Then we'll go to Finnagan's."

He stands, unbuttoning the black and gray flannel he's wearing.

"Put this on."

Stella's eyes go wide, but she says nothing.

Taking the flannel, I slip it on.

"Come here." He kneels down in front of me, buttoning the front before rolling up the long sleeves so I can still use my hands.

Peeking over the top of his head, I make eye contact with Stella, and my cheeks burn. Her lips are rolled into her mouth as she watches him. He's not even a little bit discreet.

"Better." He growls and gestures for me to walk ahead of him.

"What the fuck?" She leans in as we walk out the door.

"I don't know." I shrug. I'm just as lost as she is.

His truck is parked on the street right outside the restaurant.

"We're parked in the lot around the corner." She starts, but he is already leading me around to the passenger side.

"We'll meet you there." He opens the door, waiting.

I give her an apologetic nod and climb inside.

He reaches in and buckles my seatbelt again.

When he slides into his seat, he starts the truck but doesn't move. He just sits with his hands on the wheel, staring straight ahead.

"So," his gravelly voice finally fills the silence. "You wore those fucking child's shorts because you thought I was watching you and wanted to see if you could catch me?"

"Yes," I whisper.

"Well, you caught me. Now what?"

"I-I don't know. I didn't think that far ahead."

He hums. "That was risky, baby."

"Are you going to punish me?" My throat feels tight.

He groans and lets his head drop back. "You sound like you want it."

"No." I shake my head, but my thighs clench together too. That naggy, fluttery feeling in my belly makes me feel squirmy.

"Yes, you do. I'll take care of you, Ace. Don't worry. Let's go make your toes pretty. Worry about the punishment later."

I'm worried about the punishment now.

"I ate all my food." I point out as he pulls the truck onto the street.

A loud, genuine laugh spills from him. "Did you think that would save you?"

"I hoped."

He reaches over, sticking his hand so far up my thighs he's almost inside my underwear. "Not a chance. What nail place?"

"The one in the shopping center on Monmouth Ave." I wiggle against his hand, but I don't whine.

With one hand on the wheel, he navigates us across town. The whole time, he's squeezing and releasing my leg.

It's maddening. My pulse thumps in time with the strange rhythm.

"Red polish." He slips easily into a parking spot, the truck rumbling to a stop.

I nod and sigh—relieved—as he removes his hand.

As we walk toward the nail salon, he holds my neck again. It feels like a leash.

We're almost to the end of the row of parked cars when a

group of three people crosses the street to walk up the same row. At first, I hardly notice them. But as they get closer, they morph into familiar faces.

Oh, god.

Blake Miles. Kelly Tran. Jonah Williams.

If he notices them, he doesn't show it.

They stop dead in the middle of the street. All of them look shocked.

"Noah fucking Gaines." Blake Miles is the first to react.

Kelly looks like she's going to cry.

"I hear you got out. You fucking–" Whatever he was about to say is cut off by a car honking for them to move.

"Just because they let you out doesn't mean that you deserve it! You haven't paid your debt to society, you fucking waste of breath. You should never be allowed to walk around with normal people again! You–"

"Let's go." Kelly grabs his arm. "Let's just go, Blake. Please."

My knees wobble as we cross the street and step under the awning around the building.

"Are you alright?" I turn to him.

"Ace, Parker Moreland's friends are the last people on earth I care to have, judging me. They were friends with that piece of shit low-life. Who are they to talk?" He tips my chin up. "I'm fine."

My mind races. He thought Parker was a piece of shit?

I think that, but no one else seemed to.

"Let's go." He opens the door to the nail salon. "Forget them."

SIXTEEN

"ARE you sure you don't mind?"

"Oh, my god, Stella. Go!" I push her out of the kitchen toward the door.

"But..."

"Go! I'm a big girl. Enjoy your hot date." I wiggle my brows at her. I think I'm convincing enough. She won't go if she can see how nervous I am. She deserves to go on a date even if she's being weirdly secretive about who she's seeing.

"Ok, I'll text you!"

When she's gone, I lock the door, making sure the deadbolt is secure.

Creeping back to my room, I pull my curtains aside and peek outside.

Nothing.

I'm being paranoid.

It could be that work was rough this week or that the last few days have been an emotional rollercoaster, but I'm exhausted. Slipping into my pajamas, I stop to stare at my red nail polish.

He sat there the whole time, watching the woman do my pedicure.

Crawling into my bed, I pull the cover over my head and try not to let every creak in the dark scare me.

Today was a weird day.

Even hours later, I'm trying to process everything that happened.

He admitted to me that he follows me. There wasn't even an attempt to lie. Then he got on his knees in a restaurant to button his shirt around me. And he said bad things about Parker Moreland.

This is why I'm so tired. My brain is swimming in too much information.

A sound in the dark.

It's soft, but it cuts through the silence.

My body freezes under the blankets–listening.

It's the crunch of gravel.

Sitting up, I listen again.

There are white rocks surrounding the building–they would go right below my window.

Again.

There's no mistaking it. Whoever is there isn't even trying to be quiet.

My legs barely support my weight as I slide off the bed, my feet hitting the ground hard. Walking around the side of my bed, I pause in front of my curtains.

With trembling fingers, I move the curtains, just a crack.

Someone is standing outside. His huge shadow punctuated by the streetlight behind him.

"Open the window, baby. Or I'll break it." His voice is low and muffled through the glass, but I know his voice.

Clicking the locks open, I step back as he slides my window up and cuts the screen open.

"Why did you lock the deadbolt?" He climbs inside with ease.

"Um," I swallow hard, my eyes focused on the knife in his hand.

"Baby?" He clicks the blade closed, folding it into the handle before sliding it into his pocket.

"Stella's not home," I whisper.

"I know."

Of course, he knows.

"Get in bed." He pulls his hoodie off, throwing it on the floor before pulling his boots off too.

For a moment, a false sense of security calms my racing heart. Maybe we'll just sleep like we did last time.

"Tell me about your fiancé." He slides into bed beside me.

"What?"

"Why are you marrying him?"

"I–"

"Don't say because you love him. I know that's not true. Tell me why." His hand creeps up my leg, stopping on my thigh.

"He's stable." My voice wobbles.

He hums.

"What are you doing here?"

"Is it the money? His family has more money than any of them could ever spend." There's no judgment in his voice.

"I mean. Yes, and no." I cringe. "He is the nicest boyfriend I've ever had."

"That doesn't really mean shit, Ace. Better than a string of fucking losers is still bad."

"He's not a loser." I defend him even though the words feel like a lie as I say them.

"Really? He got into Harvard because his dad donated enough money to build an astronomy lab. He was too stupid to realize that it wasn't as cool as he thought it was, and he wouldn't shut up about it senior year. He's a rich frat boy who wants you because he can control you. You're beneath him." He pauses. "Socially. So in his mind, he can treat you however he wants because you'd be stupid to leave."

I'm offended. Anger spreads through my chest. I'm grateful for the dark so he can't see how red my skin is.

"Fuck you, Noah."

"You're not going to marry him."

"Fuck you!" The volume of my voice is much louder this time.

"You know you're too good for him. He might be rich, but you deserve better."

I scoff. "Oh, really?"

"Yes." He's not angry. There isn't any sarcasm or malice in this tone.

"I know him better than you do." I know this is weak and also untrue.

"I doubt that. Is his family nice to you?"

Fuck.

"No," I whisper. "They hate me."

"Why do you say that?"

I haven't even told Stella about this, but for some reason, the words just spill out. I can't hold them back. It feels like a release—like I can breathe again. Someone else has to know what they said.

"He didn't defend you?" His voice is different—deeper, raspier—angrier.

"He wasn't there when they said it." I defend him again.

"Ace." He growls. "If you told me that anyone in my family said that about you, I would never speak to them again. Contact would be severed effective immediately. Open your eyes."

"Noah..."

"When was the last time he made you come?"

Gasping, I lean back against the headboard, trying to create more space between us. "I–he–"

"When?"

"He hasn't." The words just come out. I don't mean to say them. I don't want him to know that.

"Never?"

"It's not his fault. I think I'm broken."

His head tilts to the side. I can barely make out his eyes watching me in the dark. "Why do you say that?"

"I mean, I've never–" I gesture vaguely over my stomach.

"You've never come?"

Too embarrassed to speak, I shake my head and cover my face with my hands.

"Never?" He sounds bewildered.

"No." I squeak.

"Oh, baby. We're going to take care of that right now."

I drop my hands to look at him, but it's too late. He yanks me down by the legs, pulling me closer to him. A click –then a glint of something shiny.

The fabric of my pajama pants cut away like ripping paper. It offers no protection or resistance.

"Noah!" Panic crawls up my throat, wrapping around my neck.

He pries my legs open. "Keep these open, Ace. I want to look at it."

"I–" I can't watch. Covering my face again, I try to take a full breath. It's so hot in here suddenly.

"Holy shit." He whispers. "I've been thinking about this for so long. Fucking dreaming about it. Do you know how fucking perfect you are? It's beautiful."

"I–" My voice cracks. I don't feel beautiful anywhere. Especially there.

"Candace. I can't tell you how many nights I stayed awake, coming over and over again, just thinking about this moment. It's so much better than I imagined." He picks up my leg, starting with my foot, and he presses kisses everywhere. My toes. My heels. My arches. My ankles. Then he moves up. My breath gets shallower with each kiss. By the time he reaches my knee, I think I might pass out. "When I finally fuck you, I'm not going to be gentle. Do you understand? I'm going to wreck this perfect pussy. After I fill you with cum, you're mine. We'll save that for when you give that motherfucker back his ring."

My mouth gapes open, then closes. There isn't a satisfactory response to that.

"Tonight. You're being punished. I'm going to make you come so many times you're going to lose your voice from screaming for me to stop." He reaches over his shoulder, gripping his shirt and yanking it over his head.

The tips of his fingers bite into my tights as he holds them open against my instinct to snap them shut.

"You can put your legs up on my shoulders if you want to, but you keep them open, understand?"

I'm asphyxiating.

My skin feels hot to the touch, and I'm dizzy.

"Ace. Say you understand."

"I understand." I choke.

He hums and leans down, kissing and nipping at my thighs. The little bites make me jump–just hard enough to sting.

When he gets to my broken pussy, his breath fans over it, and he kisses it, hard. Gasping, my hands jerk and flail around, landing fisted in my sheets and his hair. I have to hold onto something.

Between kisses, he takes long, slow inhales, smelling me. "Holy fucking shit." He grumbles to himself.

His tongue moves, doing things my brain can't even comprehend. I'm nervous, and my mind is racing.

But something happens.

Slowly, as he works his mouth up and down, in and out, in tight little circles–the thoughts start to disappear. My mind is quiet. The fear is gone. The nervousness. It's quiet.

And something else is there. A knot. Building slowly but surely in my stomach.

It's coiling tighter and tighter until my thighs tremble.

"N-Noah!" Panic spreads through me, but he doesn't stop.

I try to fight it–whatever it is–but I'm losing.

"Give it to me, Ace." He growls, making obscene sounds as he feasts. This feels like one of those nature documentaries where a lion is ripping into a gazelle, head shaking, tearing apart—wild. I'm the gazelle.

He seems almost out of control. Like he couldn't stop if he tried.

Anyone listening would think he was eating the best meal of his life. It's hard to feel gross while he is so thoroughly–and vocally–enjoying it.

Pinching my eyes closed, I try to calm the frantic feeling in my chest. I can't escape. I can't stop this. It's crashing down on me–a wave that's going to pummel me into the sand–and I'm trapped. I can't outrun it.

"Noah!" I sob. "Please!"

He sucks my clit into his mouth, and the tight coil bursts. My eyes roll behind my eyelids, and I feel weightless.

"Fuck, yes." He almost sounds relieved.

My back arches up, and sounds, just broken words and cries, pour out of me.

I bring my arm up, slinging it across my face and biting into it, but he reaches up and grabs it. "Those are mine, and I want to hear them. Don't fucking muffle it."

"Oh, my god!" I pant, barely catching a breath before my body starts to tighten again. Another can't come this quickly, can it? "It's so..." Good.

The words clog my throat, but that's what I want to say. It's so fucking good.

Staring down at him, I watch through blurry eyes. This is so unexpected. Seeing his face between my legs makes my stomach churn. The desperate, needy feeling is starting to grow.

"Oh, fuck." He groans and drops his head. Only for a second, but it gives me a chance to look at him.

His shoulders are shaking, the muscles trembling beneath his skin.

"God damn it." He grunts and dives back in.

I don't know how much time has passed. An hour? The entire night? He flips me onto my stomach and eats me from behind. He has me sit on his face. He bends me over the bed and kneels behind me.

I'm hoarse. My muscles ache. My clit throbs. Every part of me is too sensitive.

"I can't take any more. Please!" Tears well up in my eyes. I'm overwhelmed.

"You'll take as many as I want to give you."

"Wait, please!" The wave that built before is more like a tsunami now. My nerves are frayed–ripped open and exposed to the air.

"Noah!" My spine arches unnaturally, my body attempting to run. I scream a hoarse, broken sound as one more orgasm sends me into oblivion.

"You are fucking delicious." He finally releases me, climbing into bed and dragging my carcass up with him.

His face is wet. His neck. His chest. He's soaked.

I'm limp in his arms, my head on his arm. "I can't believe I came." I'm delirious.

"I did too."

"You did?" I'm able to muster up enough strength to open my eyes.

"I told you, I've been thinking about this almost exclusively for ten years."

"Ten?" I gasp.

"Your body is so responsive. How was he unable to make you come?"

"Well, he never did *that*."

"You're telling me he looked at the delicious pussy and didn't want a taste? If I had any respect for him, I'd have lost it all." His grip around me tightens.

"Do you really like it?" I still can't believe it.

"Baby, I came in my pants from tasting it."

SEVENTEEN

NOAH

SHE'S EXHAUSTED. The sleepy smile on her face has my cock raging. I made her come. I thought that would be enough–that it would put out the fire. It didn't.

I need more. She came so many times. Each one was more torturous for me than the last.

Rolling her onto her back, I sit between her legs.

"Noah." Her raspy whisper makes me twitch.

I could sit and stare at it forever.

Fuck, my insides are churning.

"Shhh." I pull my belt off and toss it. I have to come on her. It's feral. Primal. My baser instincts demand it. I'm going to mark her as mine. My scent. My cum.

Unbuttoning my jeans, I pull it out, letting it hang between us. Her eyes are barely open, watching me warily.

Slipping two fingers into her, I spread them and feel the resistance.

Fuck. I need to feel it around my cock.

Leaning over her, I drag the tip through her wet, swollen skin.

She jumps, and her hands grip my shoulders—her nails biting into my skin, breaking it.

"Just the tip, baby." I press slightly. Just a little bit.

If I just pushed a bit further.

Fuck.

She can't handle it tonight. I want to brutalize her. I want to own it. I can't fuck her like that right now.

A dark itch burns in my spine. Take her. Make her yours, finally.

My voice shakes as I drop my head down into her neck. "Tell me to stop, Ace." My arms tremble with the effort of holding myself back.

Pulling away, I meet her eyes.

"You have to tell me; otherwise, I won't be able to stop myself. Say it." I'm getting desperate now. I'm almost there. One thrust and I'd be buried inside of her. "Fuck!" I press forward with more pressure this time. "I want to feel you wrapped around me. I want to put so much cum inside you that it's still dripping when you stand up in the morning."

She's so wet. Absolutely drenched.

I need it.

My arms shake violently now, holding myself back.

"I'm throbbing."

This time, when I push forward, I feel the give, just a little bit. I'm right there. Oh, fuck.

"Stop me!" I am yelling now.

"Stop." She whispers, and I pull back.

Taking my cock in my fist, I pump it against her. "I'm going to come all over your pussy."

Her eyes go wide, but then they trail down my body, looking between us. I watch as her lips part and her breaths go shallow.

"Look what you do to me." I'm so close. "Do you want it?"

Please, baby.

When she nods, my hips flex and I spray her with cum.

It hits me so hard and fast that I almost fall onto her.

Leaning back, I watch it dripping. I made a mess all over her. If she weren't so exhausted, I would lick her clean.

Dropping into the bed beside her, I grab her, pulling her into my side. "Don't ever let him fuck you again."

"What?" She whispers.

"I mean it, Ace. I'll kill him."

A shudder runs through her, and I wait for her to ask. But she doesn't.

EIGHTEEN

"NOAH," I whisper, my hand moving over his bare shoulder. His skin is hot beneath my touch, his breathing slow and steady. He's completely at ease. I explore the dips and plains of his muscles. Memorizing him.

I'm trapped. He's crushing my chest; the full weight of his body is resting on top of mine.

"Noah, wake up." I'm too warm. Not just from the heat of his body, but the flashes of memory from last night.

Something is wrong with me.

I guess my body isn't broken; it just requires a feral animal between my legs.

Guilt sits like a ball in my throat, choking me.

I think he might actually be crazy, and for some reason, I'm playing into his delusions. But when he looks at me like that, the fear that usually creeps up my spine when intimacy is on the horizon is simply not there.

I feel safe and wanted.

Noah was hungry for me, not just to actually taste it, but

just to look at me—to touch me. I've never felt anything like it. I was the center of his entire world.

He had to hold himself back. His hands trembled as he touched me.

I'm not used to men treating me with restraint.

He didn't take anything. Only gave it. Repeatedly. It was like he didn't just want to use me for his own pleasure. He cared about mine. He gave me so much of it, I had to beg him to stop.

He shifts in his sleep, his arm tightening around my waist. I don't move.

I should.

For several minutes, I wait—letting myself feel safe beneath him.

But Stella could come in at any moment.

"Noah," I whisper. "I—"

My phone rings, and panic courses through me. Shit. He's back in town. I forgot about that.

"H-Hello?"

"Hey, babe. I'm going to swing by in a few hours and pick you up. I'm thinking dinner and a movie?" Colson's voice bursts loudly through the phone.

Noah flinches, turning his head toward the phone with a deep scowl.

"Um, right. Sure."

"Wear that little red dress I like so much."

I don't even have time to respond before he hangs up.

"No."

"No?" My heart races.

His jaw clenches. "Call him back and tell him you already have plans."

"I can't do that!" I'm suddenly afraid of what he might do.

"Why?" His voice is low and dangerous.

I don't have an answer.

Why can't I? I don't understand it myself. I just feel stuck. He's right here—giving me an out.

Noah studies me for an endless moment, and then his expression hardens into something horrible.

"You know what?" He sits up, staring down at me with hatred in his eyes. "Go. Go on your date. I promise you'll miss me by the end of the night."

I already know I will.

He stands up, taking all of his warmth with him. He's tugging on his boots. He's leaving.

"Wait—" I sit up in bed, but he doesn't stop.

Stalking toward my closet, he disappears before coming out with a black lace dress. "Wear this."

"Noah—" I hate the way he's looking at me. This anger is different from any he's shown before. This is real.

"See you tonight, Ace." He slams my door so loudly it hits the frame and bounces open again.

I sit there, staring at it.

The choice should be simple.

But it's not. I'm standing on a path, frozen at a fork in the road, and I don't know which way to go.

Sliding out of bed, I feel cold. Empty. And sore. My stomach muscles ache, and my clit feels raw and swollen.

I limp into the bathroom and turn on the shower, stepping under the hot spray.

As I wash away the evidence of last night, I fight back the urge to cry.

I'm ripped apart. Both physically and emotionally.

I'm going to wear the black dress. If he's watching, maybe that will send him a signal that I'm sorry.

Taking my time, I do my hair and makeup carefully.

He will notice the effort.

Standing at the sink, I stare down at my ring. For a moment—just a split second— an intrusive thought pops into my head. What if I just dropped it, and it fell down the drain? I would never have to look at it again.

Putting it back in the box, I step away quickly before I do something stupid.

Just as I finish clasping the straps to my heels, my phone pings.

I'm outside.

Disappointment flickers in my chest.

I don't know what I expected. He isn't going to come to the door or get out and open the car door for me.

Only Noah does that.

When he sees me, his smile falters. It's only barely noticeable, but I see it. He's irritated that I'm not wearing the dress.

Climbing into the tiny cab of his fancy little car, I give him a tight smile.

"Hey," he leans over and hugs me. "You look hot."

"Thanks." I cringe.

He weaves through traffic, speeding the entire way to the movie theater. "You should have seen it! Bodhi was so drunk! They had to call an ambulance! He ended up having alcohol poisoning."

"Cool." I listen to him talk about Vegas and the boys.

"I was so blackout drunk that I don't even remember going in!" He laughs. "Apparently, I spent twelve grand!" He tells me about the various strip clubs and high-stakes poker rooms they visited.

"Did you win anything? Or—"

"Nah, but you win some, you lose some. It's more about having fun." He leans over and places his hand on my thigh.

"Thanks for being so cool about that, by the way. Colby's chick found out we were at a strip club and threatened to break off the engagement if he didn't leave immediately. She was location stalking him! Can you believe that?"

"No." I swallow down my feelings. While he was out throwing money at hard-working women, I was being devoured by a man who claimed to own me. So, I don't have a leg to stand on here.

I can't picture Noah at a strip club. The way he looks at me–it just doesn't fit.

He pulls into a parking space, still talking about Vegas. Now, he's moved on to the buffets and room service they enjoyed.

"What movie is this?" I look at the dark, ominous poster hanging next to the ticket kiosk.

"Ronnie said it was amazing. It's going to completely change the way you think about the double standards in society when it comes to masculinity! Men have to be perfect and can't speak a word about a woman, but women have built entire platforms on man-hating!"

"That sounds..." Awful.

"It's critically acclaimed!" He buys the tickets and places his hand on the small of my back to lead me inside.

Within fifteen minutes, this artsy movie has me ready to doze off. It's exactly the kind of pretentious film Colson likes—critical thinking, deep metaphors, long shots of people staring out of windows while a narrator speaks in voiceover. Deep and cerebral.

I find my eyes wandering around the theater.

There are more people here than I think this movie deserves.

Leaning on my elbow, I rest my head in my hand. My eyes feel heavy.

But then something at the bottom of the steps leading to the rows of seats catches my eye. I jolt upright, and my palms start sweating.

He's here.

He's leaning against the wall, arms crossed, watching me.

Watching us.

It takes all of my self-control not to excuse myself to the restroom. If I go down there, he's likely to drag me away.

I can't focus on the screen. The movie is nothing but flickering images and irritating background noise.

Colson's arm drapes over my shoulders, and my body tenses.

Images flicker through my mind on a reel. His hands. His eyes. His mouth. His tongue. The tattoos that cover his skin, rolling in the dark.

Pinching my eyes closed, I can see him as clear as day. His voice echoes in my mind. All the dirty things he said—the sounds he made.

I shouldn't be thinking about that.

I shift in my seat, but it doesn't help. I feel him when I move, which only makes it worse.

The memory is burned into my skin.

He's still watching. I can feel his eyes pinning me down.

When he moves, my breath catches in my throat. He walks slowly up the steps—leisurely. He knows exactly what he's doing to me.

If this is a cat-and-mouse game, I'm the mouse, and he's already got me trapped.

He stops on the step right beside me, so close I could reach out and touch him. But then he continues.

Trying to be inconspicuous, I look over my shoulder as subtly as possible.

He's two rows behind us, sitting on the aisle seat. Just one seat sits between us.

When will this torture end?

Pulling out my phone, I look up the movie online. It's one hundred and twenty-nine minutes long! Why? What could they possibly have to say about the current double standards of militant feminists for another hour?

"Isn't this good?" Colson leans over. "I relate to this so much. You have no idea how careful I have to be at work so that I don't offend the women in the office."

I hum. How hard is it not to offend someone? "It almost feels like satire."

His brows pull together. "What?"

"I'm kidding."

Sneaking another glance at my phone, I don't let myself pout. He hasn't texted me. He's punishing me again.

Last night's punishment was far more enjoyable.

The movie eventually ends. At one point, I thought I would die in this chair.

"Hungry? I want to try this new place, 'Crudo.' I had to name-drop to get a reservation for tonight."

"Oh, sure." I'm barely listening. He's standing at the end of the aisle, inches away from me.

His eyes move down my body in the low light. I feel it, a rush of goosebumps on my skin as if he were touching me physically.

Following Colson out of the theater, I keep looking back. He's in the same place, watching.

I keep waiting for something to happen. This punishment is so much worse. My insides are tied in knots.

At the car, I stop, turning around to scan the street.

There he is. He nods, a subtle gesture, but I know he wants

me to get in the car. I hesitate only for a moment, just looking for one second longer.

"What are you doing? Come on." Colson yells from inside.

"Right, sorry." I slip into my seat.

"So, you know we're going to Cancun next month, but the boys are trying to get together for one more bash before Colby's old ball and chain makes him stay home. We were thinking something big, maybe Barcelona."

"Huh?" I haven't been listening.

"Barcelona. Spain?"

"I know where Barcelona is."

He rolls his eyes and continues talking about their plans.

As he merges onto the freeway, he cuts across four lanes of traffic. Reaching up, I grabbed the handle above my door and hold on for dear life.

Red and blue lights flash almost immediately behind us, and the sound of sirens blasts.

"Are you serious? What the fuck?" He yells and slams his fist against the steering wheel.

He crosses back through the lanes, much more safely this time, and stops the car on the shoulder.

"Unbelievable. Fucking speed traps!" He yells again. He's really worked up for somebody who just broke at least a few laws. "The least he could do is hurry the fuck up." He looks impatiently in the rearview mirror.

When the officer finally approaches the car, he is in a terrible mood, and I'm feeling nervous.

"Do you know why I told you over?" The office officer crouches down to look into the window.

"I have no idea." He rolls his eyes.

"You cut across several lanes of traffic without using a signal, and you were going 95 in a 75."

"Just hurry up and write the ticket." He scoffs. "We have plans tonight."

My cheeks burn as I look at the officer.

"Are you alright, ma'am?"

"Yes, officer, I'm fine."

He looks sympathetically at me, then turns his attention back to Colson. "I could take your car into my possession tonight."

"What?" His screeches. "That's bullshit!"

"I'm going to cut you a break. I just want you to know that in the future, if you drive that fast, you could have your car taken on the spot."

When we're finally allowed to drive away again, the mood in the car is sour, to say the least.

He keeps grumbling under his breath.

"Why didn't you wear the red dress like I told you to?" He snapped at me out of nowhere.

"Oh, well, I—"

"You just can't fucking listen, can you?" He growls. "I haven't seen my fucking fiancée in a week, and I just want to take her out and see her look pretty, and you can't even do that for me."

"I'm sorry—"

"Why aren't you wearing your ring?"

"The diamond feels loose." I lie. "I was afraid that it would fall out."

As we pull into the parking lot, I notice Noah's truck immediately. With our little police detour, he beat us here.

My palms immediately start sweating.

The restaurant is small and modern, with a bar stretching along one side of the intimate dining room.

I spot him instantly. He's sitting at the bar. His big tattooed frame looks at a place.

I know he's mad at me and he's punishing me, but seeing him here brings me comfort.

When we're shown to our table, Colson orders a drink before she even has a chance to hand us our menus.

I'm frazzled and distracted. He orders me a mojito again. And some kind of raw fish dish for dinner.

He barely speaks to me. It isn't until his third drink that he starts to loosen up. "You know, you were right. My brother pulled me aside to talk to me about marrying you. My family is worried that I'm being reckless!" He laughs. "He thinks I'm pussy whipped!" He rolls his lips into his mouth to keep himself from losing it. "You don't even give it up! We've only had sex four times in a year!"

Looking around, I sink down in my seat. The people at the table on either side of us can hear him.

"Once we get married, I expect you to do your wifely duty." He suddenly looks more stern.

I'm horrified. The glances from the other couples make my blood rush in my ears.

"Excuse me, miss." The server comes over. "The gentleman at the bar sent this over to you. He says he's an old friend?" She looks nervous.

It's a big, fancy house made lemonade.

"Whoa, what the fuck?" Colson sits up straighter, searching the bar.

"It's Noah." My insides jitter. "Stella's big brother." I remind him gently.

"No way, the fucking murderer?"

"He's not a murderer!" I whisper across the table. "I told you he got out."

"Why the fuck is he sending you a drink?"

"I'm sure he's just being friendly." I still haven't turned to look at him.

"That motherfucker. That's downright disrespectful! You don't send someone else's girl a drink like that!" He snarls.

When I finally pluck up the courage to turn around, he's looking right at me. If he's still mad, it doesn't show.

He tips his chin.

"Are you finished?" Colson snaps at me. "Or are you going to stare at him all night?"

"I'm not staring."

He's drunk and angry tonight.

"Ace." Noah's voice from behind me makes goosebumps roll down my arms.

"Thanks for the drink." I try not to smile too big.

"Ace?" Colson sneers, getting worked up. "Who the fuck do you—"

"I think you should let me take you home." Noah might as well not see him at all.

NINETEEN

NOAH

THIS DRUNK MOTHERFUCKER thinks he's going to drive her home?

"What? You're not taking her anywhere." His voice is all bravado, but I hear the shake beneath it. Even tipsy, he fucking knows. He's not so macho when a real man is present.

"You're drunk."

"That may well be, but between the two of us, I'm not the one who killed someone with a car." A smirk slowly curls at his lips. He's proud of himself for that one.

She gasps. Her hand claps over her pretty mouth. "Colson!"

My vision tunnels.

Rolling my neck, I clench my fists to keep them from grabbing him by the collar and dragging him outside. I could curb-stomp him before he even realized he was at death's door.

Leaning in, I press my hand to his shoulder, keeping him seated. "You have no idea who I am." I make sure my voice is low enough that she can't hear it. "Killing him was the second-best thing I ever did. I'm barely controlling the urge to add another body. And your name is at the top of the list."

Closing my eyes, the erratic sound of his breath makes my skin tingle. Images of his mouth open against the curb while I step down on his skull send a rush through my spine. I see it in perfect clarity—his teeth scattered across the pavement, blood pooling in the cracks, his skull caved in under my boot.

A rush shudders through my spine, sharp and electric. Fuck, I want to do it.

"Get the fuck off me, man." He tries to push my arm away.

"Keep acting up. Please." I grit my teeth.

Then her voice pulls me back from the abyss.

"Noah?"

Soft. Hesitant. Sweet.

I exhale through my nose and force myself to take a deep breath and relax, force myself to let go before I snap his neck in front of all these horrified onlookers.

Holding out my hand to her, I'm on the edge. "Let's go, baby."

"Baby?" Colson grumbles.

She slips her hand into mine, and my cock twitches. Good fucking girl.

The diners in this fancy restaurant look like they've seen a ghost as we walk out.

"Does he know that you don't like mojitos, or is it a power play thing? He orders it to control you?" I pull her into my side.

"I don't know." She shudders. "I don't know which is worse."

"Let's go get you something to eat." Half a plate of raw fish with lime wedges isn't enough.

She doesn't object.

"Thank you for stepping in." Her voice wobbles.

"I punished you enough." Opening the door to the truck, I press her against the side, our bodies shielded. "You look fucking gorgeous tonight."

Her face lights up. My angel.

My hand shakes as I place it on her throat. The restraint–holding myself back–is getting harder by the second. Her slender neck and soft skin against my tattoos gives me ideas.

My skin itches. A deep, painful torture I'll only escape when my cock is buried inside of her. I need to claim it—to own it.

I tighten my grip. Her breath hitches, eyes wide—but she doesn't flinch—doesn't pull away.

My blood boils.

"I'm losing control."

"Of what?" The slight strain in her whisper makes my cock ache.

"So pretty." I squeeze harder. "All you have to do is say the word. I would make sure that he never touched you again. Do you understand, baby?"

She nods, barely, but her big, wide eyes reach down into me and squeeze my tar-black heart. I would burn the world down. There isn't anyone I wouldn't take out at her command.

"You own me." I drag my lips over her soft cheek. "You know that, right?"

Her breath stutters on my lips.

"I'm taking you to eat, then bringing you home," I'm telling myself. "I can't touch you again until you're ready to take me because this time, I won't hold back."

She nods, but she doesn't understand.

She will.

TWENTY

PULLING my skirt up my legs, I stare at my reflection in the mirror. The hem barely skims mid-thigh, and normally, I'd feel exposed—nervous, even—but not tonight. Not with Noah coming.

I know I'm safe. He won't let anything happen to me. The thought settles low in my stomach, a quiet thrill rushing around my nerves.

This might be the first time in years that I actually have fun. Even though he makes me feel flushed and anxious, it's a good feeling.

Looking at myself, I feel confidence I'm not used to.

Stella pokes her head into the room. "Do I look right for the location?" She does a little spin, and her plaid schoolgirl skirt fans out around her upper thighs.

"You look perfect." She always does.

"Please, Candy! Give me a hint! Where are we going?"

"No." I duck into my closet. If she keeps looking at me with her big pouty eyes, I'm going to end up telling her and ruining the surprise.

A loud knock on the door makes my heart rate spike.

Rushing out of the closet, I make it to the end of the hallway as Stella opens the door.

"Colson?"

He steps inside, a bouquet of flowers in his hands.

"What are you doing here?" I find my arms over my chest.

His gaze flicks over me, taking in the skirt, the heels—the effort. I see the shift in his expression—the tightening of his jaw, the way his grip tenses around the bouquet. He's called a few times this week, but I wasn't in the mood to answer.

I'm shocked he actually showed up here. Usually, when we argue, he will ice me out until I come to him.

"Are you going out tonight?" His voice is casual, but his expression isn't.

"It's Stella's birthday. You were invited, remember?"

"Oh, yeah, right? Of course. Happy birthday." The words are empty, an afterthought. He turns his attention back to me. "Can we talk?"

"We're about to leave, Colson. I'll call you tomorrow."

"Just one minute." He isn't going to leave until I give him what he came for.

I exhale sharply. "Fine, but just for one—"

Oh god.

Noah and Jace walk through the door.

Noah and Colson make eye contact, and I brace myself for them to fight.

But Noah smiles.

Oh shit. That's so much worse.

It's not a kind smile—there is no offer of friendship in it. He's glad to see Colson in the way a predator is glad when its prey walks willingly into the trap.

"Ready to go?" Jace sets a little wrapped box on the table beside the door. He got her a present?

I feel like an idiot. That's who she's been seeing! It must be. Wow. I've been so wrapped up in my own ridiculous life that I missed it.

"Yes!" She grabs her coat.

"I'll call you later." I pull my coat on.

"Or I'll just come. I was invited, after all."

"Wonderful." I take the flowers and set them on the kitchen counter.

Noah's watching me, that damn lopsided grin on his face.

The excitement I had been feeling for the night evaporates. This is going to be awful.

The little Brazilian restaurant hums with conversation. I picked this place because the energy is light and fun.

Right now, it doesn't feel fun.

Not with Colson's arm around my shoulder. This feels wrong—he never does this. Maybe he'll put his hand on my thigh, but this is too showy.

It's fake.

I shift slightly, hoping he'll move his arm. He doesn't.

"You look beautiful tonight," he says, just loud enough for everyone else to hear.

Again. Not typical.

I force a smile, focusing on Stella and Jace across from us. "Thanks."

"Are you excited about this weekend?" He touches my ear, and I flinch.

"What's this weekend?"

"My cousin Cecily's wedding!" He looks shocked that I could possibly forget about his cousin Cecily, who didn't say two words to me when we sat beside each other at Christmas dinner.

"Right. Seabrook Island." I've been dreading this for months. Now, the thought of going seems like torture.

Looking subtly to the side, I peek at him.

He's sitting beside Jace, leaning back in his chair. He hasn't said anything, but he doesn't have to. His presence alone is enough to get to me.

When the server refills his glass, he nods and turns his gaze back to Colson. There's something lazy about the way he does it, like he's so completely unbothered—but I know better.

I can see it in the way his jaw clenches.

"Alright, alright," Stella is smiling so wide it's taking up her whole face. "I have something to tell you guys." She takes a deep breath, then reaches for Jace's hand. "We've been seeing each other."

"I can't believe I didn't figure it out until tonight!"

"I didn't want to keep it a secret from you. I was just nervous." She reaches across the table.

"Nervous? About what?"

She bites her lip and gives me a look that makes my heart swell. She's nervous because he's the one.

I glance at Noah, expecting some kind of reaction—something. But he just swirls the amber liquid in his glass.

Colson, on the other hand, does react.

His arm tightens around my waist, tugging me closer. "That's great!" He's too enthusiastic. It's coming across as phony and disinterested.

Stella doesn't notice. She's too busy soaking up the moment, and I don't blame her.

Noah notices, though.

I can *feel* his attention shift back to us, his gaze landing on where Colson's hand grips my waist. The ice in his glass clinks as he takes a slow sip.

Colson ignores him. He turns to me instead, brushing my hair back and pressing a kiss just below my ear. His lips linger longer than they need to. My stomach twists.

"Come home with me tonight," he—again—speaks too loudly.

I pull back, frowning. "Colson, it's Stella's birthday."

His fingers flex against my hip. "Aww, come on."

"Not tonight."

"Maybe before our trip, then." He does another fake smile.

I don't respond.

"Excuse me. I'll be right back." I quickly stand and rush to the bathroom. I need a moment away from his sudden shift in... *everything.* He's only acting like this because of Noah. It makes me feel gross–like I don't deserve his affection unless it's in a pissing contest with another man.

The bathroom is quiet, the music from the restaurant muffled through the walls. I take a deep breath, pressing my palms against the cool marble sink.

Having him here has completely ruined the night. I hope I'm the only one who's miserable. Stella deserves a good time.

I'm ending it.

This night— sitting miserably by his side— was what I needed to open my eyes.

I shake it off and head for the door.

But as I pull it open, Noah is waiting.

I barely have time to react before he pushes inside, shutting the door behind him.

My pulse spikes. "What are you—"

His hands are on my waist before I can finish, backing me up until my spine presses against the wall.

"Why are you with that asshole?" His voice is low, sharp, and angry.

I tense. "What?"

"He won't make you feel like I do. He can't." His fingers tighten against my hips. "He should be licking the ground you walk on."

"Stop it."

"He doesn't know how." His lips twitch. "It's not even his fault, really."

"Noah, please." I grip his shirt in my fist.

He hums, leaning in.

"You already know what I can do to you, and that was just my tongue. I can't wait to show you what I can do with my fingers and my cock."

"Oh..." my god...

Our faces are so close. He's never kissed me. My eyes flick to his lips, then back up.

His eyes go dark–his pupils spreading to the edge–erasing any traces of green.

I try to push past him, but he's faster. One hand presses against the wall beside my head, caging me in. His other hand slides up my arm, fingers brushing my throat before trailing up to my face.

My breath catches.

He traces his thumb over my bottom lip–slow, deliberate.

"Don't give yourself to him," his lips ghost over mine. "He doesn't deserve you. You're not going home with him tonight."

My heart slams against my ribs. Please, kiss me. I know it's wrong, but I want it so badly I can't think of anything else.

"Noah," I whisper.

"Say it."

"Say what?" I'll say anything he wants.

"That you're not going home with him tonight."

"I'm not."

"Good."

His grip tightens for a fraction of a second. Then, just as suddenly, he lets go.

The door opens, and he slips out, leaving me standing

there, breathless and shaken. What the fuck? I pace around the bathroom on wobbly legs.

When the door opens again, I spin around, my heart pounding.

"Candy? Are you ok?" Stella looks concerned.

"Oh, yeah." Not even a little bit.

"Ok, listen. I don't push you, you know that. You always tell me what you need to tell me when you're ready, but..." She chews her lip. "What the fuck is going on with you and my brother?"

"I don't know!" I bury my face in my hands.

"Hey! Whoa!" She wraps her arm around my shoulder. "It's alright."

"No, it's not. It's a mess." I force my eyes to dry. I'm not going to cry in the bathroom at her birthday dinner.

"Candy–"

"I'm going to break things off with Colson." I blurt it out so quickly that it takes us both by surprise.

"Oh, shit." She whispers.

"I can't marry him. I thought that he would be good for me. That he was the best I could do and that the things that bothered me wouldn't matter, but I can't do it!" I run my hands through my hair. "I kept telling myself he would mature with age and things would get better, but I don't think so. He is who he is. And I don't even like him." It feels like a weight is lifted from my chest as I say the words out loud. "He doesn't like me either." Noah's words swirl around in my head. He thinks I won't leave because I'm lesser than him.

"Thank god." She looks up at the tiled ceiling and lets out a sigh. "I hate him. He's such an asshole."

"I know he is." My shoulder slump. "I thought since he was nicer than Jamie and Luke that he was good."

Her mouth tips down at the mention of my previous boyfriends. "I love you, but you pick the worst guys."

"I do." I can't argue there.

We walk out together, her arm over my shoulders. Each step feels heavy. I just have to make it through tonight. Then it will all be over.

My feet scrape the ground, and I stumble slightly when the table comes into view. He's drinking a beer.

He hates beer. He never drinks beer.

"Hey, what's going on?" She turns.

"Nothing." I shake my head.

One last night. Just don't breathe.

Reluctantly taking my seat beside him, I lean away slightly.

The room spins slightly as the smell hits me in the face with the force of a brick.

"Colson, can we talk outside?" The words fly out of my mouth. I wasn't gonna do this right now, but I can't sit beside him for a single second longer.

The beer sealed the deal.

"Sure," he has a cocky smile on his face as he tips his chin to everyone at the table.

He reaches for me, but I pull away, walking as quickly as I can.

Outside, the sun has set, and there is a chill in the air that wasn't there before. But it's good. I need it. My skin is over-heating.

"Colson, we can't get married." I rip the band-aid off with merciless quickness. I can't beat around the bush, not right now.

"What?" His voice is already loud. There's no build-up to it instantly, from zero to one hundred.

"I'm sorry but—"

"There is no fucking way that you are breaking up with

me," he says loud enough to cause the couple coming out of the restaurant to stop and turn toward us.

"Listen, it's—"

"This is unreal! I was going to make you a Barrington! Do you know what the fuck that means?"

"Colson—"

"No." He shakes his head.

"No?"

"No. You have to come with me to the wedding this weekend. We rsvp'd eight months ago. You picked a meal. You're not going to humiliate me in front of my entire family. You have to come to the wedding."

Guilt presses down on my chest.

"In high society, you don't do things like that, Candy. You don't back out of events like this at the last minute. They're paying 300 grand for this wedding. You're humiliating me! You have to come. You owe me that much, at least!"

"Fine. I'll go to the wedding. But I want my own room." I fold my arms over my chest.

"Alright." He nods.

We stand awkwardly, staring at each other. "I'm going back inside."

He nods again, stepping toward me. "We'll be back together by the end of the weekend. Whatever this is—" He gestures to me. "You'll be over it when you see the life I'm offering you."

"What?" No—"

He gives me a smile that makes my stomach feel queasy and walks away, disappearing into the parking lot.

I didn't agree to go to the wedding so that he could try to win me back somehow; that's not an option. It's not on the table.

"Come back inside, baby." Noah's steady voice comes from behind me.

"How long have you been there?"

"Long enough."

He takes Colton's seat beside me. Slips into it effortlessly, like he belonged there the whole time.

"Sorry, Candy. I spoiled the surprise while you were gone." Jace looks only slightly apologetic.

"We're going dancing!" Stella squeals.

Her happiness and Colson's departure brighten my spirits again. The night can be salvaged.

TWENTY-ONE

THE CLUB IS HOT.

So many bodies packed into such a small space that it's suffocating. The air is sticky and smells like too many different kinds of perfumes and alcohol mixed with sweat.

Stella pulled me out onto the dance floor as soon as we got here.

My skin is damp with sweat, my hair stuck to my neck. I'm not tipsy, but just on the edge. The world feels looser, less frightening.

Noah hasn't moved from his place at the bar. Every time I look, he's there, standing guard.

The devil himself couldn't hurt me tonight.

I'm free.

Spinning around, the sensual beat of a song I vaguely recognize starts to thump through the speakers.

Beckoning him with my finger, I sway, waiting in the center of the crowd.

He walks through the room like he owns it. Even drunk and stumbling, people step out of his way.

"Dance with me!" I take his hand and spin again.

He tugs me, pulling me into his body.

He feels like a hedge, like a protective barrier—a shield—nothing can get to me if he's here.

"I don't remember the last time I had this much fun!" I sway against his body.

The lights flash, illuminating his face. He looks beautiful, bathed in blue light with his signature almost smile.

He moves with me, running his hands over my body, but his expression never changes.

"Are you having fun?" I lean up on my toes.

He reaches down, pulling me up into his arms. "Now I'm having fun."

He moves slowly, barely swaying.

"Was it the beer?" He leans into my ear.

"What?"

"Something upset you tonight. Was it the beer?"

Pulling back, I watch the way his eyes study me. He doesn't miss anything. He sees it all.

"I don't like the smell."

I feel his response vibrate in my chest, his low hum zapping through my body. God, he makes me feel things–things I don't understand.

There is an undercurrent of fear–not that he'll hurt me–not ever. But that he'll hurt others. He's so intense that it over-whelms me. The way he looks at me...

"Why haven't you kissed me?" The words spill out before I can stop them. The confidence from a few shots coursing through me.

"You want a kiss?"

"We've done other things."

"What things, baby?" His lips graze my cheek.

"You–" I look down between us.

"Feasted on your pussy like it was my last meal?"

"Yeah, that." Oh, god.

"You want me to kiss you?" He shifts so that he's only got one arm around my lower body now. When I tighten my thighs around him, he rolls his neck and grabs my throat, slamming his mouth into mine in one swift motion.

This isn't a kiss. He's devouring me again. My mind. My soul. My heart.

My fingers sink into his hair, pulling him closer, but it's not close enough. I need more. I need to crawl inside his skin, need to feel every breath, every shuddering exhale as our lips part, only for a second, only to let the world tremble around us before he drags me under again.

He groans into my mouth; the sound reverberating down my spine, curling around my ribs, tying knots inside me that will never be undone. His hands grip my neck, his fingers sliding over it, memorizing it, making it his.

I kiss him back like he's the only thing keeping me alive. Like he's air, and I've been drowning.

I have been.

The lights flash around us. The world continues on. People dancing, laughing, loving on all sides, but we're the only two here.

The universe tilts, the ground unsteady beneath us, but it doesn't matter. Nothing matters except the way he breathes into my lungs, the way he tastes like the only thing that could ever save me.

And when we finally break apart, when he presses his forehead against mine, panting, eyes dark and desperate, I know I'll never be the same.

I should have expected it. How did I not see it coming?

He only touches me with possession, like I'm the only one

in the world. When his hands are on me, I feel safe. The kiss was the same. He is the only man who won't hurt me.

"My woman." He runs his hand up the back of my hair, settling it into the hair at the nape of my neck. He tugs right at the root, forcing my head into the position he wants.

I feel myself nodding in agreement.

His.

"That was a mistake, baby." He grits his teeth. The grip on my hair tightens. But I hardly notice.

"What?" My heart lurches in my chest, and my lower lip wobbles. A mistake?

He leans in, sucking my lips gently. "We haven't kissed yet because I never enjoyed kissing. But that..."

I feel a shudder roll down his spine.

"That rewired my fucking brain." He uses his grip on my hair to pull me forward to plant his lips on mine again.

The room spins. We're stagnant in a shifting crowd; they roll around us like waves.

I never liked kissing much, either. Kissing leads to other things—other things scare me.

But with Noah, it's not the same. Other things don't scare me.

"This is mine." He licks my lips. "This is mine." His hand moves from my hair to my throat. "This is mine." He pushes his hips forward between my legs.

The tortured sounds he makes as he touches me, rubbing his face into mine—I feel like he wants me to absorb him—like skin to skin isn't close enough. There is a desperation in the way he presses forward.

I know he's holding himself back. He wants to do things to me that I might not be ready for. But the truth is, I don't know what I'm ready for anymore.

My chest feels tight when I think about all the things he's said. But that doesn't mean I'm not willing to try.

"Noah." My whisper is swallowed up by the music. "Take me out of here."

His eyes are dark, pupils blown out under the strobing lights. He carries me outside, moving through the crowd with only enough care to make sure no one hits me.

The air outside hits my skin, a much-needed break from the intense heat.

"Can I say something?" I know I can. I'm not asking permission, but I have to get this out before I lose my nerve.

He stops walking, tucking in beside the building to give me his undivided attention.

"The other night, in my room." I take a breath and stop chewing my lip. Just say it. "I want to reciprocate."

He doesn't move. For a second, I think he somehow didn't hear me.

"You want to suck my cock?" His words come out slowly.

"Yes."

I do. I've never actually wanted to before, but it was a way to get out of having sex. This time, I want to.

His grip on me tightens, and his eyes dart around.

"Go to the truck," I whisper. I feel bold, like I'm holding all the cards.

He closes his eyes and leans in, pressing his forehead into mine. "Are you sure?"

"I'm sure."

"I'm not going to be gentle with you." His hand comes up to my neck. "I'm going to fuck this pretty throat."

Swallowing against his hand, I nod. I'm not backing out now.

He shifts me in his arms and walks purposefully toward the truck.

"You're going to take the whole thing." His voice sounds rough—strained.

"Ok." I straighten my posture. I can do that.

He has us inside the truck with dizzying quickness. Straddling his lap, I take a moment to get ready for the task I asked for.

Tracing my fingers over the tattoo on his neck, I watch the way his chest rises and falls with his quick, shallow breaths.

His eyes never leave mine as I study his face, every mark, line, dip, and curve.

Unlike my previous experiences, he doesn't rush me. He doesn't even touch me. The pace is mine to set.

Leaning in, I kiss him—just a soft, sweet touch before I climb off of his lap.

Moving to the center of the bench seat, I lower myself so that I'm on my knees beside his legs.

My fingers shake under his unblinking gaze. He watches as I open his belt and pants.

Lifting, he helps me tug them down. It springs free from his boxers and bobs above his stomach.

For a moment, I just stare at it. My opponent. He's big.

Thinking back to when he said he would wreck me, I believe him.

The tip is swollen and shiny.

His hands clench like he's searching for something to hold on to.

He's panting through his parted lips.

"Fuck." His hips flex forward. "Touch it, Ace. Put your hand around it."

Reaching out, I close my fist around the base. My thumb and middle finger almost touch; it's just barely too thick.

"Worship it. Kiss it. Lick it." His jaw is locked tight. He chokes the words out through gritted teeth.

Leaning in, I pump my fist once, and he lets out a sigh, like he's been waiting for eternity for relief.

Pumping my fist again, I lick him. One long strip from the top of my fist up over the tip.

Moving my fist and my mouth together, I work up and down, earning sighs and moans from him that make my pussy twitch.

"Move your hand. Swallow it." His voice is soft but commanding.

Moving my hand away, I take a breath and hollow out my cheeks, moving down further.

His hand comes into my hair, and the other to the side of my face. He guides me up and down, using no force or pressure.

"That's it. Take the whole thing." His voice is tight, laced with frustration. "Fuck! You're such a good girl. You look so fucking pretty with my cock in your mouth."

Slowly, almost so that I don't realize it's happening, he moves my head faster.

I gag when he moves farther into my throat, pushing my nose into his lower abdomen. But he doesn't stop.

"Take it." His thighs flex, his body moving—seeking out what he needs. "Ah, god, Ace!" He calls my name. "Just like that!"

My throat is raw; drool and tears run down my face as I struggle to keep up. The sounds he made while he was between my legs pop into my mind.

When I moan around him, he grunts, and his fist flies up into the window. Glass shatters and sprays all over the seat.

"Fuck, don't stop! Do it again!" He's begging.

My pulse pounds in my clit, begging for some attention.

Glass crunches beneath his feet as he gasps and presses his heels into the floorboards.

He starts to say something, but the words are cut off by, "Oh, holy fuck!" A throaty sound spills into the car as I work myself further. I can taste him on my tongue.

He is almost there.

His hips lift faster, fucking into my mouth. Looking up, I watch the cords in his throat flex and ripple as sounds—gasps and expletives— fall from his slack jaw.

He grips my hair tight, a sharp prickling spreading over my scalp. His body shudders, all of his muscles contracting at once. Once, then twice.

On the third time, he goes completely rigid. He sobs out something, and I feel him releasing in my throat. He swells— thicker as he pumps cum onto my tongue.

My body throbs as I watch him. It's the best thing I've ever seen. I can't look away—afraid to blink and miss even a fraction of a second. When he releases my hair, I slide back slowly, letting him fall out of my mouth.

I'm a mess. And so is he. There is drool and cum all over everything.

And blood.

Blood?

Jerking back, I realize his hand is cut open and bleeding.

"Oh, my god! Noah!"

"It's fine, baby." He rasps. "Get up here. Sit that thing on my face. Let me take care of you."

"Noah! You need stitches."

"Fuck my hand. Give me your pussy." He grabs me, pulling me up onto the seat. More glass crunches as he moves down, putting my legs around his neck as he bends.

I feel his fingers as he slips my panties to the side.

"Did sucking my cock do this to you?" He sweeps his finger through it.

Before I can answer, he buries his face so far between my legs that I can't even see his eyes.

I'm so needy and desperate that it only takes a few licks for my back to arch off the seat.

"Give me all of it." He demands moving his mouth over me with such a fast rhythm that my vision blurs. Helpless moans leave the cab of the truck and disappear in the dark.

His hand comes up, wrapping around my throat, and that's all it takes.

I give him all of it. I couldn't hold back if I wanted to. Again, then again, and one more time for good measure. He rips pleasure from me–violently–like he owns it.

When he finally stops, I can't breathe. My lungs feel tight, and they burn with the effort of each inhale.

"I'm coming with you to that wedding." He presses a kiss to my cheek.

My eyes fly open, and I jerk my head up to look at him.

"What?"

"You didn't think I would let you go there with him by yourself, did you?" He runs his thumb over my lips.

"Oh, my god! Your hand!" I sit up. "I completely forgot about it!"

"It's fine." He shrugs it off.

"Noah! There's blood everywhere!"

"If I take you home, will you clean me up?" He leans down and kisses me again–pulling the air out of my lungs.

"Y-Yeah. I will." I'll do anything he asks.

TWENTY-TWO

LAST NIGHT, I woke up to the sound of gravel outside my window again.

He pried open my window and came in.

When I asked him what he was doing, he said, "You look so pretty when you sleep. I like to watch." I couldn't help but wonder how many times he had done that in the past. But I didn't ask.

Now, I'm sitting next to Colson while he drives us toward the coast. When he saw me, he tried to kiss me.

Things have been awkward since.

Sitting here, I find myself looking around for Noah. I tried to tell him where we were going, but he just smiled and said, "I already know."

Colson reaches over, resting a heavy hand on my thigh. "There's a group dinner tonight. I brought you a dress." His fingers tighten slightly, just enough to make me notice. "Relax, we're going to have a good time."

I can't relax.

He's acting like I didn't break up with him. Like, this is just another road trip. Like we're still his and hers.

I feel like I'm suffocating.

I need to get out of this car.

"My mom and grandma want to talk to you about wedding plans."

I shouldn't have agreed to this. I know that.

But we had already RSVP'd. It feels wrong to back out–like I'm as trashy as they think I am. I didn't want him to be embarrassed in front of his entire extended family.

Now I'm here, my skin prickling while he touches me.

"I mean," I clear my throat. "We should tell them, Colson. I don't want them to spend time–"

"Candy, be for fucking real. You're not breaking up with me. That was some kind of fucking tantrum because–"

I shift in my seat, forcing his hand off my leg. "Colson, we're not together anymore."

His fingers tighten before I can push him away completely. "Don't start."

"No, I *will* start," I snap, yanking my leg out of reach. "You keep acting like nothing happened, like I didn't end this. But I did. We broke up." I know he's surprised because I am too. I don't usually confront anything head-on.

His jaw clenches, knuckles whitening on the steering wheel. "You're being ridiculous."

I let out a humorless laugh. "I broke up with you. That's not up for debate."

His grip tightens on the wheel, and the muscle in his jaw twitches. "You're still here, aren't you? You still got in the car with me."

"Because you guilt-tripped me!" My voice rises, the pressure in my chest growing so that it's harder to breathe. "You said I'd embarrass you in front of your family! I didn't want that."

His eyes darken, and for the first time, real anger flashes across his face. "After everything I've done for you? You're really going to sit there and act like I'm some asshole?"

I scoff. I'm not acting.

"You're not ending things like that." He shakes his head like that's his choice to make.

"You keep moving between insulting me and claiming we're still together. I don't understand why you're so upset. Half the time, it seems like you don't even—"

His hands slam against the wheel. "Because I love you, goddammit!"

Silence fills the car, heavy and suffocating.

He exhales sharply, shaking his head. "You're making a mistake. We belong together."

I look out the window, swallowing down the fear clawing up my throat.

We don't. More than ever, I see that now.

An hour of complete silence follows. When we finally reach the resort, I want to scream.

"Don't say anything to them." He grits his teeth as he pulls the car up to the valet.

As I step out of the car, I look around for Noah. Where are you?

Several members of his family are in the lobby when we walk in.

They're faces light up when they see him, then fall when they see me. It only occurs to me right now, as I stand in front of them, that in order to save him from humiliation, I signed myself up for it.

It's for two nights.

His aunt and grandmother stop talking when I dare to step

near them. The disgust on their faces is clear. Different aunts, uncles, cousins, and distant relatives whisper about me—I can feel it. The poor girl Colson is slumming it with.

His brother is the first and only one to speak to me. He leaves me standing here, making the rounds.

"Candy." His voice always holds a mocking tone when he says my name.

"You know, if you think Candy is cheap or trash, you can always call me by my actual name. Candace." I smile sweetly.

I've always liked my name. Only they have ever made me question it.

"I never said it was cheap." He looks confused, probably by my sudden ability to speak up.

"Sure. Right. Of course not." Not to my face.

"Let's go upstairs and get ready." Colson slings his arm around my shoulder. His aunt is watching, the disapproval etched into her face. She's not even attempting to hide it. It's there, clear as day.

"Great." I hold my head high as we cross through the lobby. There is something about knowing that I won't ever have to see any of them again after this weekend that feels freeing.

Who cares if they don't like me? Now that I'm not trying to fit in, the pressure—the desperation—of wanting them to like me is gone. I feel free.

I'm sure it's all in my head, but it feels like he knows. He feels the shift in me as soon as it happens. The way he's holding me—the tightness in his grip—it's too much.

"What floor?" The elevator attendant seems to sense our tension immediately.

"Twelve." Colson snaps. The fake smile he had in the lobby disappears as soon as the door slides closed.

"Both of us?"

He rolls his eyes.

"You didn't get me my own room, did you?"

"Obviously not, Candy."

Staring down at my feet, I bite into my cheek. I've done some stupid shit in my life—made some really questionable decisions and was reckless where I shouldn't have been. When Parker died, I spiraled for a while—floating through each day with a kind of carelessness that made Stella afraid for me.

This feels even worse than that. This was fucking stupid.

What the actual fuck am I doing here with him?

His family might be in the upper echelons of high-class society, but they are rude, cruel, and elitist. Why was I so concerned with their feelings?

When the doors open, the attendant steps out, extending his hand to us. Colson follows, stepping out onto the twelfth floor.

My legs don't move.

"Come on, Candace. Now." He growls.

"I'm going to walk on the beach."

"Right now?" His eye twitches.

"Yeah." I'm not going into that room with him.

"We have to get ready. The whole family is meeting for dinner in forty-five minutes." His head tilts slightly.

The attendant is focused on the floor, his shoulders tensing up by his ears.

"What room are we in? Give me a key, and I'll be up in a bit."

"1242." He pulls a key card out of the sleeve. Without a word, he turns and walks away.

I let out a shaky breath and back further into the elevator.

Reaching into my purse, I find my phone. I want to call him —just to check.

The ride down is much faster.

"Thank you." I step out into the lobby. The back wall opens to panoramic views of miles of private beach.

His mother and father are seated on wicker deck furniture on the back patio with cocktails in their hands. I don't know the others, but I know they won't be welcoming either, so I pretend not to see them.

I'm not going to spend any more time than necessary talking to any of them.

The view is deceiving. It looks like the sand should be just a few steps away, but the path to the beach is much longer. When I finally get there, I pull my shoes and socks off and wiggle my toes in the slightly cool sand.

Walking down to the water, I walk parallel to the breaks, letting the water lap at my ankles.

Once I've passed the cabanas in the sand, I'm alone.

The air feels slightly damp and salty. It reminds me of summer vacations at Myrtle Beach. This is much more peaceful.

From somewhere behind me, far in the distance, I hear my name.

Spinning around, I expect to see Noah. But it's not Noah.

"Shit."

Just up the beach is a restaurant. The deck sits in the sand, overlooking the water. As he makes his way through the sand, I make a plan to get him to come sit there with me.

A public place. Safe. Visible.

God, this is so uncomfortable. I'm not walking back, and he's taking forever to reach me.

So we're in an awkward staring situation while he walks.

"Why the fuck did you come all the way out here? Jesus Christ!" He huffs.

"I'm just walking."

"Well, come back now. We need to get ready for dinner.

This is fucking ridiculous, Candace." He hasn't calmed down at all. In fact, he might be more agitated now. And I think he might have had a drink.

"I told you I wanted my own room. I'm not comfortable being in the same room with you."

"You're not comfortable?" His head tilts. He looks up from under his eyebrows, and I take a step back. The hollowness in his eyes makes my skin crawl.

"N-No." I shake my head.

"What do you think I'm going to do to you?" He steps forward. "We're getting married. I would never hurt you."

"Colson." I hold my hands out in front of me. What he said and the look on his face didn't match. He looks like he wants to hurt me.

His hands are clenched by his sides, and his jaw muscles are tight.

"Come on." He holds his hand out. "Let's go. Right now."

"I don't want to go back yet. Why don't we go sit at that restaurant?" I gesture to the deck.

"We have dinner plans with my family." He punctuates each word.

"I'm sorry." I step back again. My eyes dart over the beach. We're alone.

"Sorry?"

"I'm not going back with you."

He lunges forward and grabs my arm, yanking me hard.

"Let's fucking go. You're coming to this fucking dinner if I have to drag you back. We're going back up to our room, and you're going to put on the fucking dress I bought you. Then you're going to sit at the table with a fucking smile on your face and your fucking mouth closed." He drags me through the sand.

I twist my wrist, trying to pull away, but his grip tightens. Panic rises in my throat.

No one can see us.

No one will hear me if I scream.

And I don't know what he'll do if I fight back.

"Colson, stop." I keep my voice soft, hoping it helps somehow.

"God damn it." He shakes me, pushing me down to the ground hard with my wrist still in his grip. When he drops down into the sand beside me, my mind goes haywire.

No. Not this.

"Stop!" I scream at the top of my lungs. Someone, please hear me! "Help!"

"Help?" He sneers, grabbing one of my legs with bruising force and pinning me down. "Stop acting like I'm some monster that's going to hurt you."

"You are hurting me." From my view down here in the sand with his red, angry face above me, holding me down so that I can't escape, he looks like a monster.

I struggle against his hold, trying to roll so that I can get away.

"Stop!" He pushes himself between my legs.

"Colson!" I don't even recognize the sound of my voice. It's raw panic. "Please!"

"Shut up!"

"Help me!" I scream again. My voice disappears in the wind, gone before anyone can hear me.

"Candace, I swear if you don't shut up!"

"Colson, stop! This is—"

He lifts his hand, and I pinch my eyes closed, flinching. He's going to hit me.

I brace for it.

But then he releases me.

Opening my eyes, I scramble up and realize what happened.

He didn't release me. Not on his own, anyway.

Noah's got him pinned face down in the sand with his knee in the center of Colson's back.

He's flailing and struggling—just like I was—but it's like Noah doesn't even notice. His face is eerily calm.

"Noah!" I struggle to my feet. "Noah! Please!"

He can't hear me.

Colson is thrashing, his arms swinging at nothing, trying to get free.

"Noah, you're going to kill him!"

"Yes."

"No!" I crawl toward him. "You'll get in trouble! Please!"

His eyes flick to mine, the darkness fading slightly as he looks at me.

He stands slowly, letting Colson go. "This engagement is over." His voice is so eerily calm that it sends a chill down my spine.

Sitting up, panting, and wiping the sand from his face, Colson looks panic-stricken. But he has to say something. It's just not in his nature to be quiet. "You don't have any say in that. What the fuck are you doing here?"

"Give him a ring, Ace."

Colson chuckles. Not like he thinks this is funny. But like he doesn't think I'll listen.

My whole body is shaking. Everything feels blurry and out of focus.

"Give him the ring, Ace." His voice is softer this time. He holds his hand out to me, waiting.

Slipping the ring off my finger, I put it in his hand.

He drops it on the ground next to Colson. Leaning down, his large frame looming over him, he grits his teeth. "If you ever come around again, if you try to make contact —a single text message—I will fucking kill you."

TWENTY-THREE

I DON'T REMEMBER the walk from the beach to his truck. He might have carried me. My body feels weightless and heavy all at once, like I exist in two places—then and now. I've stepped out of my skin, and I'm watching this unfold from somewhere far away.

My mind is disconnected from it. I'm telling my body to do things, but it's not following the commands. I've lost control.

I'm checking out. The ability to focus comes in and out. I'm outside on the beach, then I'm in the truck. Reality is weaving itself into a tangled knot. I don't know if I'm in the past or present.

Sitting in the cab of his truck, my body shakes. I hold my own hand, trying to stop the trembling, but I can't.

Noah shoves the key into the ignition, but we're still in the parking lot. His hands grip the wheel so tight his knuckles turn white. His breathing is ragged, too loud in the silence between us. The world outside the truck is taunting me. It's beautiful. The water. The slight tinge of orange starting to streak across the sky.

How could something so ugly have happened here?

"Stay here." His low voice rumbles, clipped with rage. He pushes his door open.

"Wait!" I grab him with both hands, my nails digging into his skin. "Please don't leave me!" My voice is unrecognizable. I sound small and scared–like a child.

His jaw clenches, muscles ticking beneath his skin. "Ace. He's going to learn today. That was the last time he ever touched you. Ever."

My stomach knots, coiling inward to a painfully tight ball. "Please, I don't want you to get in trouble."

He doesn't respond immediately. Just sits there, his body vibrating with barely contained fury. I can feel it radiating off him, burning in the air between us. My fingers tighten on his arm, desperate. If he walks away right now, I might shatter. I need him here.

"Please," I whisper again. One last attempt to keep him with me. I'm barely holding on. If he leaves, I'll lose everything.

Finally, with a rough sigh, he jerks the door closed and shifts the truck into drive. The engine hums beneath us, but we're silent.

The road stretches out ahead, taking us home. Trees line either side in that way that always makes me feel like we're somewhere magical. But right now, it's not. There is no magic.

My mind feels fractured. Did that just happen? The memories blend together. Six years ago and just now. Indistinguishable—melted—a nightmare of both experiences twisted into one.

The past claws its way forward, dragging me under.

A hand around my wrist. Fingers digging into my skin. The crushing weight of a body pinning me down. The taste of copper in my mouth.

I gasp, lungs seizing, the world rolling violently. My chest constricts, a dull knife pressing inward. A hand wraps around my ribs, squeezing tighter, tighter, tighter—

I can't breathe.

The road in front of us looks darker–blurry. Shadows creep into my vision. I'm so hot. But cold.

The truck jerks suddenly, skidding slightly as Noah veers onto the shoulder of the road. The tires crunch against gravel, and then everything is still. The only sound is the engine idling and my own ragged, panicked gasps.

"Ace." His voice is softer now, but I can barely hear it over the rush of blood in my ears.

The seatbelt feels like it's strangling me. The strap is pressing against my throat. My hands claw at it, at my chest, desperate to pull in a breath that won't come. My body is shaking so hard my teeth clatter. I fold in on myself, arms wrapping around my middle, trying to hold myself together before I come apart completely.

Noah moves fast. The click of his seatbelt, the shift of weight as he turns toward me. A hand on my knee—warm, grounding. I flinch and pull away.

"Hey," his voice wraps around me. "Look at me, baby."

I squeeze my eyes shut tighter. If I open them, I'll still be there. I'll still see his face. Hear his voice. Feel his hands on me—

I can still feel the sand all around me.

I'm not in the gazebo.

I'm not on the beach.

The past isn't here, not right now. This is real. This is happening. I'm with Noah.

I know that. But it won't let me go.

"Breathe with me, Ace." His tone is firmer, more insistent. "In for four, hold for four, out for four."

His hand is still on my knee, not gripping, not holding me down—just there. Solid. Steady.

I try. My breath stutters and catches, but I try. I can't do it.

"Try, baby."

In for four. My lungs fight against it, refusing to open up.

Hold for four. My hands clench into fists.

Out for four. The darkness inches in closer.

"That's it," his warm lips press against my temple. "Again. You're doing so good. Take another breath for me."

We do it again. And again. And again. Until finally I'm able to take a full breath without feeling like a weight is sitting directly on top of my lungs.

I open my eyes and blink away the tears. The truck's headlights cast a glow over the trees, the empty road stretching endlessly in either direction. It feels like we're the only two people left in the world.

Noah's watching me, his brows drawn together in concern. He doesn't ask if I'm okay. He knows I'm not. Instead, he reaches up, brushing damp strands of hair from my face, his touch so soft it grounds me in reality.

"Come here." He pulls me up into his lap.

He's holding me too tightly, but it helps. It's soothing.

"I'm not going anywhere." His heartbeat is steady, a gentle thump in his chest that makes me feel safe.

"Thank you for coming."

"I'll always come for you, Ace. Nothing will keep me away."

My eyes droop, all the emotion draining from me, leaving me exhausted.

"Go to sleep. I've got you." His voice starts to sound distant.

TWENTY-FOUR

NOAH

SHE FINALLY STOPPED SHAKING. I think she's asleep.

My brain is on fire. The only thing keeping me from hunting him down right now is the weight of her in my arms. I can still feel the tremors in her body, phantom aftershocks of terror. His terror will be real. It will be endless.

I'm going to fucking kill him.

My fingers tighten in her hair. If I could have ripped his eyes out of his face and shoved them down his throat, I might be able to relax.

But it wouldn't be enough. Not nearly. He hasn't paid for it. He hasn't begged yet.

He will.

His days are numbered. He is marked. Death is coming for him.

The sound of her scream is burned into my skull, playing on an endless loop. The sheer, raw terror in it. A sound that he caused. That sound belongs to him now. He'll hear it inside his own head, over and over, just like I do.

I'll carve it out of his lungs myself. And when there's

nothing left of his voice but a ragged gurgle, I'll rip his throat open and watch him drown in his own blood.

Blood bubbles up in my vision. I see it everywhere—dripping from my hands, splattered across the walls, soaking the ground where his dead body falls.

Closing my eyes, I picture him gasping for his last breath. The way he'll claw at my hands, trying to stop the inevitable.

My pulse steadies, but I don't sleep.

I'll sleep when he stops breathing.

TWENTY-FIVE

IT'S STILL DARK when I blink my eyes open. We're stretched across the seats in his truck, his arms around me.

He runs his fingers through my hair. "Hey, Ace." His voice sounds tired, but I know I didn't wake him. He was standing watch, guarding me.

"How long have I been asleep?"

"A while."

Normally, I would scramble off his lap and apologize for inconveniencing him, but I don't have to with Noah.

He doesn't see me as an inconvenience. I can feel it.

"I'm going to bring you back to my place." He isn't asking, but I nod like he's giving me a choice.

Without letting me go, he slides behind the wheel. The engine hums to life, and he pulls back onto the road.

"I never want you to see him again." His arm tightens around me.

Maybe it's left over adrenaline. Maybe I'm lashing out. Because my life is out of control. But something about this particular demand upsets me.

"I have things at his house. I—"

"No."

"No?" I crane my neck to look up at him. "Noah—"

"You aren't to see him again."

The words hit me–hard, sharp, and disorienting.

"I was engaged to him. This isn't going to be that easy." Frustration simmers in my chest.

"You were never going to marry him." He scoffs like the very idea is a joke, stepping harder on the gas. The truck lurches forward, tearing down the empty street.

I don't know where this anger is coming from. Noah saved me. He didn't do anything wrong. But a raw, acidic, wild fury is flowing through my veins, and he's the only one here to direct it to.

"Don't tell me what to do, Noah."

He laughs, but it's hollow, laced with something frayed and dangerous.

"My whole life just imploded. Maybe you're right–we would never have actually married each other, but–" My words cut off as my lip trembles. It's not grief; it's rage. Rage at being cornered by life again, stripped of choices. Helpless. Always helpless. How many times do I have to find myself in that position?

"If there is anything at his place that you need, I'll get it." He doesn't look away from the road. There is no room for negotiation in his voice.

He's not listening.

I don't want Colson. That's not the point. I just want to claw my way out of this invisible cage.

"I'm so sick of feeling powerless," I whisper, almost ashamed to admit it.

"You're not powerless." His voice is softer now, but he still doesn't understand.

"I am! He... and now you're just—"

"Don't ever fucking put me in the same sentence as him." He slams his foot down on the brake in the middle of the road. He isn't yelling, but his voice is seething.

"I'm not comparing you!" I shout, voice cracking. My chest is too tight to breathe properly. "You wouldn't understand." The words tumble out faster than my mind can sort them. "You don't know what it's like! You don't know what I've been through."

His knuckles go white on the steering wheel. "I'm the only one who knows what you've been through." He grits his teeth.

"What?" My head spins. He can't mean...

He exhales, a long, slow breath. "Ace, you still think I hit him by accident?"

My stomach drops, the pieces falling too fast for me to catch.

"Noah. What are you saying?"

His laughter is empty, a dark, violent edge to it. "I couldn't find you that night. I tore that fucking party apart." His hands tremble on the wheel. "Then everyone said they saw you with Parker."

A chill settles in my bones. The cab feels too small.

"I found him in the bathroom." His voice is dangerously calm. It doesn't match the barely there restraint in his body. "He was trying to wash blood off the front of his fucking khakis. When I grabbed him, he said you were in the gazebo." He rolls his neck, eyes unfocused, staring out into the darkness. "I saw it on his face. He was afraid. I knew what he did."

"Noah..." I barely get his name out. My pulse is a frantic drum in my ears.

"By the time I got there. You were gone." He turns slightly, his face almost unrecognizable. "I followed him for twelve days."

My breath catches. I'm going to pass out.

"Twelve days," he repeats, voice dipping lower, nearly reverent. "I waited for the right moment. I planned it. I made sure no one would question it."

"It wasn't an accident," I whisper, numb.

"No," he says. "It wasn't."

"You murdered him."

"He had to pay for it. I had to make sure you knew that he could never touch you again." There is no hesitation or remorse in his answer.

I don't know what to do. "But—"

"I killed him, Ace. On purpose. After planning it for weeks. I wish I could have given him a slower, more painful death, but I couldn't figure out a way to make it look accidental. He deserved worse." He holds eye contact.

Reaching back, I tug the handle to open the door.

I don't have a plan. My feet hit the ground, and I run, darting across the road into the tree line.

It only takes a moment for the slamming of a door to send a cold rush of adrenaline through my chest.

"Where are you going, baby?" He calls out, his voice steady —easy.

I press my back against the rough bark of a fallen tree, forcing myself to breathe slowly, to quiet the sharp, ragged gasps. Squinting in the dark, I search for something–somewhere to hide. But there's nothing in here but trees and shadows. Just us, in the middle of nowhere.

"Come on out, Ace." There is a hint of something in his voice–amusement? Is he enjoying this?

Pressing my back to the bark, I look around in the dark. Of course, we're in the middle of fucking nowhere.

He murdered him.

He murdered him?

Why would he do that? How? Noah Gaines—serious, reserved, careful Noah—did that?

"Are you sure you want to play this game with me, baby? I've been watching you for so long. I know you better than you know yourself. You're excited. Aren't you?"

My heart is racing and I can't catch my breath.

No.

No, I'm not.

Except—I am.

A cold rush floods my veins, tangled with heat and anticipation.

I feel it.

He killed him for me. As punishment for hurting me—for taking something that didn't belong to him.

He was protecting me.

"Are you going to make me find you?" He's closer now.

Ducking down, I weigh my options.

"There isn't anywhere you could hide that I wouldn't find you."

The words themselves are frightening—a threat. But...

I could try to run around, find my way back to the desolate road. Or I could come out and see what happens.

"Come here." His hands are on me before I can decide.

"Let me go." I thrash in his grip.

"Never." He wrestles me to the ground. The leaves and dirt shift around us.

"I'm afraid of you."

"No, you're not." He pins me with his knees, holding my arms down. He looks almost relieved as he stares down at me.

No, I'm not. Even with the confession he just made, I know he won't hurt me. He's one of the few people I trust not to.

His breath ghosts over my cheek as he presses his forehead to mine. "I'm glad you know."

I freeze.

"What?"

He nods, his grip on me tightening. "I've been waiting for you to know. For you to see me."

My back presses harder against the dirt, but there's nowhere to go. His thumb brushes my cheek, tender like he hasn't just confessed to premeditated murder.

"You don't ever have to be powerless again." He licks my lower lip. "Not while I'm here."

Tears sting my eyes, but it's not just fear—it's exhaustion— years of weight on my chest crumble, and I can finally breathe. Then he takes my mouth with so much force, my lips sting.

My lips move against his, opening and letting him in.

He groans, a sound I'm starting to recognize.

"No one is ever going to hurt you, Ace. I won't allow it." He whispers against my lips. "He's going to pay for what he did. I promise you."

His mouth trails hot, open-mouthed kisses down my jaw, across my neck, biting just enough to make me gasp.

"Don't kill him." I'm doused in ice-cold reality.

He stills, forehead resting against mine. "He doesn't get to do that to you and live." His voice is so calm—so final. It's already settled in his mind.

"But you'll get in trouble. You can't—"

He cuts me off with his lips again. He's hungrier this time, almost frantic.

He groans like it's killing him to stop. His hands roam everywhere, touching my skin.

"While I was inside, you were the only thing that kept me sane. I'm never letting you go."

Heat and need spread through me. God, he makes me feel things that I never thought I would feel.

The fear and doubts I always have when I find myself in

this position are gone–they evaporate. When he looks at me, I'm not disgusted.

"Noah." I flex my wrists, desperate to touch him.

"I'm bringing you back to my apartment. If you want me to fuck you in the forest like an animal, I'll do that, but not our first time."

He stands, pulling me up with him. When he lifts me off my feet and carries me through the trees, my mind goes blank. A kind of catatonic wave washes over me.

The truck is still running, idling abandoned on the side of the road as the sun starts to rise.

He sets me down in my seat, reaching around to secure my buckle. "Let's go home." His lips graze my temple, soft and sweet–shockingly so for a man who has just admitted to murder. I can't move. My mind is drifting, floating.

All this time, I held the secret in. Years of hiding it, carrying the weight alone. But I wasn't alone. He knew all along.

Slipping out of my seatbelt, I slide across the seat to tuck myself into his side. He opens his arm, making space for me.

"Thank you," I whisper. I'm not positive about what I'm thanking him for. I think I know.

"Always."

TWENTY-SIX

"ACE?" His fingers graze my neck, holding my head steady as he slides out of the truck.

"We're here?" I lift my head, looking around the dark parking lot of the small apartment complex.

"You fell asleep."

How? I drop deeper into a spiral. What does that say about me? He confessed to murdering someone—on my behalf—and I not only fell asleep immediately after, but slept like a baby.

"Come here." His voice is low, almost a growl, as he lifts me effortlessly, my legs instinctively locking around his waist. The moment we step inside his apartment, a quiet dread seeps into my skin.

We stop in the kitchen, and he sets me on the counter as he thoroughly scrubs his hands. Twice. He doesn't explain, and I don't ask. I just watch until he's finished, and he lifts me up again.

He lowers me onto his lap as he drops onto the couch, leaving me straddling him, my knees pressing into either side of his hips. His hands rest loosely on my thighs.

My eyes dart over him—he's tense, every muscle drawn tight like a predator barely leashed. His jaw ticks, and he rolls his neck like he's trying to shake something off. A low, guttural growl vibrates from deep within him.

I should move. I should slide off him and put distance between us. But there is this warm feeling curling low in my belly.

Placing my hands flat on his chest, I feel his flexed muscles twitch.

He lets out a short breath. "Take control right now. Go ahead. Do whatever you want to do." His grip tightens, just enough to make me feel how careful he's being. "But don't mistake my restraint for mercy." His hips move, shifting slightly to take pressure off the bulge in his pants. "I'm not going to be gentle with you." His eyes are locked on mine.

My breath catches.

His fingers slide up to my waist, slipping under the hem of my shirt to touch my bare skin. "I'm going to touch *everything* they thought they could own." His voice drops into a growl, and each word makes my pulse flutter. "I'm going to make sure there's not a single inch of you left that doesn't belong to me."

He leans in, lips grazing my jaw. "After today, you're mine." He leaves a trail of light kisses up my jaw. "Forever."

Shivering, I press in closer. Running my hands up, I let my fingers explore his neck, then his jaw, and his lips.

"Tell me how much you want me." His head falls back.

"I want you." I almost can't say the words.

"How much, baby? Does it ache?"

"Yes." Heat spread through my face and chest. I've never participated in dirty talk before. My fingers tremble as they bring them up to his neck, holding onto him. "Noah." I cringe. "I don't...can you just–"

"Do you need me to do it, baby?"

"Yes."

His hands slide up my legs, pulling my skirt up as they go. "I'm going to make you feel so good."

My breaths are coming out in fast, shallow pants. A flush of excitement sweeps over my skin.

He shifts us, rolling so that my back is leaning against the armrest of his couch. And he's between my legs.

When he kisses me, it's like he's trying to suck the life from my body—like he's trying to consume me. It's like he can't get enough. We aren't close enough. He wants more—deeper.

His fingers graze over my hand, taking them gently and placing them on his thigh. "I want you to feel confident, Ace. Undo my pants. There isn't anything you can do with me that I won't like." His voice is so soft—soothing. But my nerves are frantic.

Swallowing the urge to cower away and curl into myself, I bring my hands to his belt.

"Look at me, baby."

I lift my eyes to his. There isn't any impatience in his expression.

"Focus on me, go ahead."

Taking a breath, I open his belt. When I try to tug it out of the loops, it doesn't budge.

He smiles, reaching down and yanking it. For him, it cracks like a whip that he tosses quickly to the floor.

"Now I want your skirt off. I want to see and feel everything."

Lifting my hips, I pull my skirt down. He takes over at my thighs, pulling it off and tossing it.

"Keep going." His eyes are still on mine.

The muscles in his arms flex as I slowly drag the zipper

down. Mustering all the confidence I can find, I hook my fingers into the waist of his jeans and tug.

He's so hard. Not just... there. His stomach, his legs. Everything about him.

His arms cage me beneath him as he leans forward and stands up. "Keep going."

The little bit of false confidence I had last time was due to the shot of liquid courage. Right now, my doubts are creeping up my spine, whispering in my ear, holding me back.

Tugging, I watch as he bites into his lower lip. His jeans slip down his thighs, and he helps me guide them all the way down.

My pulse hammers hard, a mixture of excitement and nervousness.

He steps out of them, kicking them aside.

I watch his shirt come up over his head, falling to the floor with the rest of the clothes. He's completely at ease.

My insides are fluttering and squishy.

His fingers trace my skin as he goes for the hem of my shirt. I'm so nervous, I have to take a break from the intense eye contact.

"No," he takes my chin gently. "Don't close your eyes. Stay here with me. Don't run away from it."

"Noah." Everything is too much. I feel too many things.

"I'm going to take such good care of you." He slips my bra straps down my shoulders. "Lie back and let me look at you."

Shit. This isn't the first time he's done it, but it doesn't feel any less vulnerable.

"Spread your legs wide. Put this one here." He takes my ankle and guides one leg up to the back of the couch.

Before he comes back to sit between my legs, he tugs his boxers down.

My eyes go wide. It looks bigger than last time.

"I'm going to use your pussy to edge myself. You're going to come, over and over again, before I let myself fill you up with cum."

I can't remember the last time I took a breath.

"Will you let me try something, Ace?"

"What?" The darkness in his voice scares me enough to zap some life back into my body.

"Do you trust me?"

"Yes."

"Surrender yourself to me."

"How?" My voice shakes.

He sits up between my legs and brings his hand down, touching my sensitive skin.

"Noah?"

"Relax, baby. I'm not going to put my cock inside yet." His voice wraps around me, easing the tension in my muscles. "Just trust me."

He rubs my clit, and slides one of his fingers into me.

Staring directly into my eyes, he spits between my legs. My body jumps as it lands.

"Keep these open." He takes my other ankle and places it on his shoulder. "I'm going to put my whole hand inside."

I jerk forward, a natural instinct to run. His hand is huge! There is no way that could possibly fit...

But he starts rubbing tight little circles against my clit, and I let my head fall back again.

"Such a good girl. You're going to take it, ok? I'm not going to hurt you. Trust me, and it won't hurt." His voice is so soothing and calm.

I can't speak; my voice is gone. So I nod.

His thumb moves in slow, deliberate circles, coaxing sensations from me I can't hold back. My body betrays me, hips twitching, thighs tense as heat blazes in my belly.

Then, he pushes deeper, curling his finger inside me, and suddenly the world tilts and my vision goes blurry.

"Oh, god." Fear moves up my spine.

But he's right there. "You're safe, Ace. You're with me. Give it to me."

As I shake around him, my body surrendering to the unstoppable force, he adds another finger.

With each orgasm, my body loosens. Forced into submission. He guides me through each wave.

"Ready, baby?" He whispers.

"No." I whimper.

He presses forward slightly, and I take a panicked breath. It doesn't hurt–I don't think so anyway. It just feels so strange. Full, with so much pressure.

His head falls forward, and a shudder runs through him. "Holy shit."

Loud, panted breaths heave from his chest. And his cock leaks between us, dripping down the sides.

"Fuck." He chokes and moves his hand. "Look, Ace."

I don't know what he did, but it makes my entire body jerk. He moves down, licking my clit while moving his hand again. It's the smallest, most subtle motion, but it reverberates through me like an electric shock.

Gasping, I blink back tears. I can't look.

"You're doing so fucking good. My couch is soaked. You're making a mess everywhere, baby." He moves again, and it's like an explosion, a ripple that spreads through my body so quickly it makes me scream. It came so abruptly, with so much intensity, that I can't even place the sensation. Good? Bad? I don't know. It's a paradise of torture, pain, and pleasure.

My vision goes black. When he slides his hand out and crawls up my body, a sob creeps up my throat, and I can't hold it back.

That was something entirely new.

"Come here," his voice thick with something tender and aching. He pulls me into him, cradling me like I'm fragile and precious, like holding me is the only thing keeping him steady. His arms wrap around me fully, anchoring me against his warm chest. He seeps into my skin. "You are so beautiful."

His lips trail softly over my cheek, soft and slow, until they reach my tears. He licks them up with the kind of care that makes my heart ache—like each drop is sacred. "Are you ready to be mine, Ace?"

There's a subtle tremble in his voice, like the question costs him something–like he's holding back.

"I'm ready." I think I'm ready.

I've never been asked that.

He moves me to his lap, letting me straddle him again.

"Look how bad I want you." He looks down between us. He is so swollen and red, standing straight up. "I'm aching, baby." His chest muscles jerk. The tattoos on his skin are pulled tight as he trembles slightly.

"Noah!" I gasp. "What is that?"

A little red tattoo tucked into his side catches my attention. I've never noticed it before.

"The ace of hearts." He rolls his hips, sliding his cock between my legs and pushing it up.

All at once, he's inside of me.

He chokes on a moan and brings his hand up into my hair. "Oh, fuck." His damp forehead drops against my lips. "I fucking knew it." He rasps.

My nails bite into his shoulders as I steady myself against him.

"God damnit. It's so good, baby. I knew it would be." A little gasp huffs past his lips.

His hips move, thrusting up into me with bruising force.

"Look." He growls. His eyes are glued downward. "Look how your tight little pussy is taking me so well."

Peeking down, I watch him slide out, then back in.

"Fuck, you're grabbing onto me, pulling me back in. Do you feel it?" He moves again.

There are too many thoughts and sensations hitting me all at once. "When did you get that tattoo?"

"A few years ago." His lips twitch, barely a smile, before he rolls us, pinning my back to the couch. His knees his the floor, and now he's in the perfect position to put power behind each stroke.

He's so deep I can't breathe. Each thrust knocks the wind out of me.

"Fuck!" He grits his teeth. His hand presses flat against my stomach, pushing down slightly. I can't keep my eyes open. The feeling alone is too much. The visuals make it more than I can take. "This is my fucking pussy now. Say it!"

"It's—"

He speeds up, rocking into me with so much force it makes my hips ache. It's raw, unrestrained—fucking brutal.

"Say it." His hand comes up to my throat, squeezing just enough to ground me in reality.

"It's yours," I whisper.

"What is?"

"My—"

"Say it, baby. Whose pussy is this?"

"Noah." My voice wobbles. "It's yours."

"Listen," he says, slowing down, his thrusts almost gentle. "Do you hear how wet you are for me?"

Beyond the ragged sounds of my breath, there is a slick, wet sound—our skin, the friction.

He stares down between us, watching himself slide in.

Then he abruptly slips out, rolling his neck. "Not yet." He

grits his teeth. "I have to feel you. I need you to come all over my cock before I can come, baby." He's struggling–fighting against the urges in his body.

My breath catches as he slides back in.

"You're doing so good, Ace. Take it. Let me do this for you."

The desperation in his voice does something to me. It quiets the fear in my brain, the doubt, and the nervousness. This is different. It's Noah. Not Parker or Colson.

When he reaches up again, gripping my neck, the pressure in my body spreads. "Noah."

His body tightens, a scowl taking over his face. With determination on his face, he pounds into me, a relentless, violent pace. This has got to be as fast as he's capable of going. He's using it all.

Everything blurs. His body. Mine. I feel so connected to him, so desired and cared for, that my mind drifts. My head is empty of everything outside of this room. It's just him. He does this for me. The loud noise in my head obeys him and bends to his command. He wants me to feel pleasure—so I do.

"Oh, shit." He moans. "Just like that. You're strangling me, baby."

Forcing my eyes open, I look up at his face. He's already watching me, so much pleasure carved into his expression.

This time, when I feel myself falling over the edge, it doesn't feel like falling, but soaring. The ground isn't pulled from under me. I jump. It's my choice.

My spine curves, bowing toward him.

He sobs, a pain-filled moan–and his pace finally slows. He pulls out again. "I want one more. Then, I'm filling you up."

"I-I can't."

He smiles, a wicked, knowing grin. "One more." He presses

in slowly. "Every time you move tomorrow, I want you to remember my cock buried all the way inside you."

Like I could forget.

Making the mistake of watching his face, the hot pressure in my stomach ripples outward, upward, spreading everywhere.

Clamping my teeth into my lower lip, I watch the waves wash over him.

"Touch me, baby. Put your hands on me." He begs before pressing our lips together. Kissing him feels strangely intimate. More so than any other thing. He's inside of me right now, but when he kisses me, he's taking the breath from my lungs and breathing it into his own. It's hungry—he is—for me.

Wrapping my hands around the back of his neck, I hold him closer, clinging to him. Riding out every roll of his hips.

It's been rough. My hip bones will ache, and my thighs will be bruised tomorrow. He said he would claim it, and he has.

But now, he's gentle. Each thrust is a slow roll that hits so deep it makes my legs twitch.

Building higher and higher, he forces me up. It's too vulnerable. I'm too open and exposed.

He'll keep it safe, though. My heart. My body.

He'll kill for it.

"Oh god, Noah!" This one catches me completely off guard. The room spins as he presses into me further.

"Fuck...fuck! Candace!" He growls through clenched teeth. And finally... I feel him twitching—jerking inside of me. He rolls and grinds himself into me like he's trying to get deeper. "Holy shit."

I don't know if he's ever called me by my given name before.

His face drops into my neck, and he sucks my skin, leaving

little marks. I'm barely conscious. All the energy in my body was drawn out and drained. He took it.

Wrapped in his arms, I trace my finger over the tiny red heart tattooed on his side. As my eyes get too heavy to keep open, I feel his lips on my temple.

"Sleep, Ace." His voice sounds as tired as I feel. "I've got you."

TWENTY-SEVEN

NOAH

I NEED MORE. That wasn't enough. It'll never be enough.

I could be inside of her and still be starving for her. I could devour every inch of her skin, every sound from her throat, and still be ravenous. I need to have more of her to consume her. My cock, my fist, I can't get deep enough. I want to be up all the way inside, in her heart, in her head. I want to own it.

She's lying here, soft and warm in my arms, and it feels like holding sunlight. I fucking knew it would be. It's all I thought about for years, but I had no idea how good it would be, truly.

She is oxygen. Water. The sustenance I need to live.

I claimed it all. And yet, I want more. More of her sighs, her cries, her body writhing beneath me. More of her scent soaked into my sheets, my skin, my mouth.

She let me do everything. I knew she would. Her wet, pink pussy opened up for me, inviting me inside. She clenched around me, milking my cock. Greedy girl took every last drop.

She's mine.

Mine.

Every part of her, even the things she keeps hidden from

the world, the pieces no one else will ever touch– I've already claimed them. I own them. She doesn't even know how deep I've sunk my claws into her. She's sleeping so peacefully–with no idea that I'm stitching myself into her soul.

I'm carving myself into her bones–straight to the marrow– with every breath.

I can't stop looking at her. Whatever she looks like right now is my favorite thing. Her wild, tangled hair? Perfect. Lips swollen and bitten? Perfect. Every freckle, every curve, every trembling breath—perfection. She is it. My "type," just her.

I'll take it all. Every mood, every flaw, every sharp edge, and soft place, she thinks she hides from me. I'll take her anger, her fear, her joy, her love. I'll drown in it. Gladly.

I've chained myself to this hunger–this aching need– and I'll never beg for release. She's seeped into my blood, into every cracked, broken corner of my being, and there's no cure for it. I don't believe that I have a soul–she fills that space now. The void that used to be there is gone. It feels good. Whole.

She shifts in her sleep, and I almost lose my mind. The barest brush of her knee against my leg feels like lightning striking my chest. I want to wake her up just to take more. To kiss her until she forgets her own name, until the only thing she remembers is me.

My name on her lips.

My hands on her body.

My cum in her throat and dripping from her perfect cunt.

My mark on her soul.

Flexing my fingers, I hold back the urge to roll over on top of her.

I'll have her in every way a man can have a woman.

Wrapping my free hand around my cock, I hiss. This will never be good enough–not anymore.

She needs sleep. Let her sleep.

My eyes roam her naked body, and my fist pumps my cock, slow and lazy, just reveling in her warm skin.

Right now, between her legs, my cum is dripping. Holy shit. The thought makes my blood churn.

Harder and faster, I watch her chest moving. Every breath makes the ache worse. The pressure in my stomach is unbearable.

She moves, and her hair slips back behind her shoulder. Her neck...

"Ah, fuck..." I lean up, not enough to wake her but to spit on my cock. It's not as good as her mind-numbingly wet, hot, tight.... Shit. It will do for now.

The little marks I sucked into her neck are showing. Three of them.

God damn it.

They look so good. I want to wrap my hand around her throat, just a little bit, a little squeeze.

The way her breath catches and her eyes go wide...

Grunting, I bite into my lip. I have to be quiet.

I'm going to come all over her. Make a mess on her skin.

The pressure throbbing in my cock builds until my hips thrust up, seeking her out. My mouth falls open, slack.

My mind wanders back to when my fucking fist was inside her. When I rolled my knuckles and she came, gushing all over my couch and legs. That's all it takes.

"Ah, Ace!" I groan, watching my come land on her hip and stomach.

Now, maybe I can sleep. I need to rest. I have to be in top form when I rip the spine out of Colson Barrington.

TWENTY-EIGHT

WHAT THE FUCK is wrong with me?

The words pulse in my head, loud and insistent–a headache right behind my eyes. In the light of day, the events of early this morning seem vile. It's like waves crashing down on me. And I'm drowning in them.

Parker Moreland was a predator, a disgusting excuse for a human being. But still... we don't just kill people. There are laws, consequences, and lines you aren't supposed to cross.

Noah crossed them. For me.

He killed Parker.

Then I had sex with him.

He confessed to murder, then I had sex with him...

I'm spiraling.

The memory of his hands all over my body is so real, I feel them–the ghost of his touch grazing my skin. Goosebumps roll down my arms.

He touched everything.

And I let him.

I don't know what's worse—the blood on his hands, or the

fact that after hearing about it, I still chose him. Or maybe it's that part of me felt safe for the first time in years, curled against a murderer.

My eyes drift to him, lying peacefully beside me. His handsome face relaxed now. The dark, brooding intensity is gone, replaced with peace. He almost looks gentle. Almost.

My stomach twists. This is Noah—Stella's brother.

Oh, god! Stella! I can't believe I just let her big brother do those things to me!

I *just* broke off an engagement. My heart is still bleeding from that wreckage, and yet, here I am—curled up on his couch in his arms like I belong here.

What the hell am I doing?

Tears burn in the corners of my eyes, but I blink them away.

For every feeling, there is an equally strong, equally valid contradicting emotion. I'm at war in my mind.

I've never felt truly cared for–loved–by a single man that's touched me. Not until him.

But that doesn't change what he did...

Shame and satisfaction. Fear and peace. Guilt and calm. Anxiety and relief. Despair and hope. I can't make sense of any of it.

Sitting up, I slowly, carefully, climb over the back of the couch.

"Oh, shit." My stomach muscles ripple as soon as I stand. Every part of me hurts.

He said he wanted me to remember him every time I moved. Mission accomplished.

Wincing, I pull my skirt up my legs and look around for my discarded bra and shirt.

Where did he put my bag?

It's in the kitchen on the counter. He must have set it here when he washed his hands. That makes sense now... he had plans for his hands.

My cheeks burn as I remember it.

Pulling my phone out, I cringe. Twenty-eight missed calls and thirty-six messages.

Taking a deep breath, I call him.

I'm shocked that he answers on the second ring.

"Candy! Where the fuck are you?" He sounds relieved.

"Home."

"Look, the wedding is in five hours. I'll come get you. There is still time."

"No, Colson, listen—"

"I'm already home. I came back last night. I'll be at your place in thirty minutes."

"Colson, you're not listening. I'm not coming back to the wedding. I still have a key to your place. I'll come by and get my stuff while you're gone and leave the key. Go ahead and enjoy the wedding, I—"

"Candace." The icy calm in his voice makes my breath catch. "You're coming with me to that fucking wedding. I was able to cover for you with my family. They think you were sick last night."

"I'm not coming—"

"I wonder how the police would feel about your little convict friend assaulting me." He hums. "My uncle Jeff is a lawyer. I could head down to the station with him. We could probably have that piece of shit back behind bars before the wedding!"

"W-Wait. Colson, don't—"

"What was he doing there anyway, Candy? The only thing I can think of is that the attack was premeditated. What other reason could he have had to be way out there? He was so hostile to me at Stella's birthday dinner. And when he showed up at our date. Honestly, it sounds like he's stalking you. I'm sure Jeff could help you get a restraining order." I can hear the smirk in his voice.

"No. I—"

"Be here in thirty minutes or I'm making the call, Candy. Let's see how quickly the police arrest that piece of shit. You know I'm a betting man. I'm going to wager very quickly."

"Ok, ok, I'm coming. Don't call the police!"

Frantic, I order an Uber before realizing that I don't even have shoes here.

Fuck it.

As quietly as I can, I run outside. The morning air is cold and damp, but I hardly notice it.

If I do as he says, he won't call the police. Deep down, I don't believe that, but I have to try.

His family would be devastated. I can't sit back and do nothing. The chances he's bluffing are almost none.

As I slide into the back of the Uber, I hear my name.

Shit.

"Go, please!" I bite into my cheek.

"Ace?" He yells again. He's shirtless and barefoot, rushing down the sidewalk.

Turning, I ignore the way my chest feels tight as the driver pulls out onto the street.

Twenty-two minutes. That's how much time I have to straighten myself up.

My hair is wild, equal parts sand and knots. My skin feels dirty. I'm covered in sweat and... unmentionable bodily fluids.

Digging around in my bag, I find an almost empty body spray, chapstick, gum, and a comb. This is what I have to work with. It will have to do.

I feel like the driver is judging me. He knows what I did.

Rushing to smooth myself out, I try to ignore the sense of

dread. Each rotation of the tires is bringing me closer to Colson.

I have to keep Noah out of jail. This would be the second time he went to prison for me.

Oh god. The guilt in my chest multiplies tenfold and presses on my lungs. Stella will be devastated. The last time he went in, she was unrecognizable for weeks. This would ruin her.

I'll put on the best act, an Oscar-worthy performance.

When the car stops outside of Colton's townhouse, a pit tugs at my stomach, and nausea rolls through me.

"Thank you." My throat is dry.

He turns and looks at me, a strange expression on his face. I'm frozen, and he doesn't speak, but it looks like he wants to. Maybe he can see my hands trembling.

Closing the door, I hurry up the driveway. The sooner I go in there, the sooner this is over.

He's standing in the doorway, waiting for me as I walk up the pathway. I never realized how secluded the view of his doorway is from the street.

"You fucking whore." He grabs me as soon as I'm within reach. "What the fuck, Candy!"

"Colson—"

"You have hickeys all over your fucking neck! You let that fucking convict do this to you?" He pulls me into the small bathroom just inside the door.

Oh shit. Hickies? Looking in the mirror, I see three small purple spots on my neck.

"You don't leave me!" He screams, the veins in his forehead bulging. "You are fucking trash! You come from a family of low-life scum! A person like you doesn't leave a person like me! You should be licking the fucking ground I walk on! I plucked you out of the fucking gutter, and you're acting like you didn't win the lottery. Get on your fucking knees!" He shoves me down with so much force that my knees buckle and I fall. "Beg for my fucking forgiveness!"

"Colson, I'm sorry that—"

"You know what? You don't look sorry! Beg, Candace." He pulls his phone from his pocket. "I have my uncle's number pulled up—ready. If you don't start acting a little more fucking remorseful, I'll call him."

"Please don't do that."

"Put my fucking ring back on." He tosses the box at me. "You aren't ending this engagement, and he sure as shit isn't. This is none of his fucking business. He isn't going to step in and involve himself in this."

"Ok." My entire body trembles violently as I slide the ring back onto my finger. "You're right, I'm sorry."

"Did you fuck him?" He takes a step forward. My heart hammers in my chest. I have to get out of here.

What we did was so much more than fucking.

If I can get out of this bathroom, there is a guest room beside the kitchen. I'll lock the door and climb out the window.

"No," I whisper. "I didn't."

"You won't even fuck me! You flinch when I touch you. In one year, we've only done it a few times! You're a fucking prude, but you're out cheating? With a criminal? What—"

Using his long tirade as my chance, I bolt. As fast as my legs will carry me, I run out the door and through the house. With everything I have, I sprint into the guest room and push the lock.

The door shakes under his fists. "Open this fucking door!"

He rattles the handle and hits the wood so hard I'm afraid it will shatter.

My legs wobble as I run to the window.

The loud pounding stops abruptly. A single thud vibrates through the floor.

Then there is a soft tap.

"Ace?"

My heart leaps up into my throat. "Noah?"

"Open the door, baby."

My legs move on their own, running back to the safety of his voice.

When I yank the door open, the look on his face makes my heart skip. He's angry. At me. I

Still shirtless, his chest is heaving as he scowls down at me. "Go wait in the truck." His jaw clicks.

"Noah, I–"

"Right now, Ace. Go."

With gentleness I wasn't really expecting, he places his hand on the small of my back and ushers me forward.

Colson is lying on the floor. For a moment, it crosses my mind that he's dead, but then he groans. I stop, my body locking up as I stare at him. He looks so much smaller than he did a few minutes ago.

"Go, baby." Noah's voice snaps me out of the frozen state I'm stuck in. "Outside."

My legs wobble like Jell-O as I try to step around him.

"Candace!" Noah shoves me forward, but it's too late. Colson kicks my legs out from under me. But he doesn't let me fall.

I stumble as he releases my arm. "Go, Ace!"

"Fucking whore!" Colson growls as he pulls himself to his feet.

Noah groans a pleasured sound. "Keep talking. I would love to kick all those pretty veneers out of your fucking face. Call her a name again!" The smile that tugs at his lips is terrifying. "I'm going to crush your skull." He starts dragging him down the hallway. He looks massive—like a monster pulling Colson to hell.

The screaming makes my chest feel tight. Colson's gasped cries for help are like a punch to the gut.

"Noah, please." I whimper. "Please, let's go."

"No, baby. He needs to learn his lesson."

Colson grabs the doorframe, holding on for dear life as Noah pulls him into the bathroom.

I should go outside. I'm not strong enough to hear whatever is about to happen.

My hand shakes as I reach for the doorknob. But before I can fully open it, there is a loud crash from behind me.

Colson barrels out of the bathroom, blood gushing from his nose, a bloody towel bar in his hands. He lifts it above his head as he races toward me. He's going to hit me.

Ducking, I cover my head with my arms. A sharp pain radiates through my wrist, and then everything is a blur.

Colson runs outside, and Noah scoops me up in his arms.

TWENTY-NINE

HIS GRIP on my hip is tight as he holds me on his lap. He's speeding.

"If he broke your wrist, I'm cutting his hand off, Ace." How does he say things like that so calmly? There's no emotion in his voice. It's just a statement–a fact.

"Noah." My lip trembles as I stare up at him. His jaw is set so tight he's going to crack his teeth.

He doesn't respond. No reaction whatsoever. His fury wafts around him.

"I don't think it's broken." It actually might be, but I don't want him to be angry.

The truck screeches to a stop in front of the emergency room doors. He gets out, abandoning it in the drive lane.

"Noah! You can't—" He doesn't care. So I stop.

"We need a doctor!" He shouts into the quiet room. I can walk. There is nothing wrong with my legs, but now is not the time to argue.

"What's happening?" a nurse runs around the reception desk.

"I think her arm might be broken." He sets me on my feet, gently holding my swollen arm out toward her.

"How did this happen?"

I freeze like a deer in front of a speeding car. "I—I—"

"She was hit." Noah doesn't hesitate.

"By what?"

"A towel bar."

The nurse looks taken aback but gathers a stack of papers on a clipboard. "We will call you back soon."

The vein in his neck pulsates, but he doesn't say anything. Taking the clipboard, he guides me to a seat and starts filling it out quickly.

"Um, I can—"

"I know all of this." The anger in his voice makes me shrink back.

"My social security number?"

"Yep."

Well, then.

We sit in total silence as he scribbles on the forms furiously.

When he's finished, he stands without a word and slams them down on the reception desk.

"Noah." I know he's mad, but I have to keep trying, knowing that he won't speak to me, is eating at me. It's like acid in my throat that I can't stop picking at.

"Stop, Candace."

Yikes. Candace. That's a bad sign.

"Please."

"Candace." He rolls his neck. "Don't pout your fucking lip."

I try not to, but my chin wobbles.

"God damn it, baby." He scrubs his hand over his face. "Don't cry."

"I know you're mad at me—"

"Why would you go back there? It took four fucking hours for you to run back. Why, baby?" His hands snake into the hair at the nape of my neck.

"He said he would call the police and have you arrested," I whisper.

His eyes flutter closed, and the tension in his jaw finally relaxes. "Ace, why wouldn't you just tell me?"

"I panicked. You can't go back to jail!"

He wraps his arm around me, pulling me toward his chest.

"Look at me." He tips my chin up. "Next time, just talk to me."

"I'm sorry. But he's dangerous."

"Yeah, no shit." He growls.

"I mean to you." I let out an irritated huff of breath. "His ego is wounded, and he doesn't like to lose. He has enough money to hurt you."

"Well, then I'll kill him. Problem solved."

A panicked laugh bursts out of my mouth. "No! You can't do that!"

"Sure, I can, baby." He's completely serious. "And take that fucking ring off." He growls, kissing my forehead.

My mouth gapes open and closed like a fish. I can't think of a single thing to say. Before I get a chance to scrape enough of my melted brain back together to formulate a response, the door at the end of the waiting room swings open.

"Candace Kennedy?" A nurse in navy blue scrubs calls my name.

Slipping the ring from my finger, I drop it into my bag as we follow her down the hallway. "I'm Carly Smith, the triage nurse. Let's have a look at that wrist."

She examines it carefully while asking me questions. The whole time, her eyes keep looking quickly at Noah. She's trying to be subtle, but I notice it every time.

"Can I have a moment to speak with her?" She asks, her voice calm and polite, but I recognize the tension in it.

"No." His head tilts.

"No?" Her brows shot up into her hairline.

"I'm not leaving her alone. Ask her what you need to ask her. I didn't do this to her." He doesn't falter. Being viewed with suspicion doesn't rattle him.

"He didn't." I jump in to defend him.

Her eyes narrow slightly as she looks at me.

"Dr. Stevenson will be in soon. This needs an X-ray."

When we're alone, he moves to sit on the bed with me, his arms wrapping around my waist.

"How did you know where I was?" I lean into his chest.

"I have your phone location." He is completely nonchalant.

"Noah!" I try to sit up, but he tightens his hold.

"Ace, what kind of stalker would I be if I didn't know where you are at all times?"

"You would classify yourself as a stalker?" Did he really just say that?

"Yes." He doesn't hesitate. "How else am I supposed to keep you safe?"

"That's insane!"

"Yeah." He's still too calm.

"Noah, you can't—"

The curtain is pulled back, and several people step inside.

"Candace, I'm Dr Stevenson. What happened here?" He sits on the small rolling stool and wheels toward me.

"I was hit with a towel rod." As I say it, I realize that I'm going to have to explain. That, by itself, leaves a lot of questions.

"Can you tell me who did this to you?"

"My ex." I don't mean to shudder, but my body trembles.

He hums, "We're going to take you down to get an X-ray. I can't say with certainty until I see the films, but I think there is a bone fracture."

"Ok." I inch my hand toward Noah. "I've actually fractured this wrist before."

He looks up. "When was that?"

"When I was nine. It was an accident." My stepdad accidentally pushed me out the kitchen door, and I fell down the back steps.

"Alright, let's get you down there." He smiles and stands. Behind him, the nurse rolls a wheelchair into my very crowded little section. "If you want to wait here, you're welcome to, or you can go back to the waiting room." He turns to Noah. "We can't have anyone but the patient in the radiology department."

"Noah." I spin around, wrapping my arm around his neck. "I'll be alright, I promise. I just want to finish this so we can go home."

He swallows, and his jaw clenches, but he nods. "I'll be right here."

I press a quick kiss to his cheek before settling into the wheelchair.

They push me down the hallway and into a large elevator.

As soon as the door closes, Dr. Stevenson kneels down beside me. "Candace, are you safe at home? If he did this to you, we can help you."

"He didn't. I'm safe with him."

"We are required to report suspicions to the police."

"Ok. I understand that, but it wasn't Noah."

He sighs like he doesn't believe me, but nods his head.

Luckily, the X-ray process only takes fifteen minutes because my whole body is drained. Maybe telling Noah how sore I am will put him in a better mood.

"This is a simple fracture." Dr. Stevenson shows me the

film and points to a clear line in my bone. "You'll be in a cast for six to eight weeks, but I suspect you will heal fine. Your cast will take about thirty minutes to apply, then you can be on your way."

"Great." The relief I feel as they push me back into my curtained-off area is short-lived.

The police are here. Noah is sitting on the bed, completely relaxed, talking to two officers.

"Noah." I start to stand.

"Hold on, Miss Kennedy. We have a few questions for you." One of the officers steps between us. "I'm Officer Kurtis. Can you tell me what happened today?"

"Listen, I know you're just doing your job and they had to call you, but—"

"You don't have anything to be afraid of. We're here to protect you."

I don't know why this makes me laugh. "My ex. The one that did this." I hold up my bruised, swollen arm. "Is a Barrington. If you really want to help me, you'll drop it."

"Which Barrington?" He doesn't look surprised. In fact, he looks irritated.

"Bennet, Riley, Camden?" He starts naming members of the family.

"Colson."

"Ah, the baby. We haven't had the pleasure of dealing with him yet." He rubs his hand over his face. "Look, our job is to escalate this situation to ensure your safety, but—"

"Sweeping it under the rug is the best thing to do." I cut him off.

The atmosphere in the room is suddenly very different. I can see a visible change in the staff here. They aren't looking at Noah like he's a predator anymore.

"Take my card. I'll write out this report, leaving his name

off. That way, in the future, if you need or want to file anything against him, this is there. Please call if there is anything we can do."

I take the card from him, the useless slip of paper that I will not be using. "Thank you."

When my cast is finally finished, I take Noah's hand. This has been an overall decent experience, but I can't wait to get out of here.

"You need to eat." He collects my bag and the paperwork the nurse gave me. "We'll stop and get your prescription and then food."

"Ok." I'm not going to argue with him.

He's being soft with me, gentle. But there is something about the way he moves, like his muscles are coiled beneath his skin like a spring about to snap. He's tense.

"Noah." I slide across the bench seat in his truck. "I'm alright. I know it's a bad situation, but—"

"He broke your fucking bone, Ace. Do you know what I'm going to do to him?" He chuckles like the thought brings him joy. "I'm going to break all of his bones. I'm going to remove his bones."

"But—"

"It's actually a good thing that his fucking family owns half the town. If he were in jail, I couldn't get to him. He thinks he's free, out living his life. He has no idea what's coming for him." His hands turn white against the steering wheel.

Under any other circumstances, I would take this as angry venting, but not with Noah. He's not just saying things to make himself feel better. He means every single word.

The truck pulls off the street, idling on the shoulder of a secluded country back road.

"How sore are you?"

"What?" I know exactly what he means, but I'm taken aback.

"Your pussy. Can you take it right now?" He turns, his eyes meeting mine with so much intensity I feel instantly hot.

"Here?"

"Out there." He gestures to the expanse of trees lining the road.

"In the forest?"

"I can't stop thinking about it since I said it. I want you on your hands and knees. I'm never going to hold myself back from you again. When I want you, no matter where we are, I'm taking you. The only exception being if you're too sore. Are you?" He runs his hand over the front of his pants.

"No." No sound comes out.

He reaches down and picks up my shoes from the floor of his truck.

"Run. I'm going to catch you, and then I want you on your knees."

Opening the door, I jump out and run.

Having my arm in a cast is slowing me down. It's heavier than I'm used to, and I'm afraid to swing my arm.

The sound of his door slamming closed behind me sets my blood on fire.

THIRTY

NOAH

RAGE AND EXCITEMENT course through me. When I catch her, she's done for.

On a baser level, I understand why she would rush back to him after hearing him threaten me. She was trying to protect me. The instinct to protect is one I can actually understand.

What I can't wrap my mind around is the fact that she didn't wake me up and let me handle it.

She's going to learn today. That will be the last time she makes that mistake.

She'll learn the hard way. I'll carve the lesson into her bones if I have to. She thinks she can make choices like this—thinks she gets a say in what happens to me? To us? No. She doesn't. She forfeited that the moment she became mine.

I can still taste the betrayal like blood on my tongue. My mind races with visions of her on her knees, tears in her eyes, whispering apologies I may or may not accept.

Maybe I'll make her beg—make her prove her regret, her loyalty. If she can prove it.

"Where are you, Ace?" I walk into the tree line. "Come out, come out, wherever you are!"

A twig snaps somewhere in the distance.

"I think you want me to catch you." I hum. "You can't wait until I find you."

Stopping, I close my eyes, listening for her.

The wind rustles through the leaves, and I hear her. There was a spark of excitement in her eyes when I told her to run.

My fucking girl. She wants to play. She's ready for it.

"Be a good girl and come out for me, angel. I'll go easy on you if you come out." I call out with no intention of going easy on her. I'm going to fuck her into cock-drunk oblivion.

I play along, letting her run and hide. Taking my time so she thinks she has a chance.

Another twig snaps. There she is.

Walking around the trunk of a large old tree, I find her crouching, eyes wide and wild.

Yanking my belt out of my pants, I toss it to the ground. "Up on your knees. I'm fucking your throat. Then, if you're a good girl, I'll fuck you. Show me how fucking sorry you are that you went back there."

She comes up on her knees.

Pulling my aching cock free, I grip her hair and rub her face against it.

"What did you do wrong today, baby?"

"I should have told you that he was threatening you."

"Are you ever going to run off without telling me first?"

"No." Her voice wobbles.

"Are you sorry?"

"Yes." She nods earnestly.

"Show me."

She reaches up, but I tug her head gently. "No hands, baby. Use that pretty mouth."

Her mouth drops open, and she stares up at me, slightly bewildered and shy. But she sucks me in any way. "Good fucking girl." I'm already a mess. That's all it takes.

She works me in and out of her mouth.

My hips start to move, thrusting farther into her throat. "That's it." My muscles and joints start to feel loose. "You're doing so well. You're really sorry, aren't you?" I fuck faster, holding her head immobile as I thrust harder, pushing deeper each time.

Faster.

Harder.

Deeper.

I should come. I know her mouth has to be tired. But this is a punishment, and I'm enjoying it so fucking much.

"Is your pussy wet, Ace?" I taunt her. I know it is.

Her watery eyes go wide, and she tries to nod.

"Is it aching for me? I bet it's so swollen and clenching, searching for me."

She moans around my cock, vibrations like electric currents spread through me.

Jesus Christ. The rage in my veins moves back—never gone completely—but, for the time being, pushed aside.

The look in her eyes makes me feel like god himself. She's probably dripping between her legs. She would let me do anything I wanted right now. I can see the fear—not of me—of herself. Confusion and doubt swirl around in her big doe eyes.

"You love this, don't you?"

There it is. The doubts. The fear.

"Hey," I jam my cock into the back of her throat and pause, holding it there. "You're safe. There's nothing wrong with this." I rock out of her slowly. "You belong to me. I want you like this. My perfect, pretty girl that only acts like a whore for me."

She swallows around me, and my body jerks. "Are you my whore?"

She moans.

Yes. She is.

"Tell me how sorry you are." I grit through my teeth.

A tear drops from her lower lashes, rolling down her cheek to mix with the drool on her chin.

She looks sorry. She can't say it, her throat is full of cock, but her eyes say it for her.

"Fuck! Are you ready? You want me to flip you over and fuck you now?"

She moans again, and my cock stiffens before I unload down the back of her throat.

"Take it all," I growl.

And she does. Of course, she does.

Pulling away, a string of drool hangs between her lips and the head of my cock. Her lips are swollen and red, and her chest is heaving.

"Any clothes you're still wearing in five seconds are being cut off." I yank my shirt over my head.

She sits, momentarily stunned.

"Five, four–"

She springs into action, ripping her shirt over her head and dropping her skirt into the dirt around her knees.

Too slow. Pulling the knife out of my pocket, I flick it open.

"Freeze." I grab her by the strap of her bra and cut it right between the cups so that it falls open. "You can't support your-self on your wrist, so put your face in the dirt."

She hesitates.

"Right now, baby. I'm going to make you feel so fucking good."

Her eyes are still unsure, but she shifts her body, using her uninsured hand to support herself as she lowers her cheek to the dirt.

"Arch your back. Let me see you wide open for me." I stroke my cock and watch her.

There are bruises on her ass and thighs— my fingertips. I want to dig into her skin again.

Kneeling down behind her, I watch her wiggle impatiently.

"You want me to touch you, Ace?"

"Please, Noah."

"How bad do you want me?"

"So bad, please." Her voice is raspy—strained from my cock.

I glide my fingers over her pussy and press my middle and index fingers into it with force.

She squeezes around me immediately, and my mind goes into overdrive. All I can think about is sinking into her. It's animal–raw, and primal. I have to have her.

Curling my fingers twice, I slide out of her and line my cock up.

There is no easing in. I'm balls deep immediately.

Her knees slip, and she lets out a whimper. A little fucking sigh.

I drag my hips back, and she clenches as tight as a fist around my cock.

"Baby?" I grunt. She's about to come already. "You love being chased and fucked outside in the dirt, don't you?"

"Yes." She pants.

One more, that's all it takes, and she comes so hard I almost black out.

She cries out my name, taking fistfuls of dirt in her hand, clawing at the ground.

"Don't run away from it. We're not even close to finished."

THIRTY-ONE

"WAIT RIGHT HERE." He sets me on the counter beside the sink. "I'm going to get a plastic bag to wrap around your cast."

I nod, or at least think I do. I'm hardly conscious—practically comatose.

I'm covered in dirt. There are leaves and twigs in my hair.

Even in this state, I just want to crawl into bed. Dirt and all.

"Let me see your arm." He gently wraps my cast up and starts to remove his clothes. This perks me up a bit.

My eyes move to the little red tattoo. Even after everything, I can't believe he has that. Without realizing it, my fingers come up to brush against it.

"You like it?" His lips pull upward.

"Yeah." I do. It's kind of unhinged that he's had it for years. But I do like it.

"I want to get another one. I've been saving this place on my arm." He rotates his arm, showing me the blank space on his forearm.

"What are you going to get?" I follow him into the warm shower.

"Your eyes."

"What?" My head jerks up, water slipping down my face.

"I want that pretty mouth on me somewhere, too."

"Noah! You can't!"

"Why not?" His head tilts to the side.

"I mean, I don't know." I guess he can actually. Who's going to stop him?

He chuckles as he picks up the soap and starts washing my body, slow and deliberate. His touch is different now—softer, like he's memorizing me. It's not hungry, it's careful. The dirt circles the drain at our feet, but his focus stays on me.

His fingers trail down my arm, careful not to wet my cast. When he kneels to glide his hands over my thighs, there's something almost reverent in the way he touches me, like I'm fragile.

"Why are you looking at me like that?" His voice is quieter now as he pulls the showerhead down. "Tilt your head."

I do as he says, closing my eyes as the warm water rushes through my hair.

"It's weird when you're so soft." I feel myself blushing.

He hums and runs his fingers through my hair, massaging my scalp. "I can be soft sometimes. But I don't think you actually want that."

I fold into myself, my mind racing with too many thoughts. He's right. I like his roughness. But it feels wrong.

"What he did to you and what we do are not the same." His voice drops, firm but gentle. He tilts my chin up, forcing me to meet his gaze. "Do you understand me?"

The moment shatters as a door slams. My stomach drops.

"Oh no, Stella's home!" Panic rushes in.

"It's alright, Ace." He smiles, rinsing my hair.

"No! This can't be how she finds out about us! Walking in on us in the shower is—"

"She won't say anything to you."

"Noah, it's not just what she has to say! It's about how she feels. She's my best friend. I care about—"

"Candy?" Her voice comes through the door.

"One minute." He barks out sharply before I can say anything.

"Oh, my god." I feel nauseous.

She doesn't say anything, but I can picture her face in my mind—confused and uncomfortable.

I scramble out of the shower, heart pounding. "I need to get dressed." I rush into my room.

He follows behind me, a towel wrapped low on his hips. He's not rushing to get dressed at all.

"Noah? You here?" A male voice—Jace. Great. As if this wasn't bad enough.

"Yeah."

"We need to talk, man."

"One sec." He's still the picture of serenity.

I try to pull my leggings up, but my hand is shaking, and with only one available, I can't do it. Without a word, he steps in, tugging them up for me, his fingers grazing my skin in a way that shouldn't make me blush in the middle of a crisis.

By the time we step into the living room, Stella is curled up on the couch, her legs draped over Jace's lap. But the moment she sees my arm, she's on her feet.

"Whoa!" She rushes toward me, her eyes wide. "What the fuck happened to you?"

Jace jerks his chin at Noah, and they disappear into the kitchen.

"Um, well. A lot has happened." I flop onto the couch, unsure where to start. "There's a lot to tell."

"Okay." She sits back down, watching me carefully. "Are you alright?"

"Um, I think so." I shrug, suddenly feeling emotional. "I don't know if I've actually processed it yet. Colson and I broke up."

"Oh, shit." Her eyebrows shot up into her hairline. "He didn't do that to your arm, did he?"

"Yeah. It's just a simple fracture. I—"

"Just?" She gasps. "Just a simple fracture? What the fuck?"

"I know." I'm so embarrassed.

I know she's not judging me, and her anger isn't directed at me, but I can't help the way that I feel.

"So..." She looks at her fingers, fidgeting. "You and Noah?"

I swallow hard. "Um, yeah." I force myself to look at her. "I'm so sorry, Stella. I should have told you sooner. I didn't want you to find out like this, but I didn't know how to bring it up. And for a while, I didn't know what it was or—"

"Candace!" She grabs my shoulders. "I'm not mad at you. I won't lie. It's a little weird." She laughs. "But I love you. Maybe you'll be good for each other." There is a hopefulness in her eyes that eases the panic in my chest.

"How are things with Jace?" I change the subject, taking the heat off of myself.

"I'm going to marry him." A rosy blush spread across her cheeks. "He's perfect."

I blink. "Wait, what?"

"I'm serious." She looks like she might float away. "He's steady and dependable, but just bad enough to keep it exciting. We mesh really well together. He puts up with all of my shit."

I've never seen her like this. Everything feels lighter now. The clouds that were lingering above me are finally starting to disappear.

"It's weird, right? Jace and me. And now you are with Noah. He's with my best friend, and I'm with his."

"Baby, we have to go." Noah steps into the room, still only wearing a towel.

"Oh, ok, I–"

"I'll help you put your shoes on."

"Wait? I'm coming?" I thought he was leaving.

"I'm not leaving you here."

"Is everything alright?"

"Not really. I'll tell you about it on the way."

My mind immediately goes to the worst possible place. We're going to have to flee the country. Colson and his family called the police, and Noah is going to get thrown back into prison if we don't leave right now. I don't have a passport.

"Ace. Calm down." His hand on my lower back only slightly eases my panic.

Stella and Jace are rushing out the door, too. Maybe this doesn't have to do with Colson.

"See you there," Jace yells over the hood of his car.

Noah nods. He's not frantic in the way that I am, but the ease from before is gone. I can see tension in him.

After making sure I'm securely buckled in, he throws the truck in reverse, peeling out of the parking lot with a little too much force. The tires screech, but he doesn't seem to notice—or care.

"Take a breath." He reaches over and squeezes my thigh. "Our club is..." he hesitates, tilting his head like he's searching for the right word. "We launder money for a few businessmen around the city."

"What?"

"Let me finish."

Rolling my lips into my mouth, I wait for him to continue.

"I used one of my contacts to fuck with a few Barrington

businesses." A slow, amused chuckle rolls from his chest, but there's no humor in it. "People like that don't learn unless you rip into their wallets. Money is the only thing they care about. So I had a few of their launderers taken care of."

I'm stunned. I want to interrupt, but my mouth won't move.

His grip on my thigh tightens, just enough to make sure I'm still here, still listening.

"We have a friend in a high place. He just called to warn us —apparently, we're about to be raided. The bar's clean, but I want to remove a few personal things before they get there."

The cab feels like it's shrinking. My head spins.

"You launder money?"

"Yes."

"For who?"

"A few politicians. They take bribes and dodge taxes. We clean that money up for them and, in return, they make sure we don't have any problems."

The silence in the cab is loud—blaring.

"And you went after the Barringtons?"

"Yes. People like that are always dirty, Ace. That's how they get so rich. They have under-the-table deals, too. Unfortunately for them, there was an anonymous tip that led to the city councilman they bribed to be investigated. He panicked and cut them loose. They might actually have to pay their taxes this year." He smiles, staring out the window. "My guardian angel was watching out for me."

"But what if they find out?"

"Oh, baby." He smiles. "I'm betting on it. I made sure they only had to pull a few very short strings to find me."

"Why?" My heart thumps against my ribs.

"Because I want them to know I'm coming for them." His fingers squeeze my leg tighter—not painful, just more.

"But—"

"He can't outrun it, baby. It's his time."

His hand shifts, his thumb stroking slow, lazy circles against my leg—gentle, affectionate, like he isn't talking about tearing a man's life apart piece by bloody piece.

"He broke your wrist. I'm not just going to kill him, I'm going to burn his entire fucking world to the ground piece by piece first." His voice is so calm. So still and assured. There's no hesitation or fear in it.

His thumb stills.

"By the time I get to him, he's going to be begging for death just to find a moment of peace from the constant fear of waiting."

"N-Noah."

"This is just step one, baby. They are retaliating by having the DEA come out. We don't have any drugs on the property. We don't deal, we don't use, there will be nothing there. This is just for show. They're sending me a message. But they don't know what I know."

"What do you know?"

"That there isn't anything I won't do. Everyone has a limit, Ace. I don't. As long as you're safe, I don't give a shit about anything."

"Don't say things like that."

"Why not?"

"Because." I don't know what to say. Because even though it makes my heart feel weird and my stomach clench, he's not supposed to feel like that about me–about anyone. There are rules and laws–morals. He can't go around hurting people who hurt me.

The truck comes to a smooth stop outside the club. He turns in his seat, facing me. "Candace, there isn't anything I wouldn't do for you to protect you. To make sure the people who hurt you pay for it. I fucked up before. I wasn't paying close enough attention. I won't ever make that fucking mistake again. Do you hear me?"

"I hear you." My voice wobbles.

"Good." He presses the release on my seatbelt to pull me toward him. "Stella is going to sit with you here. I don't want you to be inside in case they come early. We'll be quick." He grabs my neck and kisses me. The kind of kiss that stops everything.

When he pulls away, I'm breathless, and my lips are swollen.

The way he looks at me. It makes everything–all the frightening, wrong, dangerous things fade away.

"Stay here."

"I will."

"I'm taking you home with me tonight."

"I don't have anything! I have to be at work tomorrow. I–"

"I have all of your things at my house. You can get ready, and I'll drive you home to get dressed."

"What things?" We just left my apartment. Everything was there.

"I bought all of your potions and creams. I have them."

The man who just finished talking about how he plans to slowly torture someone, then kill him, bought my skincare to keep at his house?

"What about pajamas?"

"We won't need any clothes, baby."

THIRTY-TWO

HE HAD TO LEAVE. He promised to come right back. But even one second alone is too long.

I don't look different. Staring in the mirror, I'm the same woman as before.

My arm is in a cast, and there are fresh bruises on my hips from Noah's hands. But I'm still the same.

I'm not sure what I expected. A magical cure that would fix it all. I would be whole and normal.

When I'm with him, he doesn't let me feel ugly or used. But he's not here.

The voices creep back in.

They're louder now. They taunt me.

How could I let Noah do those things to me? How could I enjoy it?

Some part of me, a fairytale part that believed in true love and soulmates, thought that maybe one day the feelings would just go away.

But without him here to scare away the shadows, they're back. I feel looming over me.

Dirty. Dirty. Dirty.

A wave of nausea hits me, and hot tears burn a trail down my cheek. I'm disgusting. I let Noah do things to me that...

And what's worse, I like it.

Parker could see it, sense it somehow.

Guilt and shame press on my chest, and it feels too tight to breathe.

The things Noah does to me... I consented to them. I wanted them. He makes me feel like I could be safe, like it might be alright for someone to touch me.

But now my mind burns, screaming that I don't deserve good things.

Turning on the shower, I set the water to the highest heat and wait. I'll burn the shame off my skin.

When steam fills the bathroom, I step into the shower, wincing as the water pelts my skin.

Alone, I let myself cry. I'm safe to let it out. No one will hear it. No one will know.

Keep it secret.

Hunched over, I wrap my arms around my chest and sob.

It pours out of me. Hatred for the world and for myself. Thoughts are popping into my head so quickly that I can't grasp a single one.

It's war in my mind.

I'M SAFE WITH NOAH. I'm not safe at all.

He cares about me. No one could ever care about me.

I'm disgusting. I'm dirty. I'm used.

He thinks I'm beautiful. He thinks I am someone worth saving. No one can save me.

.   .   .

THEY HIT me one by one, a thousand little cuts that leave me bleeding out.

"Ace."

I barely hear him over the ragged sounds of my breath, the stream of the water, and my blood pounding in my ears.

"Candace." His voice is so soft.

I forced my eyes open to find him standing outside the shower. The light bends around him, his body tense.

"Why are you crying?"

I don't want to tell him. If I open my mouth, everything might spill out.

He steps into the shower, wrapping his arms around me.

"Tell me." He's not as soft this time. He's demanding it from me.

"Why do you want me? You could get someone who isn't ruined. Someone who–"

"You aren't ruined." He says it with so much conviction I almost believe it.

"I am." I shake my head. "I'm disgusting, Noah." My voice cracks.

His jaw flexes. "Don't ever say that again. You survived, Ace. There's nothing disgusting about that."

"The things we do..."

"There isn't anything wrong with the things we do, Candace. You are allowed to feel pleasure. You deserve it."

"No, I don't." I grip his shirt in my fist.

"If it takes the rest of our lives, I'm going to change your mind on that." He peels back, holding my face in his hands. "Leave that with me. I'll take it. I don't want these thoughts in your head anymore. Will you trust me?"

"It's not that simple."

"It is. Give it to me. I'll take it."

"But..."

"You're mine now, Ace."

I feel myself nodding, hypnotized by the deep green of his eyes.

"Give it to me. Take a breath, does it feel easier?"

A little bit.

"It's my fault." He whispers. "I should have been there to stop him."

"It's not your fault!" I gasp.

"I was supposed to protect you." He weaves his fingers through my hair.

"You did." The words come out before I can stop them. Speaking them out loud is accepting what he did.

He lifts me into his arms and carries me out of the shower. Our bodies ease into his bed, dripping wet. I curl into him, truly safe.

"Next time you feel like this, call me. I can't take care of you if I don't know about it." He is somehow soft and stern.

"I will."

THIRTY-THREE

"I'LL BE HERE." He presses a quick kiss on my cheek.

"I know."

I expect him to linger, maybe walk me all the way to my desk, but he doesn't. Instead, he turns away at the door.

"Good morning, Miss Kennedy!"

"Good morning." My voice is steady, my smile automatic. I walk the same path I do every morning, past the same desks, and the same people who believe in things like law and order. Justice. Right and wrong.

I don't belong here. I'm a fraud.

I shouldn't be allowed to work here anymore. Not with what I know.

Because I don't just know the truth—I've accepted it.

He confessed to murder, and I slept with him.

He told me that he's a money launderer. I didn't even blink. There wasn't even a second that I thought I should walk out the door.

And worse? I don't even feel bad about it.

That should terrify me. It should make me sick.

But it doesn't.

It only makes me wonder if I ever really believed in justice at all.

What's wrong with me?

I'm more emotional over the fact that I don't feel anything. It's confusing.

Without the weight of his presence, my mind races with too many thoughts.

"I have a meeting this morning." Mr. Connors comes out of his office, disheveled. "While I'm gone, can you respond to the email from Don Livingston? I'll take any time he can give me, even if that means pushing prior engagements."

"Will do." I smile a fake smile.

He rushes out of the office with his files and coffee. Luckily, he was too frazzled to notice my arm. I don't feel like talking about it.

Sitting at my desk, I start up my computer with every intention of getting right to work.

But for some reason, that's not what my fingers do.

Instead of opening the mailbox and responding to the DA from the next county, I open our secured file database.

Barrington.

The keys practically type by themselves.

"Holy shit." There are at least fifty files here. Clicking on one of them, I read over the information.

It looks like Noah isn't the only person who knows about the Barrington family's crooked ways.

Apparently, the DA's office knows too. Very well.

Racketeering.

Bribery.

Tax Evasion.

Blackmail.

The list goes on and on.

Then I see another file. Locked and encrypted.

Pulling out my phone, I take several pictures of different pages. This is so very illegal.

Even as I'm doing it, I scold myself—but I don't stop. Page after page, I click through, documenting everything until I'm too nervous to continue. My insides are fluttering, and I feel sweaty as I put my phone away.

No one saw me. I'm the only person in the office, but I feel jumpy.

Every creak or hum from the air conditioner makes me jump.

I can't believe Colson's family is involved in any of this. They are so well respected. Each of them is considered a pillar in the community. They run charities and serve on different boards and committees. His mother is a part of the local community theater—she has been known to be the greatest benefactor they have ever had. They donate books to the children's hospital and host a Christmas gala for people who are struggling financially.

How can they be criminals?

Pretentious assholes, sure. But criminals?

By the time I actually start to work, a sharp twinge low in my abdomen makes me cringe. "Oh, no."

Jumping up, I grab my purse and rush to the bathroom. Please, not today!

Unfortunately, today.

It hits me fast. Cramping, heat, and the slight ache in my lower back and down my thighs. Fuck.

At least it explains the emotional landmine I've been tiptoeing through all morning.

I'm not losing my mind.

I'm just on my period.

Slumping in my seat behind my desk, I rub my hand over my face.

My computer dings–an email response from Mr. Livingston.

"Hey!" Mr. Connors walks in looking just as flustered as he did this morning when he left. His tie is crooked, and he's got a stack of unorganized papers in his hands.

"You're on the books with Don Livingston on Wednesday morning." My eyes scan over the email quickly. Just in time.

His face lights up. "You're a lifesaver! Thank you! Go have a coffee break." He smiles.

"Thank you."

I don't deserve a coffee break, but I'm taking it, anyway. I need to breathe fresh air for five minutes.

Every three steps, I check my purse for my phone. I keep sliding my hand in, needing to feel it, needing to see it. Like if I don't, it might have somehow disappeared since the last time I checked.

It's stupid. Irrational. But today, it feels like I'm walking around with a bomb in my bag—one wrong move and someone will ask to see it, borrow it, take it. And they'll know. They'll see what I've seen.

No one has ever borrowed my phone before. I've never lost it or had it stolen from me.

But today feels like the day.

Today, with all of this highly classified material on it.

The coffee truck around the corner has these crumbly streusel muffins that sound like exactly the thing I need right now.

As I round the corner, something catches in the corner of my eye.

In the parking lot across the street, Colson is leaning

against the door of his car, watching me. Through the windshield, I can see Trent sitting in the passenger's seat.

Clutching my purse, I freeze, staring at them.

My phone rings, vibrating against my chest.

Fumbling to answer it, Noah's name is on the screen.

"Noah?"

"Keep walking, Ace. I'm right here. He's not going to do anything."

"You're still here?"

"I told you I would be."

"I thought you meant you would come back when I was ready to leave." I turn and continue down the street.

"I'm right here, baby. I never left."

His voice wraps around me. A security blanket that shields me from the rest of the world. My chin wobbles, and I stop, covering my face with the back of my hand.

"Whoa, hey!"

I hear his muffled voice through the phone.

"Ace? Put the phone back against your ear. What's the matter? Why are you crying?"

"I don't know." I shrug, my voice shaking. "It's comforting that you're here. I have to tell you something."

"Are you going to the food trucks? I'll meet you there. I didn't want him to know that I'm here, but this will look like we're meeting for coffee."

"Yeah." I feel tension release all over my body. He's close by.

Rounding the corner, I see the courtyard of food trucks. He's walking from across the street. His eyes are locked on me, but of course they are. He's been watching all along.

"Noah." I melt into his arms.

"Look at me." He stares down at me, his eyes moving over my face.

"I'm fine. I promise." Just an emotional wreck.

His mouth tugs up into a soft smile. "Do you want something to eat?"

"I was going to grab a muffin." He leads me to a table. "How long have they been here?" I look over my shoulder.

"About an hour." He looks completely serene. "Sit here. I'll grab you a muffin. Drink?"

"No, thanks." I watch him walk across the courtyard to the truck.

There is something magnetic about him. Other people see it too. I recognize it on their faces. He draws the gaze of everyone in his path. Women glance up and then look again, a pink flush creeping to their cheeks. Men stand taller–his height, build, and confidence a silent challenge.

He quickly comes back to the table with my muffin and a bottle of water.

As soon as he sits, I notice Colson walking toward us. His head is high and confident, his gait purposeful.

"Colson and Trent Barrington!" Noah stands, raising his voice loud enough to alert everyone here to their presence.

This rattles them.

"What are you doing here? Come sit down!" Noah smiles, gesturing to the table.

Colson's steps falter. They weren't expecting him to draw attention to us.

They slide into the seats across the table.

"Mr. Gaines, I presume?" Trent looks at him like he's a bug he wants to squish.

"Correct."

"Funny running into you here. You were next on your list. Killing two birds with one stone, I guess." He smiles, but it looks menacing.

"What were you coming to visit me for?" Noah leans back slightly, wrapping his arm around my shoulder casually.

"Well, we just learned about your little club out in Columbia. It seems like you're doing pretty well for yourself."

If he's trying to rattle him, it's not working.

"Look who knows how to search public records," Noah smirks. "Good for you. Is there a question in there, or are you just here to congratulate me on my success?"

"We heard the DEA raided you."

"You heard that?" Noah sits up. "A little bird tell you?"

Trent hums, Colson sits forward, matching Noah's position.

"Interesting timing, don't you think?" His eyes are glued to Noah's arm around me.

"No, not really. I assume that little bird must have also informed you that they didn't find anything during their little search. That club is squeaky clean." He takes an easy sip from the water bottle. "As for the timing, I think it's pretty much spot on. In fact, I was expecting it a day or two earlier. After I gave the tip about the laundromat that your family uses as a cover for the bribes they're taking from Senators McCormack and Stillwell, I thought you would act quicker."

"Son of a bitch." Colson grumbles, breaking his confident expression and looking down at the table.

"Listen," Trent tries to act like he is unbothered, but I can tell by the way his neck is reddening that he's flustered. "You're an ant. Do you understand? A tiny piece of shit, nothing. Trash. We could wipe you out, and no one but this little bitch would even care."

The muscles in his arm tense around me, but he doesn't make a sound.

"More than anything, you're a nuisance. We don't want to

attract attention, so this is your final warning. Stop, now, or we'll be forced to act. You're playing with the big dogs now."

Noah chuckles, so low and threatening it scares me. "I'm going to cut your tongue out."

He chokes, clearly shocked. I have a feeling that's not what he was expecting.

"Apologize for what you just called her, and I might consider letting you keep it." He completely ignores the rest of it.

"Remember what I said." He stands, obviously eager to get out of here. "This ends now. The next message will be worse than a raid."

"See you soon." He calls after them as they make a hasty exit from the courtyard.

"Oh, my god, Noah! Please, you–"

His lips on mine shut me right up.

"Eat your muffin, Ace." He pulls back, licking his lips.

"I wanted to show you this." I open my phone and slide it across the table.

He looks for a moment, reading the screen. His spine straightens, and he picks up the phone, interested. He scrolls through the pictures, one after the other.

"Holy shit. Good girl." He kisses my temple hard. "I'm going to fucking bury them."

THIRTY-FOUR

"DO you think you can get clearer pictures?" His grip on my thigh is gentle as he maneuvers the truck toward my apartment. "Don't stress yourself. If you can't, you can't. I know you're a good girl, and breaking the rules is stressing you. If you can get better shots, that would be helpful, but only if the opportunity presents itself."

"I'll try." I swallow the dry lump in my throat.

"Ace, I'm serious. I won't be disappointed if you can't do it."

"I'm afraid for you." I inch closer to him. "They have so much money and so many connections. The fact that they were investigated and there wasn't a single news report about it means they buried it. How? None of them are in jail. The files are just sitting there. No one is pursuing it."

"That's good, Ace. I don't want some pesky investigator in my way." He smiles.

"I'm serious, Noah." He's underestimating them. They've fooled everyone in this town for years. Their reputation is sparkling. I'm sure they aren't going to take a threat to that kindly.

"I'm taking this seriously." He pulls into the parking lot of my complex and parks in the empty space beside my car.

Stella isn't here.

It seems like his mind is in the same place. He grabs me and slides me across the seats. In a whirlwind, we're out of the truck and he's marching quickly up the sidewalk with his mouth on mine.

"Noah, wait." My chest deflates. "We can't."

"Why?" He stops.

"I'm on my period." I cringe, waiting for his face to twist with disgust. My skin feels warm. I'm sure I'm as red as a tomato.

"What?" He lets out a surprised laugh.

"I'm on my period, so we can't..." I look down at his chest.

"Are you in pain?" He pushes the door open. "Do you have cramps?"

"No. I'm alright. Earlier, but I'm ok now."

"Then grab a towel because we're about to make a mess."

My mouth falls open. "But—"

"Towel." He sets me down. "Unless you don't care about your sheets and carpet."

"You're not grossed out?" I'm too shocked to move.

"Baby, are you fucking kidding me?" He grabs me and kisses me with so much desire that it makes my brain melt.

A burst of heat ignites in my belly. Maybe it's the hormones, but I feel needy and desperate.

"This fucking skirt is driving me crazy." He groans and rubs his palms over my ass. "I've been dying to strip you out of it since I watched you put it on this morning."

Softly— carefully, he pulls down the little zipper in the back.

My insides clench, equal parts nervous and excited.

This feels dirty and wrong.

He shouldn't want this, and I absolutely shouldn't be letting him do it. He probably thinks it's just a few drops or something. This is the first day...

My hands twitch, hovering like I might stop him, like I still have the chance to put a wall back up between us. But I don't move.

Slowly, methodically, he strips us down piece by piece.

My skirt, his pants.

My shirt, his shirt.

Layer by layer, until we're left in nothing but our underwear.

I curl into myself, trying to shield my body from him– I want to be smaller, less seen. This is too vulnerable.

"Baby." His tone is soft, but stern. "Don't cover up, don't hide."

"I'm embarrassed."

Of everything.

Of the way my hands shake.

Of the way I'm already wet, and he hasn't even touched me.

Of how much I want this when I shouldn't.

He growls, dropping to his knees in front of me, and pulls my panties down. "Open."

I don't.

For half a second, I freeze. But then I give in, moving my feet apart, just a bit.

As soon as he has access, he curls his finger around the string of my tampon and plucks it out.

"You're on your period because I didn't put a baby in you this month." He leans in, pressing kisses to the tops of my thighs. "There isn't anything to be embarrassed about. I'm not scared of a little blood."

"Holy shit." I hiss. His mouth is going to be the death of me.

"I want you every day. This," he stops, sweeping his fingers through my pussy. "This is always beautiful. There's nothing gross about it. It's a little blood, Ace."

"N-Noah." I don't want him to be upset, but I can't help it. I'm panicking.

He stands, placing my hand on his cock. "I'm so fucking turned on, Ace."

"But—"

"No." He stops me. "But nothing. I'm fucking aching for you, baby."

"But—" My brain can't think of any other word to say.

"Should we even things up?"

"What?"

He grabs his pants off the floor, and before I can make sense of what he's doing, he has his knife out and he's flicking the blade open.

"Noah, oh my god!" I scream, but it's too late. He slices the skin on his chest, a thin, shallow cut that starts to seep blood immediately. He cuts right through his tattoos like they mean nothing.

"Never be ashamed or embarrassed in front of me." He grabs my neck, dropping the knife to the floor. He lifts me up, pressing my body into his bloody chest. I feel everything—his heart pounding, his ragged breaths in my lungs, the tremble in his hands as they roam over my skin.

Slippery and wet, we kiss, our bodies mashed together like we'll die if we stop. Who knows? We might.

We're starving for it.

I need him like my next breath.

Blood spreads between us, dripping from his chest onto

mine. We're covered in it. In only a matter of seconds, my room looks like a crime scene.

His blood, mine. It's impossible to tell where it came from. An even playing field. I'm not used to that.

"Lie down." He pulls his swollen lips from mine.

I don't know why I'm surprised. Nothing should take me by surprise anymore, but I gasp. "You're not going to–"

"Yes, I am." He pushes me back gently. "Put your feet on my shoulders."

Sitting on the edge of my bed, I'm freaking out inside, but I do as I'm told.

"Legs up." He guides me softly. "Just like that."

I can't take my eyes off his face. I find myself searching for hesitation or hidden disgust. There is none. He dives in, kissing a trail up my thigh, nipping and sucking my skin.

"I'm going to make you feel so good." He makes eye contact before attaching his mouth to my clit.

I'm instantly pushed to the edge of paradise.

It only takes a moment to forget about the blood completely.

"Noah!" I arch up from the bed, my body reacting violently to his touch. I didn't expect it to feel this good this fast.

"You're so sensitive right now." He moans. "Your pussy is gushing for me already."

My mind is flooded with too many thoughts and emotions. Tears well up in my eyes as he continues to lap up everything like it's a delicacy.

My hesitation and unease melt away completely. The sounds he's making, the ravenous way he moves, like a wild animal tearing at its meal.

Deep in my stomach, a knot tightens, coiling around itself, pulling inward, closer, tighter, harder.

"Oh god, it's so good." He groans. "You're so close. Let me have it, baby. Give it to me, please."

The growl in his voice dropkicks me over the edge. Gripping the bedspread in both fists, my body contorts while he draws orgasms out of me like demons. I don't know the language I'm speaking while I scream out.

I don't remember where we are, my name, or what day it is. My brain is empty except for the feeling.

He coaxes it out of me, licking me through it. He takes every drop.

With my body still on the edge of the bed, he climbs up. He looks like a lion that just ate a gazelle. His mouth, neck, and chest are bloody, some his, some mine.

"Fucking delicious. Now I'm going to fuck you until you fall asleep." He lines himself up and lifts my legs up, putting my feet around his face. "Looks like you rolled out the red carpet for me." He gives me a shit-eating grin, staring down at the mess between my legs.

"No–"

He's inside in a single thrust.

"Fuck!" He grunts, and I shriek. I'm soaked, blood and arousal making me so slick he meets no resistance, but it still ripples and aches. "So tight and fucking perfect for me, Ace!" He starts to move, drawing his hips back and slamming them forward. "Look at me." He groans.

He's more intense with each thrust, faster and harder. My bones rattle, and my eyes roll into my head.

Brutal. Ruthless. Feral.

He lets my legs slide down around his arms so that he can lean in.

Wrapping my arms around his neck, I anchor myself to him.

"Noah!" I'm overwhelmed. "Please." My breath catches,

and tears roll down my cheeks. This is scary. Every time he touches me, I feel more.

"You're safe, baby."

I know I am. He'll take all the dirty, broken parts, and he won't look at me as less for having them.

"I fucking worship you. You say the word. Anything you need. I'll move mountains to get it. You want a big, pretty house? Pick the one and I'll put in an offer. A car? A ring? You want me to kill someone, snap your fingers, and it's done. You want a dog? A baby? I'll give you one of those." He is reverent, worshiping, soft.

His mouth—the words and the kisses don't match the rest of his body. It doesn't make sense how he can be so contradictory. His mouth is full of love. It pours out of him, but his body, he's fucking me. There is no softness there.

But I want it this way.

I like it.

"Go ahead," he says, placing his hand on my throat. "I can feel you clenching around me. Come. Squeeze me. Come on me. Make me feel how good it is for you."

Pleasure pools between my legs, building as he fucks me.

"Noah?" I whimper. I know I can ask. He'll do anything I need. He won't judge me.

"What is it, baby? What do you need to get there? You're close, aren't you?"

"Squeeze harder," I beg.

Without hesitation, he tightens his grip on my throat. My vision blurs, and I gasp against his hand. Rocking my hips, I meet his thrusts.

He sucks my lower lip into his mouth and bites. The slightly sharp sting makes me come.

My whole body shakes as he swallows the cries that rip from somewhere deep inside me, in my chest—my soul.

He stops twitching deep inside me. He sobs my name between grunts.

When he pulls out, he looks me in the eye as he moves down my body again. "Open your mouth." His voice is so rough and demanding.

I do, slowly, still trying to figure out what he's doing. My brain is only half-functioning.

He wraps his mouth around my pussy and slurps.

"Noah! I shriek from the sensation and the knowledge of what he's doing.

He comes up and brings his bloody mouth to mine.

And I take it.

A mouthful of his cum, and my blood, and arousal.

"Don't waste it." He smiles, blood in his teeth. "We're delicious together."

THIRTY-FIVE

NOAH

I CAN TASTE her blood on my tongue. Fuck. I think we just unlocked a new kink.

Her dried blood all over my cock is fucking killing me.

I'm barely holding myself back from putting my fucking fist up there.

She is so soft and small, I'm trying so hard. But there is too much rage coursing through me.

I want to rip the world apart at the seams. Every hand that's ever touched her has added to this fucking low image she has of herself.

What kind of bitches was she dating that she would feel embarrassed by a natural bodily function?

God, I want more of it.

When she wakes up, I'm going to at least taste it again.

My hands flex, the only movement I can make that won't wake her up. My muscles twitch, itching to get up and go to the Barrington residence. I want to burn it to the ground with all of them inside.

He called her a bitch.

He called *her* a bitch.

The word is like a grater against my ears. I can't stop hearing it.

Bitch.

I'm going to cut his tongue out and feed it to him.

I'm going to pluck his eyes out and piss into his skull.

"Noah," her sweet voice dives into my mind, pulling me by the neck from the depths of my turmoil.

"Yeah, baby?"

"You can't sleep?" She still sounds exhausted, that sweet, raspy, satiated lilt in her voice.

"No."

"Why not?"

"Too much to think about."

"Plotting?" A little crease forms between her brows.

"Yes."

"I don't want you to get in any trouble. I don't want you to go back to prison."

"I'll be careful, I promise. I won't leave you again."

THIRTY-SIX

I'M BREATHING as if I ran a marathon.

I've taken four pictures. There are at least fifty to go, probably more.

He left for a late meeting. I can probably take all of them before I leave for the day if my hands would stop shaking and sweating long enough to get clear shots. Doing this one-handed is hard enough, but with all the trembling, I'm really struggling.

Taking a breath, I hold my phone up. As I move my thumb to click the photo, it starts to vibrate in my hand.

Gasping, I drop the phone onto my keyboard.

"Shit."

Grabbing it, I quickly answer. "Hey, Stella." I know my voice sounds strange. It's too breathy and high-pitched.

"Hey. I have an idea I want to run by you."

"Ok."

"So, we're supposed to sit at home tonight, right? They're stressed about something at work, and they're both being weird about it. I want to go check on Jace."

Shit. Jace hasn't told her the truth about their business yet. They explained the DEA raid away as an asshole agent who wanted to make sure Noah wasn't doing anything wrong.

"Um, you know, I think we should just stay at the house." I try to sound casual. I hate lying to her.

She hums. "I'm going. You can stay home if you want to, but something doesn't feel right to me. I'll drop you off and-"

"Wait! I'll come with you. Just give me some time when I get home to get ready. Please."

"Great!" I can hear the smile in her voice.

"Ok, I'm leaving now. I'll be there in ten minutes."

"Awesome!" I drop my phone into my lap. "Shit."

Picking it up, I call him. Four times. It goes to voicemail every time. Fuck. I'll just have to stall until he answers the phone.

I don't actually want to stay home either. But if he's telling me to it must be for a reason.

Though secretly, way deep down, there is a part of me that wants to see the look on his face when we walk in.

I bet the vein in his neck would pulsate, and he would flex his hands.

Maybe I'm more into the plan than I thought.

It's not like we're going out somewhere dangerous. We would be at his club on a Friday night while they're open and full of witnesses. What's the worst that could happen?

I call again. This little rebellious streak can't wipe away years of people pleasing and fear of being a disappointment.

He still doesn't answer.

This is starting to feel out of my hands.

I'm not going to let her go out alone. If Colson is following me, I don't want to stay at home by myself either, so this is the best option. There is safety in numbers. At least this is the reasoning I'm using to justify directly disobeying his very clear and frankly reasonable request that I stay home.

I'm leaving it up to fate. If he calls me back in time, it will take me to get home, change, and drive out there; it wasn't meant to be. If he doesn't call...

Snapping as many pictures as I can, I rush out the door. I don't want her to have to wait for me.

I'll make it up to him with the crystal-clear images I managed to capture. Hopefully.

As I slide into her passenger's seat, my legs wobble slightly.

The huge smile on her face means she hasn't changed her mind on the way here.

"Oh, relax!" She reaches over and squeezes my shoulder. "This is not a big deal, Candy."

This is a very big deal. She doesn't know it, but it is.

My expression must be giving away my nerves because she laughs. "You're such a good girl. You're allowed to break the rules sometimes. Who are they to give us rules anyway?"

Oh, man. If only she knew.

"We could just buy face masks and ice cream and watch rom-coms."

"Next weekend." She looks at me flatly. "I feel like Jace is being shady. He's being weirdly secretive about this. I have to check or it's going to eat at me. Plus, you know I don't like to be told what to do."

"I know." I sigh. I can't tell her that I know.

The thrill of what Noah might do is feeling less thrilling and more frightening as the minutes tick by. He's going to be pissed.

When we get to the apartment, I try calling him again, three times, while we get ready. I opt for jeans and a basic t-shirt. A short dress will only provoke him further.

"That's what you're wearing?" Her brows pull inward.

"Yes, it is. I'm not getting myself into trouble." I pull my boot on.

"I am." She winks, tugging on her very miniature skirt.

I try to call one more time. A knot aches in my stomach when he doesn't answer again. Something is wrong. It must be. He would never ignore so many of my calls.

The hour-long drive feels never-ending. Each minute, my nervousness grows. Is he hurt? Did he get arrested? Did they get raided again?

The line outside the club is long, wrapping around the building. That's a good sign.

This time, there isn't anyone waiting to bring us inside. We have to wait with everyone else.

"What if they aren't here?" The sudden thought makes my heart sink.

"Why wouldn't they be? Jace said he would be here, working. If they aren't here, I'm whooping some ass! He better fucking be here." She skips over fear and dives headfirst into anger immediately.

"They're probably here." I try to convince both of us.

Her mood is less excited than it was before. Doubts and the long line are dampening the excitement.

The line creeps slowly, trickling down until we are finally in front of the door.

"It's free for ladies tonight." The bouncer smiles and checks out IDs.

"Great. Is Jace here?"

"The boss is in." He looks at us suspiciously.

"I'm Stella. His—"

"I'll get him a message." His tune changes instantly.

"Tell him I'll be at the bar." She steps inside, her confidence boosted and her head high. She takes a breath. "I knew they would be here."

Almost as soon as we're in front of the bar, a man makes eye contact with me from the other side of the bar top.

He starts to move immediately, bee-lining straight for me.

"Stella." I grab her hand, feeling anxious.

"Can I buy you a drink?" He is in front of me so quickly, I don't even have time to process it.

"No, thank you."

"Aw, come on! One drink!"

"She said no," Stella snaps. "Leave us alone."

"Come dance with me then."

"No."

Alarm bells are sounding in my head. "Stella, let's go to the back. To the offices."

"Wait! Come on! Don't be like that!"

This is off. It's like he was waiting for us—for me. If he were working here, he would have said so.

"Leave me alone." I push past him.

"I just want to buy you a drink and dance! Why are you being so weird about this?" He follows me.

"I don't want a drink, and I don't want to dance. Please leave me alone."

"Don't play hard to get." He grabs my arm, pulling me back toward him.

"I'm not playing hard to get!" I yank my arm away, but he tightens his grip painfully. His nails dig into my upper arm.

"Get the fuck off, you asshole!" Stella shoves him back.

I open my mouth to tell him again that I don't want anything to do with him, but I don't have a chance. Before I can speak, his grip is ripped away, and his body goes flying.

Noah's here.

And he's pissed.

The man is on the ground before he even knows what's happening. Noah is on top of him, pinning him to the ground with one hand on his throat while the other hand makes repeated contact with his face.

Three. Four. Five.

He punches until blood splatter is cast from his hand each time he raises it.

Luckily, the music is drowning out the sound of his fist connecting. I don't want to hear the crunch of bone.

"Noah!" Stella screams, but her voice is lost in the chaos. I doubt he would stop, anyway.

Jace wraps his arm around her, whispering something in her ear. Her eyes go wide, and she turns to me, reaching for my hand.

"Candy, we have to stop him!" A tear spills over her lashes.

I don't know what to do. With the loud music thumping, and the crowd gathered around to watch the spectacle, I don't know how to get to him.

"Noah!" I scream as loud as I can.

His fist stops, hanging mid-air, blood dripping from it.

He turns slowly, his green eyes look black. He's almost unrecognizable. There is usually softness in his eyes for me. Not today.

Dragging himself up from the floor, he turns to the bouncers. "Get him the fuck out of here."

His mouth is set in a thin line, his jaw clenched shut as he places his hand on the back of my neck. It doesn't hurt, but it's hard enough to make me take notice. It's trembling. He's holding back his fury.

An unspoken conversation is had between him and Jace, a moment of eye contact before he starts to walk through the crowd toward the back hallway–toward his office behind the bar.

The door to the office closes with a loud thud that makes me jump. The purple lights shining through the office reflect on his face, making him look like a violet demon.

"Candace." His voice is just a hoarse whisper as he rolls his neck and clenches his bloody hand. "Explain it. Now."

THIRTY-SEVEN

"I-I TRIED TO CALL YOU." I take a step back. "Stella was determined to come, and I didn't want her to be alone. And I didn't want to be home alone." This was a terrible idea. The look on his face is so intense, like he's going to incinerate me.

He takes a step forward, and I shrink back instinctively.

"Come here." He points to the ground in front of him.

"I tried to call you. At least twenty times." I stutter and take short steps to avoid being so close to him. My excuses feel hollow and empty now.

"Here." He growls.

When I'm close enough, he grabs me, yanking me into his arms. "When we got the message that Stella was here, I thought to myself, poor Jace. He obviously can't trust his girl to do a simple thing, like stay home when she's asked. Luckily, my good girl is at home right now, safe. So imagine my mother-fucking surprise when I checked your location only to find you here."

"I'm sorry," I whisper.

"I don't think you're sorry." He runs his bloody hand through his hair.

"I am sorry." I look up at him. In the back of my mind, I wonder if the man he beat up is alright. This might be a lot worse than just disobeying a request. He could be in real trouble.

"Did you wear this outfit hoping I would be less angry because you're not half-naked?"

"Yes."

He hums. "Do you think it worked?"

"No." I bite into my lip to keep it from wobbling.

His bloody hand comes up to my neck, squeezing hard enough to make me gasp and panic slightly.

"Next time I tell you to stay home, you're going to. Do you know how I know that?"

"How?" I can hardly whisper through his grip.

"I'm going to fuck you so hard, you'll never fucking forget it. You're never going to disregard me again."

He releases my neck and grabs my shirt, ripping it down the middle like paper.

"N-Noah–"

"No, Ace. Not right now. Take your punishment. You've earned it."

"I know." I hang my head. "I just–"

"Unbutton my pants." His eyes are so dark–it's like he's daring me to step out of line.

My fingers tremble as I reach out, popping the button open.

"I'm in a bit of a shitstorm right now, baby." He groans as he pulls his pants down his hips, letting his cock spring free. "This is really the last thing I need right now."

"I'm sorry."

"Tell me with your throat."

Immediately, I drop to my knees, looking up at him.

"Worship it. Show me how fucking sorry you are."

Opening my mouth, I keep my eyes on him, reaching for it.

"No, hands." He growls.

Right. "Sorry."

"Show me."

Kissing the tip, I flick my tongue over it. I'm going to make him forgive me. I'll take whatever he hands out until he's not mad anymore.

His fingers thread through my hair, not hard, just there, a gentle touch that reassures me. Even angry, he still wants me.

I throw myself into the task at hand. Watching his face, I forget everything else. I just want him to feel good and for his anger to melt away.

"Fuck, just like that, baby." His voice already sounds less mad. "You look so pretty on your knees."

Opening wide, I give him all I've got.

"Do you like this? You like riling me up, don't you? You want to play with the monster, baby?" He moves his hips slowly, not ramming himself down my throat.

I hum around him. My panties are soaked. He's mad, but I know when he pulls me up from the ground, he's going to make me feel so good.

My mind wars with itself. I never know which way is up when it comes to him. All the feelings mix together and conflict. Fear and arousal. Shame and excitement. I don't know what I should feel, but he mutes the chaos. As long as he's happy–I'm alright. None of the shame matters.

"This isn't a punishment for you, is it? You fucking love it." He grits his teeth.

I look into his eyes, my vision blurry.

With each drag of my tongue across the vein on his shaft, I feel my own arousal growing. He's going to fuck me so hard.

The look on his face only pushes me further into desperate territory. So handsome, but furious. His brows pulled down, his lips tugged into a frown that only breaks when he grunts or whispers my name.

Whimpering, I move faster, pulling him deeper each time.

He gathers my hair in his hands, holding it up out of my way.

"Take more."

I suck in a breath and brace myself.

He isn't forcing it; he's letting me do it. But that only makes the pressure feel worse. I have to push myself because he isn't going to do it for me.

Pushing forward, I take him all the way to the back, my throat constricting around him.

He rewards me with a groan and a slight tug of my hair.

In and out, my jaw starts to hurt, but he doesn't come. The fury in his eyes hasn't lessened even slightly.

"Keep going." He encourages me. He reaches down, cupping my jaw beneath his cock. It's gentle at first, but it gets firmer as I swallow again and again. "You want it, don't you?"

I hum. Yes, I do. I want it.

His voice is tighter, the muscles in his thighs clenching, and each breath comes with effort. He's holding it back.

My head is spinning in a haze of lust and exhaustion. My jaw aches. But I can't stop.

"Careful." He growls, using his grip on my jaw to slide my mouth around him. Forcing myself to push through it, I close my eyes. "Good girl." He shoots down the back of my throat like that's what he's been waiting for the whole time. "Surrender." His voice is so strained—gravelly.

I can't help the moan of relief that falls out of my mouth as he finally pulls himself out of it.

Grabbing my jaw, I move it slowly, relieving the ache that has settled into the bone.

He grabs me, pulling me up off the floor. "Pants down. Bend over my desk. I'm going to fuck this little rebellious streak right out of you. Next time you think about ignoring me, you'll remember this night."

I follow him to his desk, where he presses me forward, more gently than I was expecting.

"Cheek to the glass." He kneads my ass roughly in his hands. "Reach back here. I want you to hold yourself open for me."

My stomach clenches as I bring my hands back to spread myself open.

"Wider."

Digging my fingers in, I pull it open wider.

"You're fucking soaking, baby. Did being punished do this to you?"

"Noah, please." I wiggle against the desk.

"You're not going to come." He slams into me completely, with no warning. "That's the rest of your punishment. I'm going to bring you to the edge over and over again, and then I'm going to leave you needy and desperate."

The only answer I can give is a cry.

"You're already close, aren't you, baby?" He groans. "Your perfect cunt is gripping me so fucking hard. You're strangling me."

For the first time since we came into this room, he sounds like my Noah. The anger in his voice is gone–replaced with pleasure.

The legs of the desk scrape loudly as they inch across the floor from the force of each thrust.

I feel myself building toward something devastating.

"Noah!" I moan, half begging.

He pulls out, leaving my body on the edge.

"God damn it, Ace." He grunts, gripping my hips. "Stop."

"I can't," I whine. I'm not doing it on purpose.

He slides in again, slowly this time. It's catastrophic. My body shakes, every muscle flexing into a tight ball.

He thrusts his hips three times and pulls out again.

"You don't get to come!" He yells, dropping his forehead down against the sweat-slicked skin of my back.

"Please." I whimper, tears rolling down my cheeks.

"No." He presses in again. "Fuck!" He shouts, pulling out. "This is supposed to be a fucking punishment! But I can't do it. Come, fuck! Squeeze my cock, baby. Let me feel it." He slams forward, and I black out. My vision blurs as the tension snaps like an overstretched rubber band.

Relief. Sweet, perfect release that relieves all the tension in my body in an instant. I'm jello–putty in his hands.

His chest presses into my back, and he rests on top of me–in me–catching his breath.

I can't speak. My senses haven't returned to me yet.

"Barrington is following you." He casually unbuttons his shirt.

"What?" That zaps some life back into me.

"Yeah, he's having you followed. Don't do anything different. Just know that he's watching. It's going to be hard, but try not to. That might put you in unnecessary danger."

"Like coming out to the club?" I sigh.

"I should have called you. My phone was off for a meeting. I have someone watching you, too. Someone I trust."

"Who?"

He chuckles. "A friend from prison." I open my mouth, but he grabs me, helping me into his shirt. "I know that doesn't sound like you're safer in his hands, but I trust him not to let anything happen to you during the very infrequent moments when I can't watch you myself. I'll never let that happen again. Do you understand? You will never, ever, be truly alone again, Ace."

"I understand." I feel warm and safe as he rolls the extra-long sleeves of his shirt up my arms.

"Let's go. You shouldn't be here tonight."

As we walk out of the office, we're met almost immediately by three police officers.

"Noah Gaines?" One of them holds out his badge while the others wait, their hands poised over their guns. "You're under arrest for assault."

"Noah?" I panic.

"Go with Jace, baby. I'll be alright." He turns to look at me. The absolute calm in his expression startles me. He's not afraid.

"Noah Gaines. You have the right to remain silent." The officer grabs him too roughly for a man who isn't resisting at all. "Anything you say can and will be used against you—"

"Hey! Not so rough!" I feel a dizzying wave of nausea crash down on me. "Please! Don't hurt him!"

Seeing him in cuffs, being led away while they read him his rights, is sending me into a full-fledged, frantic frenzy.

"Come here, Candace. Go wait in my office with Stella." Jace's grip on my arm is firm, but his voice is gentle.

Stella is sobbing loudly behind him. The sight of her brother like this, again, is too much for her. "This is all my fault. I shouldn't have come here!"

"It's not your fault." I wrap my shaking arms around her.

"It is." She covers her face.

Inside Jace's office, the noise and chaos fade away.

"What the fuck do we do, Stella?"

THIRTY-EIGHT

"WE SHOULD GO DOWN THERE, RIGHT?" I pace around the office. "We have to! We can't leave him there alone!"

"Candy." Jace shakes his head. "This is the county jail. It's a cakewalk compared to prison. He'll be alright until we can bail him out."

"But he can't stay in there all night." My chin wobbles.

"He'll be alright. If we went down there right now, I'm sure they would turn us away. It's the middle of the night. I can tell you one thing with certainty. He wouldn't want you sitting there waiting for him. It's Friday, well, Saturday now. He will probably see a judge first thing on Monday. That's when they will set his bail."

"He has to stay there until Monday?" My heart feels like it's about to pop, like someone is squeezing it in a vise. "Will he be given a phone call? He will, right? That's the law, isn't it?" All the wheels in my mind are spinning out at the same time. I'm stuck in the mud, unable to gain traction, so I'm just spinning in violent circles.

"Yes. I'm sure he'll call you." He turns all of his attention to Stella. She's sitting in his chair, staring off into space. Her eyes are open, but she hasn't moved in several minutes. It's like she's comatose. "Stel? You alright?" he approaches her like a wild animal that needs slow, cautious reassurance.

"No." She whimpers. "I'm not alright."

He wraps his arms around her, holding her close to him, which only makes me feel how far away he is even more acutely.

"Security has been removing everyone. We're closing early. Let me take you home. I'll stay there with you tonight, then we will make a game plan in the morning." He stands, pulling Stella up with him.

He's not like Noah. No one is like Noah. But I recognize that same quiet confidence–the steadiness of his nature.

The club looks different with the lights on. Some of the magic is gone. The purple glow is gone, and only trash and spilled drinks remain.

A group of people is busy cleaning up the mess the crowd left behind. The floor is wet and sticky. There are glasses set everywhere. Litter and garbage are swept into piles on the floor. Behind the bars, the bartenders are scrubbing and washing.

"Mike is here to lock up." He calls to them. "Thanks for your hard work tonight. See you tomorrow."

Tomorrow?

I can't really wrap my head around the fact that this place will be open again tomorrow night. While Noah is in jail. The rest of the world is just going to keep on living.

Shrinking down in the back seat of his car, I wonder if Colson is watching me right now.

"It's just so wrong that he's the only one in trouble. That guy was being fucking aggressive. Noah stepped in because he wasn't listening to her. He wouldn't let go of her arm." Stella sniffles.

"Tomorrow, we will go down to the police station and tell them that." He reassures her.

We make eye contact in the rearview mirror. It's only for a second, but that's long enough for me to understand what he wants from me.

I have to tell the police about the man at the club.

Nodding, I pull out my phone and write all the details in my notes while they're still fresh.

It just feels like too much of a coincidence. Why me? Why would he come after me so specifically? It was like he was waiting for me.

Maybe he was.

A tear rolls down my cheek before I realize I'm crying.

This really is our fault. I should have talked her out of coming.

By the time we get home, I've worked myself into a panic again. Something isn't right. Never in my life has a man been so singularly interested in me. Well, aside from Noah.

"I'll be here if you need anything, Candy," Jace calls after me as I rush to my bedroom. "Seriously. Scream and I'll come running."

"Thanks, Jace. Just take care of Stella for me." I close my door and stare at my room. He isn't going to be outside watching me tonight.

My phone rings and I drop it, trying to answer it as quickly as I can.

"Noah?" I hold on to it for dear life.

"Hey, baby."

"Oh, god. Noah, I'm so sorry. This is all my fault."

"Ace, listen to me. I only get two minutes, and the call will drop automatically. I'm going before the judge on Monday at ten. Jace knows that a lot of our cash is tied up right now, but tell him that I said to use the–"

"I'll get the money for your bail."

"Baby–"

"No. I'll get it. I'll be there on Monday morning. We'll get you out. We're going to go to the police station tomorrow to tell them that the man was harassing me." I wipe the tears from my cheek.

"Tell Jace to call Harry Townsend."

"Who is that?"

"A lawyer."

"We will be there on Monday. All of us." My mind races to think of anything else I need to tell him urgently.

"Don't cry, baby. I'm alright. They got me in an individual cell. It's small, but I'm by myself. I'll meet with my lawyer tomorrow. Everything is going to work out."

I don't understand how he's so optimistic.

"Everything is going to work out?" I fight with the urge to cry.

"Yes, baby. It will." He sounds so steady and sure.

"Ok." I nod, setting my shoulders back.

"My time is ending, Ace. Stay with Jace. He'll make sure you're safe."

"I will," I promise.

The call clicks, ending abruptly before we can say anything else.

Sitting on my bed, I stare up at the ceiling. My mind turns over everything that happened tonight. By the time I have a plan outlined in my head, the sun is rising outside.

Running over to my dresser, I dig around in the top drawer until I find what I'm looking for.

Stella and Jace are already in the kitchen, looking miserable and exhausted as they silently sip coffee.

"I need to go to the pawnshop before we go to the police station."

"What are you pawning?" Stella perks up.

"He called last night. He's going before the judge on Monday morning. I want to have his bail money already. I figured this should cover it." I set my engagement ring down on the counter.

"Holy shit. That's quite a ring." Jace's eyes go wide.

Stella smiles, "poetic justice."

"I thought so." I slip the ring into my pocket. "We should go talk to the police. I thought about it all night long. I didn't want to forget any details."

Jace sighs. "Listen, I need you both to be prepared for this part. What the guy did to you in the club could be considered assault because he wasn't letting go. But that doesn't mean Noah was allowed, legally, to use that much force. Just because you speak to the police, that doesn't mean they will drop the charges against Noah."

I nod. I didn't think they would drop the charges altogether, but hearing it stings.

Stella sits in the backseat with me, her head in my lap.

"I'm scared, Candy."

"Me too."

"How am I going to tell my parents that he might go back to jail?"

"Hopefully it won't come to that."

Jace looks back at us through the mirror. "I called the lawyer while you were getting ready. He's going to the jail right now to meet with him. He said that it sounds like a simple assault case that will probably end up with a fine or a small stint, no more than thirty days."

"Thirty days." My lungs burn.

"Fuck, that makes me nauseous." Stella groans.

"Me too." I lean my head back and close my eyes.

We stop at the pawn shop first. I've never pawned anything. My mom used to pawn everything we owned at the end of the month to make rent. I never went with her. I wish I had.

"Don't take less than fifteen for that." Jace looks at me.

"I won't take less than eighteen." I am determined. It's for Noah. I can do this.

Inside, the store is empty. Shelves and glass display cases with various junk and knick-knacks are spread around the small, dingy shop. An older man and woman are standing behind the counter. They look up at me when the bell on the door rings.

"Pawning or selling, sweetheart?" The woman greets me.

"Selling." I step up to the counter and place the ring on a little velvet cushion they have set up beneath a small light.

The man clicks his tongue. "That's quite a ring."

"It is." I force my fingers not to fidget.

He picks it up, studying it while the woman pulls out a cloth bundle with tools inside. She takes a magnifier and holds it up to her eye, studying the diamond closely.

She hums. "Good cut, color, and clarity. I would say it's almost a carat and a half." After looking at it for a few minutes, she turns and whispers to the man.

"What are you asking for it?" He looks at me, careful not to give anything away.

"What are you offering?" I don't want to show my hand too early.

"Do you know how much this ring is worth?"

"Yes, I have a pretty good idea." I wait.

"We give thirty percent of the value of the item. I would say a ring this size, cut, and clarity probably costs anywhere from sixty to seventy thousand. I'll give you seventeen."

I know it costs at least seventy-five, but I'll let that slip.

"Eighteen and it's yours." I stare him down. Every cent helps.

The woman nudges him, and my heart rate spikes. I can't tell if that is a nudge in favor of my offer or against.

The silence feels long and heavy.

"Deal. She'll draw up the paperwork for the sale."

"Great." I let out a shaky breath. Hopefully, his bail is less than that.

After all the i's are dotted and the t's are crossed, I walk out of the shop with a small fortune bundled under my arm.

"I got eighteen thousand." I slide into my seat.

"Holy shit! Nice work!" Jace laughs.

"Thank you so much, Candy." Stella's eyes well up.

"Don't thank me." I squeeze her shoulder.

"The lawyer called while you were inside. We're going to pick up a copy of the police report. Noah wants us to see something."

My mind races. What could he possibly want us to see on the police report?

The drive to the station only takes ten minutes, but it feels eternal. In the parking lot, I stare at the gray brick building. He's in there somewhere, locked in a cell.

Jace takes the lead with the receptionist. He gives her the case number for the police report and the name of the detective who's been assigned the assault case.

"Does anything here look like something he would want us to see?" Jace hands me the report. My eyes scan over the pages. At first, nothing jumps out.

Then, I see it, under the listed names.

Bradley Carpenter.

"Carpenter?"

"Is that it?" Stella looks confused.

"Colson's mom's maiden name is Carpenter. I think he had a cousin, Brad."

This was a setup. A trap. I led him straight into it.

"That can't be a coincidence." She takes the paper.

Jace and I make eye contact–he knows.

"Hello, I'm Detective Wright. I heard you wanted to speak to me?"

Stepping forward, I shake his hand hard. Rage and determination join forces, propelling me forward.

"I want to make a statement about the assault at The Violet House last night."

THIRTY-NINE

NOAH

FUCKING BARRINGTON. Does he really think that I can't put together these very simple-to-follow dots? His cousin? Really?

His fucking cousin.

Either he doesn't care enough to cover his tracks. He's gotten so used to the shield of daddy's money that he doesn't even realize the monster he's unleashed.

Or.

He thinks I'm a drooling imbecile, too stupid to put the pieces together. His mother's sister's son.

Sitting on the cold metal bench, fury courses through me. I'm gnawing at my fucking enclosure. The cuffs bite into my wrists as I wait for my bumbling idiot of a parole officer to come.

She's here somewhere. I know it. They told her I would be released as soon as she paid my bail. She's waiting for me.

"Mr. Gaines." Harry's voice cuts through my silent plotting. He has a deep frown on his face. "I didn't expect to see you here."

"I'm sure you read the report. You know what happened, Harry."

"I do. But you can't beat someone to a bloody pulp for touching your girlfriend."

I'm going to do more than beat him to a bloody pulp. I'm barely getting started.

I'll give it to him. This was smart. I fell right into the trap. The charges will be dropped when Bradley Carpenter disappears, never to be seen again.

"I want to see you twice a month until this situation is cleared up."

"Alright," I hold my arms out for him to unlock the cuffs.

"Stay out of trouble, Noah. You've been given a fresh start. Don't fuck it up." He waves his badge in front of the electronic lock on the door.

I see her through the window on the door.

There's my girl.

Her tear-streaked face and tired eyes make my blood simmer.

As soon as it's open, she's running, crashing into my arms. Her body trembles as she wraps her arms around me.

"I'll see you next week," Harry calls after me.

I nod and lead her out. I need to get her the fuck out of this place. Seeing her here is making me irrationally angry. She doesn't belong in a place like this.

I don't even want to touch her with the stench of that place on my skin, but I can't help it. I need to have my hands on her or I'll lose control and end up back inside.

"Are you alright?" She pulls away just enough to look at me.

"Don't cry, baby. I'm barely holding it together." She can't look at me like that, sad and sweet, with her lips tilted downward. I can't fucking stand it.

"Clayton is waiting for us at the bar." Jace jumps into the driver's seat.

"Who is Clayton?" She looks at me.

"Just an associate." That's not a lie. Just a half-truth. Clayton holds the key to my next move. She doesn't need to know about that.

She hums. I can see the questions in her eyes, but she doesn't ask them, at least for now.

"It was Colson's cousin. He did it on purpose. This is all my fault." She leans into me as Jace maneuvers the car out of the parking lot.

"It's not your fault. You should be allowed to go wherever you want without the fucking piece of shit following you around."

"Colson is following you?" Stella spins around in her seat. The guilt on her face matches Ace's.

"Yes. So from this moment forward, when we tell you to stay somewhere—"

"We'll stay put." She hangs her head.

Her warm body distracts me from everything else. She pressed against me tightly, her trembling body hiding under my arm.

I have to keep her safe. If anything happens to her again, the very thin thread holding me to reality would snap.

I would burn the whole world down.

"I have to meet with Clayton, but after we're going to bed, so I can take care of you until tomorrow," I whisper in her ear.

She shudders. "Ok." Goosebumps spread across her skin.

My cock twitches. She is so responsive. One dirty promise and she's desperate for it.

We get to the bar too quickly, and I have to release my grip on her.

Clayton is sitting at the bar. His long, greasy hair and even longer, gangly limbs make him look like a spider.

He stands when he sees us, and Ace tenses, tucking herself into my side again.

"Go wait at the bar with Stella. This will be quick." I press a kiss to her forehead. It was supposed to be quick, but I linger–the sweet smell of her hair ensnaring me.

She turns, gripping my shirt with her free hand. "Hurry."

FORTY

"WHO THE FUCK IS THAT?" Stella whispers as I slide into the seat beside her.

"I don't know."

The hair on the back of my neck is still standing on end. He was so tall and thin. It looked unnatural. Like there was nothing but muscle and bone beneath his pale, waxy skin. Whatever business they have with him can't possibly be good.

I feel wound up tight, like all the nerves in my body are buzzing at once, making my insides flutter and twitch.

"Want a drink?" She hops off the stool and moves behind the bar.

"No, thank you." If I took a shot right now, I would throw up. Picking at the frayed edge of my cast, I stare at the hallway they disappeared down.

I'm not going to investigate. I'm going to sit my ass in this chair and wait. But my mind is racing, and sitting here feels almost impossible.

There are so many things going on around me, swirling like

a riptide that is about to drag me away, but I don't know what they are–where the danger lies. I feel helpless.

I don't know what's coming or where to look. My body wants to brace for impact, but I can't see through the fog.

I thought Noah getting out would fix it, but it hasn't.

I'm spiraling.

With each second that passes, my chest gets tighter, and it gets harder to breathe. My hands tingle like pins and needles, and my vision blurs.

Pinching my eyes closed, I cover my face with my hands, just trying to give myself a moment in the dark. If I could just make the room stop spinning.

"How long has Colson been following you?" Stella's voice sounds strained.

"Since we broke up." I don't know how much to say. I don't want to give something away that Noah doesn't want her to know yet. I don't want to drag her down into this pit of panic and despair.

"Fuck." She downs another shot. "This is a fucking mess."

"Yeah." I let out a humorless laugh. That's an understatement. This is a fucking nightmare.

"I think Jace and Noah might be dealing drugs." She whispers, pouring another shot.

"No." I hate the look of fear in her eyes. "I don't think so."

"Really? They got raided. He said it was retaliation, but now they're in a meeting with the fucking slender man! What else am I supposed to think?"

"It's Colson. And his family. They're causing trouble because of me. Colson blames Noah for our breakup, and he's using his family's money and connections to fuck with them. You're caught in the crosshairs. Jace is caught in the crosshairs. I'm fucking up everyone's lives." My voice cracks. I should have known something like this would happen. I'm pulling everyone down.

"No." Noah's voice booms out of nowhere. "You aren't. Come on, baby. We're leaving."

The creepy man slithers out of the bar as he holds his hand out to me.

"My truck is still parked outside. Let's go."

My feet move. I'm walking out with him, but I'm numb. Everything around me is happening without my consent or permission. I'm in the car. His hand is on my leg. We're driving. Stopping. Getting out.

It's all a blur.

I'm stagnant, surrounded by fast-moving parts. There is no stability, no ground beneath my feet.

Inside his apartment, my trembling legs give out.

"Whoa, hey." He catches me, bringing me down to the floor with him. "What's going on, Ace?"

"I don't know." I bury my face in his shirt. I don't want him to see me.

"What do you need?" He's so calm.

"I don't know!" I sob. "I want the room to stop spinning and for the fucking elephant sitting on my chest to disappear."

"You're panicking, baby. Take a breath for me. I'm going to fix it, ok?" His voice pulls me out of the abyss.

His arms hold me tight, wrapping me in security.

"That man at the bar, Clayton, he is a bit of a specialist. His area of expertise is niche, to say the least." He strokes my hair.

"What does he do?"

"He sets up accidents."

"Who is going to have an accident?"

"A few people." He looks at me so softly.

"But—" The panic floods back.

"No." He places his hands on my shoulders. "Don't panic."

"I can't calm down." I feel like I'm hyperventilating. I'm breathing too fast but not getting any air.

"Baby." He gets on his knees. "You need to control it. Rein it in. Take it out on me."

"What?"

"Do whatever you need to do to feel in control." The way he's looking at me, the reverence, the restraint–it's like taking a shot that takes effect instantly.

"I—" I don't know what to say. Seeing him on his knees like this grounds me so suddenly that it's jarring. My mind was scattered, but now everything is in crystal clear focus. "Let's go shower. I want to take care of you."

The chaos stills, and my thoughts are sharp.

My arm is going to make it difficult to do everything I want to do, but I'm willing to put in the work.

He follows me down the hallway. My brain is going in a million different directions, not from panic but from possibilities. I'm full of adrenaline. I know exactly what I want to do to him.

"Strip." I push down any self-doubt. I'm in charge.

He drops his clothes and waits for more instructions.

Yanking at my clothes, I quickly throw them on the floor with him.

I want to touch him everywhere, to bring him close, then make him beg. Having him–this big, strong man, whimpering for more–that is exactly what I need.

I step into the shower, and he waits, his gaze locked on me.

"Come in." I step aside, making room for him. I'm not used to being in charge. It's exhilarating.

The water cascades over his shoulders, running down his chest and stomach. I only have one hand, but I have enough determination to get the job done. Taking the soap, I lather it in my hand before giving it to him to hold while I run my fingers over his body.

Little soap bubbles run over his skin. The cut he made on his chest looks like a minor scratch now. The line is barely visible.

Thinking about that day makes me want to do it again. It was wild and dirty, but freeing. I wasn't ashamed or embarrassed. He makes me feel wanted every single time.

With slow, deliberate movements, I wash him, leaving a specific place for last.

Lathering the soap again, I hold eye contact as I grab his cock in my fist and run my soapy hand over it.

He grunts and steps forward but otherwise restrains himself.

Chewing on my lip, I try to hide how my heart is hammering in my chest. I'm not throwing in the towel this soon, but the look on his face, his body, his everything–it's almost too much.

"Bend down so I can reach your hair."

His eyes flutter closed as I massage his scalp, working my fingers through until there is a thick lather of shampoo.

"You can rinse it." My voice is hoarse. I'm struggling, but I want to do this for him, and it might be the only time he lets me.

Leaning in, I press a kiss to the little red heart tattoo.

"Now wash me." My breath stutters.

He doesn't hesitate; his hands are on me immediately, his fingers sweeping over my skin. With such tender softness, he washes my body, leaving nothing untouched. It's like he's touching something sacred.

His hand dips between my legs, and my knees wobble.

When I'm clean, he runs his knuckles over his cock, letting out a little huff of breath that makes my pulse pound. "What do you want, baby? I'll do anything you ask." His voice is soft. There is no pride or ego. Just raw submission.

"Get on your knees again." My thighs press together. Seeing him like that ties my belly in knots.

His whole body goes rigid as he drops down, leaning in to kiss my lower stomach.

Lifting my leg, I slip it up over his shoulder. I know exactly what I want.

He groans and leans in, running the tip of his nose against my clit.

"Noah!" I choke. "Make me come."

"Yes, ma'am."

He wastes no time. His tongue sweeps through my slick skin.

"Oh, god." I grip his hair and hang on tight.

He licks and sucks until I'm shaking and moaning so loudly the sounds echo off the tiled walls. His tongue makes patterns against my clit, making magic, painting pictures, creating languages, writing poetry.

"Let me hear how much you like it." He moves one hand up, sliding his finger inside.

"Put your other hand on your cock." I narrow my eyes. I think he forgot who is supposed to be in charge here.

Watching his face, I see the moment he does it. I can tell by the way his eyes flutter closed.

"Don't come yet." I grind hard against his face.

The ache builds, throbbing harder each second. I'm struggling to stay upright.

Delirious and lost in the feeling, I make eye contact with him. "Do you love me?" I hear the words come out of my mouth as he does.

He stops what he's doing, pulling away from me. Everything shifts so abruptly that I feel dizzy.

Panic rises like bile in my throat. Embarrassment consumes me, down to the soles of my feet. He doesn't. Of course, he doesn't.

"No." He stands quickly, grabbing me before I can try to cover myself or move away. "I don't love you, Ace. Love is a feeling. A choice. People fall out of love. Feelings change. This–" he gestures between us. "This is never going to change. It's forever. It's until my heart stops beating. I more than love you, Candace. I am devoted until my last breath. You are the only good part of me."

I'm speechless.

He moves my wet hair out of my face. "There isn't anything I wouldn't do for you. Nothing."

I believe it.

"Kiss me, Noah."

Our lips meet with frantic desperation. I can't kiss him enough. We're not close enough. I want more.

He carries me out of the shower, our wet bodies landing on his bed.

"Show me how you feel about me. Be rough or soft, I don't care. But I want to be able to see you."

He sits up, pulling me onto his lap. "Sit on it."

With his arms wrapped around my waist and our chests pressed together, I sink down onto him.

"Fuck," he mumbles under his breath, adjusting his feet so that he has leverage to rock up into me. "I want to fuck your heart. To be so deep inside you that I touch everything."

I'm already overstimulated. His tongue has me in a frenzy– I only need a bit more.

"I'm going to kill him, baby." He moves his hand up to hold the back of my neck, pulling my head closer to his. "I won't let him hurt you."

"How?" I feel myself building so quickly, it's frightening. My stomach clenches, tying itself into a knot.

"I have to get rid of his cousin first."

"Ok." I nod my head, agreeing.

"When this is all over, you'll never have to look over your shoulder again. I'm going to make sure you're safe."

"I know." I whimper against his mouth.

"Once I know we're free, I'll buy you a big house out in the country." He grinds into me.

"Fuck." I drop my face forward, pressing into this shoulder. "Oh my god, Noah!"

"Can I come with you, baby? Please?" He whimpers, and I start to unravel.

"No." I want to let him. But I can't yet. It's a crazy kind of high— being in charge of him like this. He could stop at any moment, he could flip me over and pin me down and do whatever he wanted, but he doesn't. He won't.

His lips part as he pants, his eyes widening. "Ace, please."

"I want to feel your weight on me, and I want you to fuck me hard. Then you can come."

The words are barely out of my mouth when he moves forward, dropping me back onto the mattress with his hand behind my head. He lets go of his weight, pinning me down.

"Open your legs wide for me." He chokes.

Planting my feet flat onto the mattress, I brace myself.

With his face pressed into my neck, he fucks into me so hard and fast that something breaks beneath us. I feel it, the sudden drop and shift of the mattress, but he doesn't seem to care, so neither do I.

"Ace!" He begs. "God damn it. I can't. You're so–" He gasps, a miserable sound.

"Noah! I'm—" the words are lost in a moan followed by a sea of cries. I'm barely conscious enough to tell him to come.

But he hears me. Wrapping one of his arms around my lower back, he holds me tightly to him.

His pace falters as he rolls through the tremors, wreaking havoc on my body.

"God—Ace!" His body goes rigid.

Out of breath and still too high to speak, we just lie in silence, wrapped around each other.

"Thank you," I whisper when enough of my senses come back to me to formulate words.

"Don't thank me, Ace. Anything you need, I've got it."

"I know."

"We broke my bed." He hums, the amusements in his voice making me smile.

FORTY-ONE

THERE IS a rock in my stomach as I walk into the office. If I thought I didn't deserve to be here before, I really feel it today.

"Miss Kennedy! Are you sure you're feeling well enough to be back?" Mr. Connors looks concerned. "You look pale."

"Oh," I take off my coat before I sweat through my shirt. "Yeah, I'm alright. Thank you."

"Today, I'm going to be receiving discovery from the defense on the Montgomery case. When it gets here, will you let me know? We're going to have a lot to go through. I think they're planning to bury us."

"I'll let you know as soon as it arrives." I'm grateful for his distracted attention. If he looked at me too closely, he would see my nervousness.

When the boxes arrive, all of my energy is spent taking inventory. They sent over two hundred and twenty-three boxes of paperwork. The county clerk seems annoyed, but I'm overjoyed. This much work means I don't have time to think about my personal life.

Hours of marking and categorizing paperwork feel like a

mental vacation. It's mind-numbingly dull and tedious, but that's exactly what I need.

Just as I start to relax, as the nervousness starts to fade—two detectives walk into the office.

Working this job for two years, I can spot a detective from a mile away.

It's not unusual to have all kinds of police presence here, the ADA meets with them often, but I don't recognize them in particular.

"Hello, we're looking for Candace Kennedy."

"I'm Candace." I rub my sweaty palms together.

"I'm Detective Thatcher. This is Detective Dunn. Do you have a moment to speak with us?"

"Sure." I look at the stacks of boxes like they can help me somehow.

"Do you know Bradley Carpenter?" He jumps right in.

"Um, no. I know who he is. There was an incident at a club in Columbus last week. I didn't know him before that."

"Can you identify these items?" He holds a few photos out to me.

Studying the picture, I'm not quite sure what I'm looking at. "This is my college diploma. And this is a t-shirt of mine."

"Would there be any reason you can think of for these items to be in Mr. Carpenter's possession?"

"What?" Panic rises in my throat. "He had those?"

"They were found in his vehicle."

"Was he in my apartment? How did he get these?" It feels like the walls are closing in on me, and the temperature in the room is rising by the second.

"Don't worry, Miss. Kennedy. He's deceased. If there was something going on, he isn't going to be able to harm you." He watches me, looking at my reaction to this news.

"He's dead?" The volume of my voice rises so much that Mr. Connors steps out of his office.

"Is everything alright?" He looks concerned as he steps toward me.

"We're just asking questions about a case. We'll be out of the way in a minute." Detective Dunn smiles at him. Maybe it's my paranoia, but she seems much more friendly with him. Am I a suspect?

They are too relaxed. I feel like a mouse in a trap. Are they trying to trick me into letting my guard down so they can catch me?

"Are you aware that he is your former fiancé's cousin?" She turns her attention back to me.

"I put that together when I saw his name on the police report."

"And Noah Gaines is your boyfriend currently?"

"Yes."

"Do you have any idea why your ex-fiancé's cousin would take personal effects from your apartment or harass you in a nightclub?"

"The breakup wasn't exactly amicable. Maybe Colson is behind it." I doubt they will follow up on that lead. "I honestly can't think of any other reason. I never met his cousin."

"I read the report from the officer on the scene, but do you mind telling me what happened?"

"I don't mind." Sweat gathers at my hairline. It's too warm in here. "I went to the club with—"

"To The Violet House?" He interrupts.

"Yes. I went to The Violet House with my roommate, Stella. Her boyfriend, Jace, is the owner. Noah works there as a bouncer and barback. When we got there, we went to the bar. I was waiting for Noah when I was approached by a man."

"Bradley Carpenter."

"Yes." I nod. "He asked me to dance, and I declined. Then he asked if he could buy me a drink. I declined again. He started to get more forceful. When I tried to walk away, he grabbed me and wouldn't let go."

He nods along, taking notes. "Then what?"

"Then Stella got involved. She told him to let me go, but he wouldn't. His grip got tighter. It was actually painful. Then Noah came and forced him to let me go."

"I see." He smiles, closing his notebook. We won't take up any more of your time. I'm going to leave you with my card. If you think of anything else or have any questions, don't hesitate to reach out."

"Right." I take it and slide it into my pocket. "I will."

I'm shaken to my core as they walk out of the office.

Did I give anything away? Do the police suspect Noah?

I didn't expect this to happen so quickly.

My mind is going to spiral, somersaulting over this information all day long.

"Is everything alright?" Mr. Connors comes out of his office, wading through the stacked boxes to sit at the conference table.

"Yes, and no." I try to smile, but my lips are dry. "I broke up with Colson Barrington, and then his cousin, who I had never met, grabbed me. Those officers told me he died, and he had some items that belonged to me in his car at the time."

"Oh, shit."

"Yeah."

"How did he die?"

"They didn't say."

He hums thoughtfully, rising from his chair and disappearing into his office. A moment later, he reappears with his laptop. A few clicks of the keyboard, and he pulls up a file.

"The ME hasn't released the toxicology or full autopsy yet,

but preliminary reports are pointing to a drug overdose. He was found in his car, parked halfway on the train tracks. Looks like he's got a history—priors for drug possession, public intoxication, resisting arrest." He turns the screen toward me. "There were drugs found at the scene."

"Oh, wow." I read over the five different times he was arrested on drug-related charges.

A wave of sadness washes over me. I pity him. With a record like this and a family like that, his life was probably not easy. I bet Colson manipulated him into this, and it cost him his life.

There is a small, naïve part of me that hopes he really did overdose and that Noah had nothing to do with it.

He told me a few people were about to have accidents. I didn't expect it to be so soon.

Deep down, I know it was him. He had a hand in it. The grim reaper-looking man from the bar did this.

Guilt starts to weigh down on my chest, pressing into my lungs.

But then I think of Noah's face. And suddenly, I don't feel guilty.

Bradley Carpenter would still be alive if he hadn't followed Colson's lead. If he hadn't laid hands on me. If he hadn't tried to put Noah behind bars. He made choices. Bad ones.

He knew what he was doing was wrong. He played the game and lost.

I exhale, slow and steady. My chest feels lighter.

Whether or not it's wrong, I don't really care.

Opening my bag, I pull out my sliced apple with peanut butter. I'm not going to give this a second thought.

Just as I finish my snack, Mr. Connors rushes out of his office. He is, as usual, frazzled and rushing, but today he has nothing on the schedule for almost two hours.

"I've been pulled into an emergency meeting. Will you clear my schedule for the day? Then you can go home." He buttons his suit jacket into the wrong buttonhole.

"Is everything alright?"

"I'm not sure." He calls over his shoulder. "Kent wants to see me right now."

Pulling up the calendar, I cancel his afternoon appointments. I wonder why the district attorney wants to meet him so urgently.

FORTY-TWO

THE SMILE FADES from my face when I step out into the early afternoon sunshine to find Stella waiting for me.

"Hey." I try not to let my face fall too much.

"Don't look so disappointed." She laughs. "He sent me to get you. They got an urgent call."

I can tell by the look on her face that something else is going on. The laugh wasn't real. She's worried.

"Um, we've been instructed to go home and grab a few essentials, then go stay with my parents for the night." She chews her lip.

"That sounds bad."

"Yeah." She nods.

I try to act like everything is fine. But my fingers tremble as I text him.

Are you alright?

I don't expect an immediate response, but I can't stop staring at my phone as I wait for one.

By the time we reach our apartment, my phone is almost taunting. Three separate bullshit marketing notifications. But radio silence from Noah.

"I'll just grab a few things." I rush out of the car. Inside my bedroom, I shove things in a bag without even looking at them. There might be four pairs of pants and no shirts. I don't have the brain capacity to care.

Did he get arrested?

I should have called him to warn him that the police were already investigating, but I was worried they might have tapped the phones or something. That's a real thing, right?

I imagine him sitting in jail right now.

Every worst-case scenario plays out in my head in rapid succession, bad dream after bad dream, each one worse than the last.

Rushing out of my room, I meet Stella in the hallway. She has a half-packed bag in her arms.

"Ready?"

"Let's go." I don't want to stay here for one second longer than necessary. After last time, I think we both want to follow instructions down to the letter.

"You have no idea what happened?"

"None." She shrugs. "He didn't tell me anything. He just rushed out of the room. Then Noah called and asked me to get you."

If Noah called her, he's not in jail. He would have told her. Probably.

"What the fuck. Get off my ass!" She sits up straighter, glaring in the rearview mirror.

Spinning around, I find a blacked-out SUV driving so close to her bumper that I can see the bugs stuck in its grille.

"Oh, no." I force down the fear that it's Colson.

"It's him, isn't it?" She slams on her brakes, and the front of their car taps hers. It's just a little bump, not even a fender bender, but it's enough to push her over the edge. She turns off her car in the middle of the street. "I'm ending this shit, right fucking now."

"Stella? What are you–"

The sound of her phone trilling through the car speakers cuts me off.

"911–What's your emergency?" A clear, calm voice answers.

"We're at the intersection of State Road 28-101 and Watson Street. I need the police right now. We're being followed by a truck that I don't recognize. I can't see the driver. They've been driving really close to my car and speeding. And when I came to a stop at the light, the rear-ended me. I'm afraid to get out of my car. Please, send someone!"

"We have officers en route. Stay on the line with me. Don't get out of your vehicle."

"Please, hurry!" She looks in the mirror.

"We have officers in the area. You should be able to hear the sirens already." The operator's voice stays steady. "What is your name?"

"Stella."

"Is anyone injured, Stella?"

"No."

"Oh my god, Stella. They're getting out!" The driver's side door opens but quickly closes when the sound of sirens fills the air.

I'm sure they weren't betting on us calling the police. They certainly weren't counting on there being a car patrolling nearby.

Spinning around in my seat, I watch as the truck lurches

backwards and then stops. There must be someone behind them. They are blocked in.

I don't mean to scream, but when they push forward, slamming into the back of Stella's car hard enough to push us forward, I realize what they're doing.

"They're trying to run! They're fleeing the scene!"

They reverse and hit her car– once, twice, three times– before there is enough space for them to pull away. They speed past us, running the red light.

A police car with sirens blaring and lights flashing flies through the intersection behind them, pursuing them.

"Stay where you are, Stella." The operator walks us through it. "Police are in pursuit, and another officer is en route to you now. Just hold tight."

"Ok."

We sit for a second. She reaches over and takes my hand.

"I was so afraid they were going to run us off the road." She looks me in the eye, her lips tipping upward slightly.

"Me too."

"They've been following us since we left home."

I hadn't noticed. But now I know what she wants me to say.

"I see the police!" She yells out, her voice full of relief.

I get out of the car as she ends the call with the operator.

The officers quickly spring into action. After ensuring we are both unharmed, they begin to document the scene so that we can move the car out of the way of traffic.

Stella moves the car into the parking lot of a gas station to finish the process.

One of the officers is in the middle of interviewing me when his radio crackles. He fumbles to turn the volume down, but the voice on the other end has already said enough.

"You're not going to believe this. Colson and Trent Barrington are the occupants of the other vehicle."

"Colson is my ex-boyfriend. He's been stalking me." I watch the color drain from his face.

The officer blinks, and his lips part, but he doesn't say anything. Just a stiff nod before excusing himself to speak with the other officer on the scene.

Stella slips away, standing beside me. "He said they were apprehended and being arrested." She whispers.

"They'll be bailed out within the hour."

"That man has a dash cam." She points to a man who stopped to talk with the officers. "He's submitting it on our behalf."

My phone buzzes in my pocket, and my heart leaps into my throat.

"Noah?"

"What's going on, baby? Why have you been sitting at the gas station for fifteen minutes?" His voice is low and steady. God. Just a word from him. That's all I need. My insides flutter.

"Colson rear-ended Stella."

There's a pause, and then a rumble—low, harsh, enraged—as if he can't keep the anger from spilling out. A string of expletives pours out of him.

"Are you alright? Are you hurt?"

The edge in his voice softens. I close my eyes, gripping the phone tighter. "We're okay. A little shaken. That's all."

"You're sure?" His voice dips lower, a gravelly whisper, as if he's trying to breathe around rage.

"Yes. Someone got it on their dash cam. They're giving it to the cops now."

He lets out a long, slow breath. "Good. Listen to me, Ace. As soon as you can, get to my parents' house. Don't leave until I get there. I'm sending you dinner. Eat all of it. I don't care if you're not hungry."

"Ok." I have to clear the sudden dryness in my throat. "I will."

There is a moment of silence, and I imagine him running his hand over his face, the tension in his jaw, his dark, stormy eyes.

"I'll come get you as soon as I can."

"Are you safe?"

He hesitates, and my heart clenches. "I'll be there soon, baby."

I don't want to hang up.

"I'll see you soon," I whisper.

"Yes, I promise."

"Ok."

Don't go yet.

"I have to go, Ace."

"I know."

"Hang up the phone."

"Ok." But I don't.

"Ace."

"I'm worried about you."

"Don't be."

"Miss. Kennedy? Can I finish taking your statement so you can get out of here?" The officer comes back.

"Yeah, sure." I fake a smile. "Bye, Noah," I whisper.

"Go straight home."

Sliding the phone into my pocket, I try not to pout.

Officer Lanester asks me about my relationship with Colson and the timeline of the stalking events. He takes the contact information for the detectives on the Bradley Carpenter case. As I say everything out loud, it hits me how fucked up all of this really is.

I've never hated Colson more than I do right now. I want

him out of my life. We're over. He needs to just bow out. But he can't.

A dark, intrusive thought pops into my head. I try to push it down, but it won't leave me alone.

He won't be around much longer.

"Do you have any questions for me?" He snaps me out of my downward spiral.

"No!" I need to get away from him. Thoughts of murder are not great at any time, but they feel particularly dangerous in front of a police officer.

When we slide into our seats, the car is tense and quiet for a few miles.

"What the fuck?" She breaks first.

"I know."

"Seriously, Candy. What the fuck? Has he done that before? I was wondering why Noah wanted you picked up from work, but–"

"He hasn't done that before, but I guess he thought he could, since Noah wasn't there."

"Big fucking man acts up when it's women alone, but he's afraid when there is a man around. What a bitch." She growls.

This situation isn't funny. Maybe it's the tension. Or the fact that I've felt like I'm holding my breath for weeks, but a snort rips from my chest.

Covering my mouth, I try to hold back my laughter, but it's impossible. "He is a bitch."

She starts to laugh too, and once we're both going, it can't be stopped.

"He really hit my car! Did he think we wouldn't call the police?" She laughs. "I bet he wasn't expecting me to brake-check him."

This momentary break in the tension is exactly what I

needed. As she parks the car in her parents' driveway, it starts to creep back in.

I can't let her see how worried I am. She knows more now than before, but there is still a lot left out of the picture.

"My girls!" Mrs. Gaines grabs us both, hugging just a bit too tightly. "Dinner arrived for you about three minutes ago. It's in the kitchen." She gives us another squeeze and lets us go. "I'm so excited that you're staying! It's been so long since you girls stayed here. I'll admit, I hope your power stays off for a few days." She grins sheepishly.

"Our power?"

"Yeah, hopefully!" Stella laughs loudly, cutting me off.

"Oh, right, yeah. The power." I'm a bit slow on the uptake today.

Stella links our arms and pulls me into the kitchen. "Sorry, I forgot to mention that. Noah didn't want to raise suspicion, so he told me to lie."

"It's ok." It's for the best that she doesn't know what kind of shit storm I got everyone mixed up in. I'm endangering her children.

A burger and fries are waiting in the kitchen for me. My stomach is tied in a knot, but I eat the whole thing.

Each bite feels more erotic than it should. I'm doing exactly as I'm told. He's going to be proud of me. I don't have to think, just do, just obey.

It's nice to turn my brain off.

When I've finished my dinner, I send Noah a picture of the empty wrappers.

No response.

As we pass by the living room, the TV catches my attention.

"Live from WKZZ Channel 5 — trusted, local, now. This is the Evening Report."

"Good evening. Our top story tonight — tragedy strikes one of the city's most powerful families." The anchor looks solemn. My mind immediately goes to the Barringtons. Did something happen to them already?

"The son of District Attorney Jason Kent was found dead early this morning in what authorities are calling a 'tragic accident.' But questions remain. We're live on the scene with what we know so far — and what's still unanswered."

The screen flashes to ambulances and police tape outside of the district attorney's house. He lives on the same street as Colson's parents.

"Yes, we're live here at the scene. The Hyde Park neighborhood is not used to this type of occurrence. All we know now is that Kent's youngest son was involved in an accident involving the electricity in their home, seen behind me."

"I bet that's why Mr. Connors rushed off," I whisper to Stella.

"How awful for them!" Mrs. Gaines sniffs.

I don't realize that I'm dialing his number until the call is already ringing.

He doesn't answer.

Stella showers. Still no answer.

Then I shower. No answer.

I'm starting to spiral. My mind is spinning in every direction. I can't keep calling. It's making me feel insane. He's going to see fifty missed calls and think I've lost my mind.

When I'm sure that she's asleep, I creep out of her room and down the hallway. His old bedroom is dark and cold. Slipping under the blankets on his bed, I close my eyes and breathe in the smell of his pillow.

Please, just tell me you're okay.

I stare at the phone until my eyes start to feel too heavy to keep open.

My phone dings in my hand, and I sit up.

Go to sleep, Angel.

FORTY-THREE

NOAH

SHE'S IN MY BED.

Seeing her there calms the chaos in my brain. Rubbing my bloody hands on my pants, I stand at the foot of the bed and watch her. The moonlight from the window illuminates her pretty face.

I don't move or make a sound, but she startles awake. It's like her body can sense mine. She can feel me.

"Noah!" Her voice is raspy and tired as she sits up. "You're back." The relief in her voice spurs me forward against my better judgment.

I need to shower, but I have to check on her first. I need to touch her skin, to check that she's uninjured.

She's wearing my fucking shirt.

Sucking in a breath, I reach for her. The smile falls from her face.

"Oh, my god!" She throws the blanket off. "You're hurt!"

"I'm not. It's not mine." My jaw clenches.

She stops, frozen.

I'm covered from head to toe in deep red blood. He

screamed. He begged. I worked for every fucking drop. "One down."

"One down?" She shivers. Her wide, frightened eyes meet mine.

Reaching out, I grab the hem of my shirt and tug her toward me.

I need to kiss her.

It's not gentle at all. She gasps against my mouth, and I press my tongue in.

"Say it's ok." I breathe the air from her mouth.

"It's ok." She wraps her arms around my neck, pressing her body into mine.

"Fuck." Slipping my hand beneath the shirt, I don't fumble around in the dark. My fingers find her wet cunt instantly. Of course, she's soaked. I wish I could take her back there and fuck her beside his body. It's too late for that now. I'm sure it's being cleaned up already. A missed opportunity.

Pulling the bloody blade from my pocket, I flick it open. The sound of the metal locking into place is like a switch in my brain.

"Get on the bed, spread your legs."

She blinks, her breath trembling before she does as she's told.

"We need to be very quiet, baby." I drop the knife on the bed beside her. "Where are the clothes you were wearing when you got here?"

"In that bag." She points to a small duffel bag on the floor. The wrinkle of confusion between her brows makes me smile.

Kneeling down, I dig through the bag and pull out her panties.

"Open your mouth."

She gasps, a sharp breath, and her body squirms. "N-Noah—"

I shake my head. "Be a good girl and open up for me. I'm going to fuck you so hard. We need to make sure you can stay quiet. Unless you want everyone in the house to wake up." My cock twitches at the thought. "Do you want them to know what I'm doing to you in here, baby?"

"No." She whispers. Her throat flexes as she swallows before opening her mouth.

"So fucking pretty." I press her panties to my face and inhale.

I can see how wet her pussy is. Soaked and dripping. Delicious.

Stuffing the wadded-up underwear into her mouth, I step back and stare at her.

This isn't enough.

"Spin around so that your feet are on the headboard."

I hear her follow instructions as I open my closet. A tie and a sock will do.

"Spread them wide." I take one of her ankles, pressing a kiss to it before tying it to the headboard.

The sock is a bit harder to work with, and I have to pull it tight against her skin. It will leave a chafed mark behind when I untie it.

Good.

I have to peel my shirt off. It dried against my skin.

She makes a sound, a muffled, desperate attempt to talk. Pulling the panties from her mouth, she comes up on her elbows.

"Noah! You're hurt! Your chest—"

"Put the panties back in your mouth and don't take them out, or I'll tie your hands."

Her chin wobbles, but she obeys.

"When I'm done with you, I'll let you clean and bandage it." I touch her cheek, wiping away the tear that slid down.

She nods her head. I knew this would help.

Fuck, my cock aches. I need to sink it into her now. The fucking pulsating is killing me.

I climb onto the bed between her legs. Leaning back, I take my cock in my fist, rubbing my thumb over my shaft while I watch her.

She's squirming and panting. Her chest is heaving with each breath.

Taking the knife, I run the blade up her leg, stopping at the softness of her inner thigh. Pressing the point into her skin just enough for her to feel it, I watch for signs of fear.

None.

Rolling my neck, I ignore the urge to drop down and fuck her now.

Patience.

"How bad do you want it?" I scrape the knife up her other thigh.

Her body trembles, a full-body tremor that rushes over her.

Pressing the point in again, I watch her eyes. She's so fucking excited. Her body betrays her.

Leaning forward, I slowly drag the knife point up her stomach and over her nipple. She writhes beneath me, her body spasming and twitching.

Reaching down, I slip my fingers inside of her, curling them against the sweet spot that makes her move like a puppet I'm controlling.

Her eyes roll back, and she jerks against the restraints.

"Shh, quiet, Ace."

A muffled moan slips through her panties.

"Look at me." I slide the knife up to her neck. "Are you afraid?"

She shakes her head. No.

Closing my eyes, I take a breath. I'm about to come right

now. The complete trust. The total surrender. Fuck me. It's perfect. She's perfect.

She doesn't question me. My command is met with immediate obedience.

"Keep your eyes on me."

She nods, and I know she's trying her best, but her eyes roll back again.

Pulling my fingers out, I position my cock at the soft entrance to her pussy and slam forward, burying myself as deep inside her as I can.

Immediately, I'm overwhelmed with the urge to fill her with cum. I want to watch it drip out of her while she's tied open in front of me.

"Fuck." I grunt. "Eyes up."

With the knife pressed to her throat, I fuck her so hard the mattress starts to inch out of place.

"You feel fucking amazing, baby. It's so good. Your body was made for mine, wasn't it?"

She nods frantically.

"Let me feel you come. Strangle my cock."

And just like that, she does. She squeezes me like a fist.

"Fuck." I can't breathe. "I'm—"

Yanking the panties out of her mouth, I press my lips to hers. Sloppy and wet, I moan into her mouth as I come so hard my heart nearly stops. I'm barely conscious as I ride out the rippling spasms that crush my body.

She whimpers and wraps her arms around my neck.

"You said I could bandage your wound." Her sweet voice silences the itch in my spine.

"I said that, didn't I?"

FORTY-FOUR

SHIFTING UNCOMFORTABLY IN MY SEAT, I look at the clock. I'm distracted.

My body is sore and achy, but my mind is overloaded with questions I didn't ask him. I should have, but I panicked and shoved it all down. Whose blood was that?

The browser pings, a new email from the lobby desk. I didn't even know they had an email address.

> *There is a package for ADA Connors at the*
> *security kiosk.*

That's...odd.

Standing, I start to turn toward his door, but decide against knocking. He's had so much on his plate. I'll grab the package and have it waiting here for him whenever he comes out.

As I make my way down the hallway, I wonder if Stanley is sick today. He always brings packages up after he takes them through security.

I have to set up a meeting with the public relations team.

Pulling out my phone, I write notes to myself. I'm going to get so much done, I won't have time to think about anything else. Mr. Connors needs to have his suit dry-cleaned. I'm sure he forgot. I smile to myself as I type out the note.

I'm ripped out of my thoughts by someone yanking me out of the hallway and into a small supply closet. The door slams closed, and I'm shoved against it.

"Hey!" I start to scream, but a hand slaps hard over my mouth. "Colson?" My voice is muffled against his palm.

"Shh." He snarls hot against my cheek. He slams me into the door and rams his knee between my legs. "Shut the fuck up."

My head shakes, trying to get free of his grip. He's pressing my lips into my teeth with so much force that he splits my lip. I taste blood.

He has my body pinned, and something cold and sharp is pressed against my neck.

"Stop it. Listen to me! This is getting fucking ridiculous, Candy." He's sweaty and jittery. I've never seen him look so disheveled. "This is going to stop now. Today." He looks around, looking behind him as if there is a chance someone else slipped into the closet with us.

His wild eyes are scaring me the most. He looks lost. He's sweating and unkempt. His pupils are pinpricks in bloodshot, watery eyes.

"I'm going to let go of your mouth, but if you fucking scream, I'll kill you. I'll slit your fucking throat. Do you hear me?"

I nod.

I don't make a sound when he pulls his hand away, I barely breathe.

This knife is different from the one that was against my neck the other night. That one didn't scare me. Noah didn't scare me. Even covered in blood, I knew he would never do anything to hurt me.

Colson looks like he wants to. I pinch my eyes closed so I don't have to look at him.

"Open your eyes! Look at me!" He barks angrily, pressing the point in harder. I barely notice it, though.

"Colson, please." My voice waivers, but otherwise I keep it calm and quiet. "This is—"

"You're going to call him right now and break up with him. He's behind the shit that's happening to my family. My dad thinks he's a middleman, but he isn't, is he? You're going to end it right now, and then he will leave us alone."

"He isn't doing any—"

"Stop fucking lying to me! You're a whore and a filthy fucking liar. I can't believe I was going to marry you."

"I'm not lying." The knife leaves my throat, before I have a moment to process the relief, his open hand cracks sharply across my face.

My head slams against the door, pain erupting across my cheek. A dull ache settles in behind my eyes.

I don't mean to cry, but the sound slips out anyway.

"Shut up. You're going to call him and tell him to back off. If he doesn't, my family is going to make sure that he never sees the light of day again. If you want to see him, you'll have to go for a prison conjugal. You disgusting bitch."

Pain pulsates in my cheek and jaw. It's hot, the bruise blooming in real time. Whimpering, I cower back.

"Don't whine." His voice changes, his finger softly trailing over my cheek. "You're not the victim here. Crying doesn't make you innocent, Candy. You made me do that." He crouches, bringing his eyes level with mine. "I'm trying to fix this. Fix us. I know you didn't mean it."

"Us?" There is no us.

He grabs my face, my cheeks breaking against my teeth. He's trying to snap my jaw. He must be. My knees buckle, but he keeps me upright. Leaning in, his lips ghosting over mine. "Call him."

"I–"

His free hand runs down my chest. "Where is your phone?"

He keeps searching, moving his fingers into places that make my eyes water–places he knows my phone is not.

"I bet you let him touch you. Are you his little whore, Candy?" He laughs, releasing my face so that he can kiss me.

My mouth is busted and bleeding, my cheeks are bleeding into my mouth, but none of that is as bad as his lips on mine.

Bile rises in my throat.

He moves his knee up. My skirt lifts slightly, and he tugs it the rest of the way up. Turning my face away, I gag. I'm so repulsed by his touch, his lips, the smell of him. It's going to make me physically ill.

His eyes narrow, and he runs his fingers over my panties, between my legs. "You were supposed to be mine. I should fuck you right now. Give you a taste of what you're missing."

I want to beg him to stop, but I think that will only make it worse. Closing my eyes, I wait for it to be over.

"Where is the phone?" He growls.

"I dropped it."

He releases me enough to look around on the floor. It's behind him on the ground.

"Pick it up and call him." When I hesitate, he slams me back against the wall. "Candy, I swear to god. Pick it up. Do you see how easily I can get to you? You won't be safe anywhere. Do what I'm asking, or I'll come back. Even your watchdog can't protect you."

There is a sound outside in the hallway. People walking by, just past the door.

I open my mouth, but he slams his hand against it again, knocking my head into the door and rattling my brain.

He leans forward, listening until the sound is gone.

Without a word, he grabs me, pulling me up to kiss me with such bruising force it makes me sob into his mouth. Then he releases me and runs out of the closet.

Frozen, I just stand there.

I listen for footsteps, waiting for him to return. Eventually, my trembling legs give out, and I crumble to the floor.

My cracked phone is on the ground beside me. I can hardly see, as I call him.

"Hey, baby–"

My cracked sob stops whatever he was going to say.

"Candace?" The urgency in his voice only makes me cry harder. "Ace, what happened?"

I can't speak. A silent sob is caught in my throat. I can't breathe or let it out.

"Candace!" He shouts.

No sound will come out of my mouth.

"I'm coming, baby. I'm coming." His breath comes through the phone fast. He's running. "Can you tell me where you are?"

I suck in a breath and try to make something come out of my mouth.

"Listen to me, baby. Jace is outside. He's going through security right now and going up to your office. Can you tell me where you are? Take a breath, Ace. If you can't tell me, it's ok. I'll kick every fucking door in until I find you."

"The closet." I sob.

"Baby, take a breath for me, ok? You're crying so hard I

can't understand you." I hear a door slam and the roar of his truck engine.

"I'm in a closet!" I hiccup.

"You're in a closet? I'm three minutes away from you. One hundred and eighty seconds. You hear me? I'll be right there."

Closing my eyes, I start to count.

"Are you on your floor or another?"

"Mine. I'm on my floor." Seven, eight, nine, ten.

The sound of his horn blares through the phone. "Jace is inside. He's looking for you."

"Um, no." I pull my skirt down. "Please."

"Ok, he won't come inside."

There is a screech, and another door slams.

A light tap on the door makes me jump.

"It's just Jace, baby. He's going to wait outside, alright? No one but me is going to come into that room." He's running again. "Here." He sounds impatient. "I'm going to the ADA's office."

I hear the muffled sound of the security agent talking.

There is a shuffle outside, and the door opens.

"Baby." He drops down to the floor, and I jump into his arms.

He doesn't ask any questions, just holds me while I sob into his shirt. I'm safe in his arms. Once the shock wears off, I sit back. Blood from the inside of my mouth is all over his shirt.

"I'm sorry about that." I touch the wet stain.

"I couldn't possibly care less about the shirt, Ace. What happened? Who did it?" He gently tips my head back, his eyes searching.

"Colson."

His eyes flutter closed, and he takes a long, slow breath. "This is my fault. I should have been here."

"It's not your fault–"

"Where is the blood coming from?" He wipes my tears away. "This isn't all from your lip."

"Inside of my mouth." My chin trembles. "He grabbed my face."

"Let me see."

Opening my mouth, I watch his face. His eye twitches, and he sucks his teeth.

"I promised you that he would never touch you again, and I failed. I know my promises mean shit to you right now, but Ace, he will never do this again. Do you hear me?" He sets his hands on my shoulders. "Did he do anything else?"

"No." I shake my head.

"Ace, are you lying to me?"

"Yes."

He nods but doesn't speak; he just waits.

"He kissed me. And touched me."

"Come here." He lifts me up. "I'm going to take you to the bathroom to clean up."

My eyes hurt, swollen from crying, with a dull ache settled in behind them.

He opens the door, and Jace nods, giving us the all clear to come out.

I've worked here for two years. I've never been inside that supply closet.

Inside the bathroom, there are occupants in both stalls. They talk, oblivious to what is happening by the sinks.

Noah quietly wets a few paper towels and wipes my face. "We're going to go back to your office. Tell Connors that you're sick."

"I can't take any more sick days." My nasal whisper makes me cringe.

The loud sound of a toilet flushing sends me rushing for the door. I don't want a single person who doesn't absolutely have to see my face to see it.

"She doesn't want to leave." He looks at Jace like he wants to rip his head off. "I'm going to go after him—"

Jace grabs his upper arm, yanking forward to tell him something quietly. "Don't go after him. Stick to the plan, man."

"Please. Don't leave me." I put my hand in his.

He sighs and rubs his hand over his face. "I'll stay with you."

FORTY-FIVE

I WALK SLOWLY up the steps into my office. He is waiting outside; he promised that he would be here when I leave work. The only reason I'm able to hold it together at all is knowing that.

He's right here.

When I slid out of the truck, he stopped me, pinning me against it while he kissed me so intensely it left me panting.

I force my fear and thoughts of Colson to the back of my mind. This is my job. He's not going to keep me from my life.

As soon as I step inside, I know things are weird.

There are nine people already gathered in our small lobby.

"Good morning." I try not to seem so confused. I should know if he has meetings set up. I'm his assistant.

While I unlock the office, I notice that they inch in closer. They each have things with them: boxes, laptops, and files. It looks like they're preparing to move in.

"I'm sorry." I spin around, keeping the door closed behind me. "Why are you here?"

"Oh," the woman closest to me looks surprised. "Um, we're support staff. We're here for the ADA."

"For what?" I'm still lost.

"The DA stepped down." One of the men says with a flat, irritated voice. "Didn't you know?"

"Um, no." I've never felt more ill-equipped to do my job than right now.

"He's taking an indefinite leave of absence. Mr. Connors is taking over while he grieves the tremendous loss of his son." He looks at me like I'm the lowest person on earth.

"That makes sense. I was just unaware." Turning back, I unlock the door and leave it open for me to follow them in. "The conference room is right here," I point. "You can set up your stuff."

"His meetings are going to have to be shifted." The condescending one looks at me over the tip of his nose. "He's taking over Kent's schedule."

The door at the end of the room opens, and we all freeze.

Mr. Connors walks in, disheveled as usual. "Oh! Miss Kennedy! Can I have a word with you in my office? Everyone else, please, make yourselves at home and begin to write up a brief on the current cases you're working on. My team is already doing the same to give to the acting ADA."

He rushes past us into his office, and I hurry behind him.

"I'm so sorry I didn't contact you. It's been a whirlwind." He sets his briefcase down before quickly closing the door. "We're going to have a lot to adjust to." He rubs his forehead.

"We are, but they have the right man for the job. I'll grab you a coffee and print you an itinerary for the week. At least you'll know what's immediately coming up."

"You're a lifesaver. Thank you."

Rushing out of the office, I ignore the chaos and grab him a coffee from the coffee cart outside. I have a purpose–he needs me. I'll deal with everything else later. Right now, priority number one is making sure he crushes this.

Noah is standing outside, leaning against the driver's side door of his truck.

When we make eye contact, I blush. I feel like I'm floating somewhere on top of the world. It doesn't even feel wrong anymore.

He came home the other night covered in blood, soaked in it. I barely blinked. My only concern was that he was hurt.

But I trust him. Maybe it's irrational. But I do. Implicitly. Completely.

Taking my place in line, I have to force myself not to look over my shoulder at him.

When his arms wrap around my waist, I'm not surprised.

"Hi." I sink into him.

"Hi, Ace." He breathes against my neck. "You look so pretty in this skirt." He presses one of his hands flat against it.

"I have a lot to tell you at lunch."

He kisses below my ear. "I'll be here."

When it's my turn to order, Noah releases his grip on me, but not completely. His hand is still resting on my neck.

"This is for Mr. Connors."

"His usual, then?" The woman smiles.

"Please."

We step aside as she makes the drink.

"Does he have a tab here?" Noah suddenly seems interested.

"Yeah, he set it up so I can get him coffee, and he can pay his tab at the end of the week."

"He's a really good guy." He sounds thoughtful.

"He is."

"He's going to have a lot on his plate." He says this like he's sure of it. "He's lucky to have you."

"What are you–"

"Mr. Connor's coffee." The barista calls out, interrupting what has become a very important conversation.

"I'll be here to talk about it on your lunch, baby. Go inside." His voice is gentle but firm. We're not talking about this now.

"Ok." I nod, taking the coffee with suddenly trembling hands.

I feel uneasy as I walk back into the office. Everyone is gathered around the television in the conference room. Even Mr. Connors.

"What's going on?" I try to smile as I hand him the coffee.

He doesn't speak, just rubs his hand over his mouth in shock.

"The body of Richard Barrington was discovered by warehouse workers at the cargo hold in Columbia." The news anchor reads in her cold, stoic voice.

Colson's uncle Richard.

"The cause of death of the esteemed local businessman has not been released, but a source is calling the scene 'gruesome.'" She continues.

My heart pounds against my ribs.

There is no world where this is a coincidence. He comes home drenched in someone else's blood, and then three days later, the body of a Barrington is discovered. It had to be him.

He put a knife to my neck... the knife.

My legs buckle as I quickly drop into a chair. Luckily, no one is looking at me.

"Breaking News!" Another anchor's voice cuts in. "We are getting word that Trent Barrington Senior, brother to the deceased, is missing. The police have been unable to locate anyone from the Barrington family this morning."

My brain is flooded with images of all of them, dead somewhere.

The room is a whirlwind of chaos.

"Miss Kennedy, can I speak with you in my office again, please?" Mr. Connors looks pale.

"Of course." I swallow the sand in my throat and follow him, holding onto the backs of the chairs as I walk past them so I don't fall.

He closes the door and lets out a shaky breath. "I'm only telling you this because you're close to the family. But I received word from an investigative journalist this morning. They are breaking a story about the Barrington family. They have evidence, credible evidence, that they are involved in a laundry list of criminal activity. The story was going to break tomorrow. Now one of them is dead, and the rest have gone underground." He scratches his head.

The phone rings at his desk, startling both of us.

Clearing my throat, I straighten my shoulders. "Assistant District Attorney Connor's office."

"Put him on now." A voice growls.

"Who–"

"This is South Carolina Attorney General Hawthorn. Put him on the phone." He punctuates each word.

"Yes, sir. Right away." I place the call on hold. "It's Attorney General Hawthorn."

If it's possible for him to get paler, he does.

"I'll be outside." I slip out to my desk. I shouldn't, but I do it anyway. Picking up the receiver, I hold my hand over the mouthpiece and listen.

"How the fuck did a source get that information? I was called by a fucking reporter who's been digging into the Barringtons. They have fucking file numbers, for Christ's sake! How did they get those? Was the leak from your office? I swear to god, Connors, it better not have come from you."

"It didn't, sir. I wasn't aware of the files until I looked into them after the reporter reached out to me." He sounds baffled. There is a moment of silence before he speaks again. "But, just so I'm understanding you correctly. You knew about the files and their contents?"

The line clicks, dead. I quickly set down the receiver. Mr. Connors wasn't involved in any cover-ups. I knew it. But confirmation is good.

I open the calendar and type out a list of appointments. I'm going to give him everything he needs to succeed while the world burns down around us.

My eyes flick to the clock. Three hours until lunch. I'll have to make it until then.

FORTY-SIX

I WALK OUT into the sunshine, the warmth hitting my face immediately.

It seems wrong for it to be such a beautiful day. There is chaos and death swirling in the air. Murder, torture, violence.

Noah is waiting for me at the bottom of the steps.

We make eye contact, and I don't smile. Folding my arms over my chest, I march down toward him.

"How much of this shit storm did you already know about, and why didn't you tell me?"

His lips twitch. "I assume you're talking about the recent discovery of a certain esteemed local businessman." He makes his voice stiff like a news anchor.

I flatten my lips into a line.

"What do you want me to say, Ace?" He steps toward me, grabbing me and yanking so that I stumble into his body. "I killed him. Then I came home and fucked you, covered in his blood. You didn't ask at the time because you didn't want the answers." His voice dips into a low growl. "Isn't that right?"

"Why did you kill Richard?"

"Because he's as much a part of it as Trent or Colson. I'm taking all of them out. They mistreated you. They disrespected you. And now, they think they can throw their dirty fucking money around to scare you." He seethes.

"I don't want you to kill people for me, Noah. I–"

"It's a little late for that, baby. The wheels are in motion. They're all going away, one way or another."

"How did you already know that Kent stepped down?"

"I had a hand in that, too." His fingers trace my jaw.

"But he stepped down because of his son–" I gasp, covering my mouth with my hands. "Did you kill his son?"

"Not personally."

Vertigo swirls through me, making my knees buckle.

He grabs me, holding me so that I don't fall. "Take a breath, Ace. We're more than halfway through this."

"But–"

"Kent is crooked. He takes bribes and lets monsters out of prison based on how much they can pay him." He smiles. "I would know."

I feel sick.

"You paid him? But you got out for good behavior."

"We did." He tucks a strand of hair behind my ear. "It was part of the deal. He came to visit me. Apparently, he found out about the club and thought I might like to buy my way out of prison early. Good behavior is bullshit. He needed to be out of the way. For years, he's been blocking anything from coming out about that family. I told that little fucker I was going to ruin him, then kill him."

I feel myself trembling, my body violently shaking against his.

"All he had to do was leave you alone, baby. I don't give a shit if they're corrupt or if all the money they make is dirty. But he fucked around and now they're all finding out." His gaze is heavy.

He runs his thumb over my lips before dropping it down to my throat. He squeezes and yanks me forward.

He coaxes a kiss from me. I can't resist him.

My mouth moves against him, needy and desperate. It's giving me comfort and security. The fear in my head fades away, and I know everything will be alright. Even with everything I know, with everything he just told me. I still want him.

"You need to eat." He pulls back, leaving me breathless.

As we walk around the corner to the food trucks, I can't help but nervously look over my shoulder.

"They aren't here." He places his hand on my neck as we join a line at a slider stuck. "Are you sure this is what you want?"

"Oh, I don't know. I don't really care."

His brow furrows. "Pick something that actually sounds good to you, Ace."

How is it possible for one man to be so contradictory? He treats me like I'm precious one second after discussing murders.

"Can we try that place?" I point to the Cuban food truck. "It's new here, but I've heard good things."

"Come on, baby." He guides me toward the other line. His fingers carefully sweep over my neck, a soft but not subtle reminder of his presence.

After we order, I lead him to the farthest table from the others. We need privacy to talk.

"What else do you want to know? I won't lie to you, Ace. But make sure you really want the answers to the questions you ask." He reads my mind as he sets my food in front of me.

"Um, the knife from the other night, the one you..." My

hand instinctively touches the skin on my neck where he pressed the point. "Is it the same one..."

He rumbles, a low growl as his hands flex and clench. "Are you asking if I killed a man with the same knife I ran over your body?"

I clear my throat. "Yes."

"Yes." His voice trembles. "I did. I flayed his skin from his bones, then pressed the tip of that same knife into your neck." His eyes are dark; the green is almost completely gone. "You loved it, didn't you? You're thinking about how much you loved it right now."

My phone starts to buzz on the table. Noah tilts his head, his expression changing as soon as he sees the name.

"Why is Colson calling me? Should I answer it?" I panic.

"Answer it." He nods.

My heart is in my throat as I click the button. "Colson?"

"Your psychotic fucking boyfriend better watch himself, Candy. If he thinks he can fuck with my family, I'll show him what money and power really look like. Tell him to back the fuck down, now. Or I'll slit your throat in the middle of his club before burning it to the fucking ground." He snarls.

He takes the phone gently, holding it up to his mouth. "Or maybe I'll slit your throat in the middle of my club. I haven't decided yet. The beach would be poetic justice, though, I think." He looks almost bored. "You know, Colson, all you had to do was leave her alone. I want you to really think about that. None of this would be happening if you had just backed off. But you put your hands on her. Now I'm going to take your hands." He ends the call and silences my phone.

"Don't answer anymore of his calls, baby."

Immediately, his phone vibrates on the table. An unknown number.

"Hello?" He answers nonchalantly.

"Is this Noah Gaines?"

"Sure is. Who is this?"

"This is Trent Barrington Senior."

"I've been expecting your call." He takes a casual sip from his water bottle. "What can I do for you?"

"Where is the key?"

"What key?"

"Don't fuck with me, kid." His voice sounds like his throat was scraped over gravel. "Just give us the key, and we can all walk away from this. This can stop right here."

"It's funny to me that you feel like you still have a leg to stand on. What are you negotiating with, Barrington?"

"Give me that fucking key or I will stomp the miserable life out of your body myself."

"I don't know what you're talking about." He slips his hand into his pocket and sets a pair of small gold keys on the table beside the phone.

"Listen here. It would be a damn shame for something to happen to that pretty little whore of yours."

Noah's mouth twists into a cruel smile. "My whore? That's interesting. Do you know where your son is? Not the bitch that just called. The other one."

There is a muffled sound, shuffling. My heart rate skyrockets as if it were me.

"Yes, I know where he is." He sounds both relieved and annoyed.

"Oh, good. That means I know where you are. See you soon, Mr. Barrington." He hangs up the call.

"What are these?" I stare down at the keys like they might bite me.

"Safe deposit box."

"What's in it?"

The lopsided grin on his face looks so young and boyish. It has no place here. "Nothing, it's empty."

"What was in it?"

"It's all of their sins."

"All of them?"

"Baby, I have everything. It's interesting what rich, old people will put in a safe deposit box. They don't understand that the world has changed. Those aren't foolproof anymore." He hums. "Finish your lunch." He leans forward, kissing my temple. "It's time for me to return these keys."

"Wait. Are you sure that's safe? What if they hurt you?"

"Let them try." He kisses me again, this time wrapping his fingers around the column of my throat.

I know what he's trying to do. He's using this kiss to distract me, and it's almost working.

"The attorney general is in on it." I blurt out. "I forgot! He called Mr. Connors this morning. I listened in. He's upset that a reporter is digging around."

"You should keep the news on while you're working. There might be some incredibly insightful stories this afternoon."

"What else do you know?"

"I know what everyone else knows. The information isn't new. They were just in too deep to reveal it."

"You had to kill people to reveal it."

He shrugs. "That's the price you pay."

"Is it too late to stop? To just walk away?" I feel foolish and naïve just asking.

"Yes. The second he put his hands on you, it was too late, Ace. This will be over when he apologizes to you."

"What if they have you arrested?"

"They can't. If I'm in jail, they can't get the contents of that box back. And they're desperate for it. So desperate that Barrington called me directly."

"Please, be careful."

"Don't worry about me, baby. I won't leave you again."

FORTY-SEVEN

"HOLY SHIT." One of the aids slouches back in his chair, shaking his head. "You think you know people?"

"I met the Barrington brothers at a few different events over the years. I never would have guessed." One of the girls stares at the news anchor, replaying the coverage with a kind of blank, bewildered look in her eyes.

For the past two hours, the local news has been a whirlwind of breaking stories. A single one would be a big deal, but this is never-ending. It's a wildfire. It was almost immediately picked up by regional stations.

And we were just informed that it will reach the national level by tonight. New York and Los Angeles are already running the story. The scandal is growing by the minute.

It has all the pieces for a sensational headline; I get it. But it's still shocking to see our little town put on the map for something so awful.

As the layers are peeled back, numbers and figures are being thrown around. Money, contracts, and bribery add up to hundreds of millions of dollars. More money than most people would see in multiple lifetimes, they are using to pay off illegal schemes.

Tax fraud, evasion, bid rigging, and collusion. It's all there.

Meetings have been canceled, and emergency sessions are being scheduled in record time. No one who works in our local government is working on anything that doesn't have to do with this case, probably for a long time.

My foot taps nervously as I wait for the end of the day. I'm counting seconds at this point. I'm practically vibrating.

I played a part in this. I gave Noah the files.

"Well," Mr. Connors comes out of his office. His usually crooked tie has been completely removed, and his sweat-stained shirt is all that's left. "I just got word. The FBI is on their way. There will be agents here by the end of the week."

Quickly standing, I hand Mr. Connors a stack of papers. "This is the meeting schedule for the rest of the week, though most of it is likely to change. The arraignment for the Stow case is tomorrow morning, then you have a pleading hearing at noon. That's all that's on the books for court this week."

"Thank you so much, Candace. You've done great work today. You can duck out a few minutes early." He gives me a tired smile.

"Are you sure?" I feel obligated to ask even though my legs are trying to sprint out the door.

"Positive. Go home. Rest. This is going to be a very long week."

"You do the same." I know he won't.

I gather my belongings as quickly as possible. Everyone else seems content to just sit here in front of the television. They don't acknowledge my departure, so I don't say anything.

When I step outside, the warmth in the air wraps around me, sticky and humid.

Noah is standing outside his truck, waiting and watching.

As I bounce down the steps toward him, a truck scratches through the parking lot, stopping behind his truck.

"Ace." His voice is loud and stern.

Everything happens in slow motion. A van cuts into the crosswalk right in front of me. The door slides open.

My body shuts down. I don't run or scream.

"Candace," Noah calls from the other side.

"Get it quietly, or we'll kill him." I hear the click of a gun.

What the fuck am I supposed to do? I can't let them hurt him.

I step into the van, and the door slams closed as the driver speeds away.

The man grabs me, not roughly or even particularly tight. His eyes meet mine, his ski mask covering everything else. "I'm going to tie you up. Don't fight or struggle. It's going to be alright."

Why do I believe him?

"Where are the contents of the lockbox?" The man in the driver's seat looks back at me in the rearview mirror.

"I don't know."

My phone starts to ring in my purse.

"Give it to me." The driver holds his hand out. His sleeve moves up slightly, and his glove is folded over, the perfect combination to show off the tattoo on his wrist. A tattoo I recognize.

"Mr. Green?" Did they think I wouldn't recognize him? I saw him at their house a hundred times. He never spoke to me, so his voice isn't familiar, but the tattoo and his eyes are definitely a giveaway. The Barrington family's head of security–this is going from bad to worse and quickly.

"Aww, shit. Shut her up." He growls. "Hello?"

"That was a mistake." Noah's voice is so eerily calm and quiet that it sends a chill up my spine.

"Look, we aren't going to hurt her. Just give us the contents of the lockbox."

"No," Noah growls. "The contents of that box are long gone. You should call Barrington and ask him where his son is. If he's interested in making a trade, call me back."

The phone beeps, the call ends.

"Fuck." He throws my phone down onto the floor. "Cover her fucking face."

"Wait! Please! I won't say anything to anyone! I—"

"Shhh," the man in the back says, putting his hands on my shoulders, steadying me. "It's going to be alright."

The way he's looking at me, I feel like I know him. I don't recognize his voice or his eyes. He pulls a pillowcase over my head, but doesn't tie it. The bindings around my wrists are really loose. I can slip my hands through them.

Either that was done purposefully, or this guy is a truly terrible criminal.

The van drives over the railroad tracks and into the fields beyond them. The road goes from smooth to the bump of unpaved gravel outside of the city.

When we finally stop, he takes my arm carefully. He doesn't shove me or drag me. "Watch your step out here."

"Who are you?" I whisper, but my question is left unanswered when Mr. Green calls from somewhere in the distance.

"Make sure you tie her up tight. If she runs off, we're in deep shit."

We walk over gravel, then grass. The buzzing sound of cicadas surrounds us. Otherwise, it's silent.

"Step up here." He leads me into a building, I think. It's still hot and humid inside, but it's darker now. "Candace, listen to me carefully." His voice dips down as he sits me in a chair. "I'm a friend of Noah's, alright? He's on his way here. Nothing is going to happen to you. Barrington isn't used to getting his hands dirty like this. He doesn't know who he's fucking with right now."

"Who are you?"

"Noah's guardian angel." He laughs.

"Oh," Noah called someone that before. I remember it. "The friend in high places."

"That's me." He touches my shoulder. "Just sit tight. He will be here soon."

I'm blindfolded and tied to a chair after being kidnapped at gunpoint. I feel so calm.

I hear something outside, someone yelling. It's so loud against the quiet stillness of this place.

Minutes tick by so slowly it's cruel. I can't move or see, I have no idea how long it's been, but it feels eternal. The darkness and stillness feel like they will never go away. Since the shouting, there has been nothing. Not a sound. I'm tired and frustrated. My eyes are heavy, but my nervousness keeps me awake.

Waiting.

A sound makes me jump, pulling a startled scream from my chest.

There is a thump. Then another.

"Fuck." It sounds like a door slamming into the wall. "Come on."

"Guardian angel?"

"Yeah, it's me." He unties me quickly. "Mr. Barrington and Colson are here and–"

"Where the fuck is Trent?" He bellows. His voice is cracked and raw.

I bet I know where he is

It doesn't seem like he's underestimating Noah now.

Knowing that Colson is here doesn't ease my mind at all. He won't help me.

I'm yanked forward hard, and the pillowcase is pulled off my head. Blinking and disoriented, I adjust to the darkness. The moon hangs low and full in the sky above a shimmering, marshy lake. Tall grass grows around us, swaying in the breeze and shielding us from anyone who might be looking. We're in the middle of nowhere.

Colson is standing with his dad, and I almost don't recognize him. He looks like hatred.

"Your fucking boyfriend has my son." I cringe and cower back as he screams in my face. "I'm going to call him, and you're going to tell him to let him go. Then we will let you go. Do you understand?"

He runs his hands through his hair. I've never seen him so unglued before.

"This is all your fucking fault." Colson seethes at me.

"I—"

"Of course you would pick a fucking psycho for your boyfriend. Does he know who he's fucking with?" His voice isn't his. He's a stranger. "People like you don't win against people like us."

"Please, just—"

"Just say what you're supposed to say." The phone rings once, a shrill sound cutting through the silence.

"Barrington."

I can tell just by the sound of his voice that his teeth are clenched.

"Noah!"

"Ace, are you alright?"

"I'm fine. I—" He tugs my arm roughly. "Um, Noah, you have to let Trent go, ok?"

"Baby," his voice is soft. "I didn't want you to have to be a part of this. I didn't expect them to have the balls to grab you off the fucking street. I need you to keep your eyes closed, ok?

You're going to hear things that sound bad. But keep your eyes closed."

I can't breathe.

"Ace, do you understand?"

"Where the fuck is my son?" Mr. Barrington pushes me down. I fall onto my knees in the dirt. "Release him and tell me where he is. I'll have her dropped off, unharmed, in the–"

"I know you're not used to taking orders. You're not used to being the one backed into a corner, but you aren't in a position to be making demands. You never should have touched her. Right now, as we speak, a private plane is taking you and several of your family members to Saudi Arabia by way of Morocco. Did you know that? No one is even going to be looking for you here. According to flight records, your plane took off forty minutes ago. You're a ghost. So don't tell me what I'm going to do. I'm going to do whatever the fuck I want. And there's nothing you can do about it. When I get there, if there is a single scratch on her, I'll kill every single one of you." The line clicks, dead. He hung up.

Mr. Barrington turns to me, rage and grief written on his skin. He pulls something up from his waistband, something black that shines in the moonlight.

When he lifts it above his head, I bring my hands up, dropping the rope to cover my face.

"This is all your fucking fault!"

I scream, but it's too late. The butt of the gun hits my forehead, just above my eye. My skin splits, and blood pours from the wound immediately.

FORTY-EIGHT

NOAH

THE MOON IS HANGING in the sky, low, almost touching the horizon.

It's so calm and quiet here. This is the perfect place to commit several murders.

My boots scrape against the gravel as I stare up at the sky, walking up the road toward the little boathouse on the shore of Lake Marion.

Yes, this is the perfect place. I can take my time extracting their screams out here, and no one will be around to hear them.

Jace is en route. One of the golden Barrington boys is bound and gagged in his truck. The heirs to this steaming pile of shit are finally going to get their inheritance tonight.

They shouldn't have touched her.

This is going to be so much worse for them. I'm going to show them what it feels like to wish for death. I might take their fingers. And their teeth. One by one.

I'll admit that they are paying for what Parker did to her, too. I couldn't give him what he deserved. That rage is still there. Tonight I'll release all of it.

I'm going to make him feel small and afraid, just like he did to her. Tonight, he learns.

Just beyond a slight bend in the road, covered by the tall reeds of grass, I hear her scream.

My feet hit the ground hard, running toward the sound before I even realize it.

The scene appears out of the tall grass like it's coming up from the ground.

She's in the dirt. Blood running down her face. Barrington is above her. With a fucking gun in his hand.

Everything shifts, out of focus. Red.

As red as the blood on her face.

I don't recognize the movements of my body. I don't see or hear anything. My mind is a blank slate, a quiet place where her voice echoes softly.

When my vision clears, the darkness receding back into the empty place where a soul should be, I'm kneeling in the dirt over something I think used to be a man.

Barrington's lifeless body looks like pulp. Like meat.

He looks like he was hit by a train. His face is mashed to an unrecognizable mass of blood and tissue.

My hands tremble, heavy like they've been dipped in lead.

My knuckles are cracked and broken. I don't know if the blood is his or mine.

"Noah." She whispers, reeling me in from the dark.

Dennis is holding back Barrington's security guard, his arm wrapped around his throat, but he's not struggling anymore. They're just standing there with their mouths hanging open.

I search for her. Colson has her. One of his arms is locked around her throat. Her eyes are full of fear.

"Let her go. Now."

He looks like he's in shock. He's not blinking.

I pull myself up from the ground. "Colson."

His eyes snap to mine.

"Let her go. Right now."

His hands release their grip on her.

"Come here, baby." I expect hesitation. I brace for it. I must look like something straight out of hell, but she rushes into my arms. She runs right to me. "Are you alright? Let me see you."

"He hit me, that's all. I'm fine."

No. She's not fine.

"It's bleeding. We need to bandage it."

It's only now that I realize I can see her because of the headlights shining on us. Jace is behind us in the van.

I turn to Dennis. "Get rid of him and tie him up, then you can go."

"I'm sorry she—"

"Why didn't you warn me? This was never supposed to happen. She never should have seen any of this."

"I didn't have a chance to call you when shit went down. I was watching her."

"Look at her fucking face," My fury echoes through the dark.

"He didn't tie my hands." Ace reaches for me. "He told me who he was and that he would keep me safe."

"Jace has your money." I need him to leave before I get angry. He is a valuable friend to have. Killing him because she has a cut on her head would be counterproductive. But I want to.

"The flight information is logged, and all of their assets are frozen. His wife will have to come out of hiding soon, and she'll be broke."

I take her chin and look at her. "Is that good enough for you, or do you want her to suffer physically because of how she treated you?"

Her eyes go wide. "That's good enough."

"Good enough." I tip my chin to him and turn all my attention to her.

I wrap her in a tight hug, shielding her face and ears from the single gunshot that rings out in the night. Her body flinches at the sound, and her grip on my shirt tightens.

Colson tries to run, but Dennis takes him down almost embarrassingly fast.

"So your guardian angel is a dirty fed?"

"Remember Jace's cousin? The one who protected me in prison? He is an informant for Dennis. We met, and he started using the club to wash his money. As luck would have it, he was placed on an assignment to help the Barringtons. Because his interests were better suited to our continued existence, he helped us instead. Loyalty is negotiable."

"Oh," she nods, her body trembling. "Is it over now?"

"I have to get rid of Colson and Trent." I have to feed them to this thing inside my chest. It's awake. And hungry.

FORTY-NINE

"BABY, you need to sit in the car with Jace."

"But—"

"Ace, the things I'm about to do to them aren't for you to see." He kisses me gently. "I want them to apologize to you. Can you handle hearing that?"

"Yes."

"Then I'll come get you when it's time for that, but wait in the car." He kisses me again. "Jace, turn the radio up." He shoots him a look before disappearing into the little boathouse.

When they pulled Trent out of the back of the van, I hardly recognized him. He was crying and screaming behind the tape over his mouth. He was already begging–sobbing.

It was probably the sight of their father lying dead on the ground.

I think I might be in shock. I watched him do that with his hands. He didn't have a weapon, a rock, or a tool. Just his hands.

The sound of bone crunching is playing in my head in a loop.

He didn't just kill him. He broke him.

Then he held me gently, cradling me, and tended to my wounds. He pulled his shirt off and softly wiped the blood from my face. He kissed me, cared for me. There was a reverence about it. He is Jekyll and Hyde.

"Are you alright?" Jace breaks the silence as he twists the heat up in the already hot cab.

"Yeah, thanks." No, not at all. Not even a little bit ok. My teeth clatter together uncontrollably.

I don't want it to, but sitting here, my mind is spiraling. When he went inside, he was so calm.

What is he doing to them in there?

Covering my face with my hands, I feel sick to my stomach.

I should be stopping this. I'm not hurting them, but I'm sitting here allowing it to happen. I'm complicit.

My legs won't move. I do nothing.

"Jace?" My chin trembles.

He turns to me, silently waiting.

"Should we stop him?"

There is a pause. A moment of consideration.

"I think we should let him finish." He doesn't look riled or panicked. There is no emotion on his face whatsoever.

Let him finish? But by then it will be too late. They'll be dead when he's finished.

"But..." I turn the volume down on the radio. The stupid, bubbly pop song coming through the speakers is making me want to put my head through the window. This is not a good soundtrack for mass murder.

A sound that can't be defined whips through the wind. It's tortured and so full of pain.

I freeze, my eyes jerking up to meet his.

"Ok, bad idea!" The volume goes back up on full blast.

That didn't even sound human. That was a wild animal calling out in the dark, dying.

My entire body shakes, trembling like I'm cold, but I'm sweating. My chest is heaving, and each breath burns in my lungs.

"It's been too long, hasn't it?" I wipe the sweat from my forehead. "Should we check on him? What if they got untied, and he's in trouble?"

That didn't happen.

I know that.

But my mind is creating scenarios to induce a mental breakdown.

For some reason, in this moment, images of Colson flash through my thoughts. There weren't many good moments. But those are all I can seem to think of. It's torture. There were five times in our year together when he was surprisingly sweet, and right now my brain chooses to remember them.

The radio is loud and cheerful. The girl is singing about how his love is making her break into spontaneous song.

My hands clap around my ears. I can't hear any more of this!

"Here!" Jace's loud voice cuts through the music as he sets his phone to play through the speakers. The song that starts is violent and angry. That's better.

One song moves into the next, then the next. The scratchy, raw voice screams through the speakers as we sit, staring straight ahead.

By the fifth song, I can't take it anymore.

"This is wrong." I stop the music again.

"What?" He can't hear me.

"I said, this is wrong. He's in there because of me. I shouldn't be sitting out here, listening to music while he's in there, taking care of everything that started because of me." My voice cracks. Fear, anger, and guilt course through me.

"This isn't on you, Candy." His brow furrows. "The Barringtons aren't good people. If they didn't do this to you, they would have done it to someone else."

"Yeah." I sniff. That's probably true. But Noah is in there right now because of me, not for anything they did to other people.

The clock on the console reads one A.M.

The adrenaline is dropping. I feel it leaving me.

At some point, the music starts to fade, blurring into background noise. My head jolts up, and I look at the clock again. Now it's after two.

"Did I fall asleep?" I look at Jace.

"For a minute."

What kind of person falls asleep while people are being tortured just a few feet away? What is wrong with me?

Jerking the door handle, I jump out of the truck and run.

"Noah!"

I hear the sound of Jace rushing out after me, but it's too late. There is a clang and a thud before the door to the boathouse flies open.

"Ace." He steps into the frame, his bare chest covered in blood. The moonlight reflects off it.

"I–" my voice breaks. "I'm–"

He drops a pair of work gloves to the ground and grabs me, pulling me into his arms. "It's ok."

"I can't sit there anymore. Are they dead?" My body shakes against his.

"Colson isn't. He has something he wants to say to you. But only if you want to hear it." His hand takes the back of my head, cradling it as he kisses my bandaged forehead.

"I don't know if I can."

"He's so sorry for treating you badly. And for hurting you. Not just the physical things he did, he's sorry for making you feel like you didn't deserve to be treated better. He knows how wrong he was, Ace." His eyes look normal again as he looks at. "Go back to the car. I'll finish up."

"Wait." I can't ignore the tug in my chest.

He did this for me. For my honor, to avenge me, to hurt the people that hurt me. I have to look.

I feel pulled in two directions at once. I need to look, but my body is actively fighting against it. I peek over his shoulder into the void behind him.

"You don't have to, Candace. If it's going to haunt you, don't." There is so much compassion in his voice that it unravels a piece of my composure. Tears well up in my eyes.

"I do have to." I can't explain it. Not looking is running away from it. I could have stopped it. I need to see what he did, or I will always wonder.

He sets me on my feet, and I take his hand.

There is a single hanging light inside the boathouse. It sways slightly, making shadows move around the room.

But it's enough.

There isn't a single safe place to look. Trent is on his knees, his hands tied behind his back. A coarse rope is looped around his neck, tied to the boat behind him, holding him upright. A string of blood hangs from his mouth, pooling in a puddle around his knees. There isn't a part of him that isn't bruised or bleeding.

Colson is tied to a chair. His head is hanging forward, but his chest is moving, shallow breaths.

"Hey," Noah taps the leg of the chair with the toe of his boot.

"No! Please!" Colson screams. His body thrashes around in the chair, pulling against the restraints.

"She's here." Noah's voice is almost soft. "What did you want to tell her?"

Colson turns his head slightly, and his busted-open face turns my stomach. "W-When you broke things off, I should have left you alone." He sobs.

"That's right." Noah nods. "What else?"

"You deserved to be treated better than I did," He whimpers. "You deserve better than me."

"That's right."

It's only now that I realize he's missing the fingers on his left hand. All of them. Gone.

A strange numbness settles over me. I don't know how I'm supposed to feel. Disgusted? Angry? Vindicated? All of it at once?

"Go wait in the car while I finish up. I just need another minute." He kisses my hair. "Tell Jace to call Clayton. He'll know what to do."

"Ok." I'm outside of my body, above the room, watching.

"You're both going to rot in prison for this," Colson spits. I guess Noah didn't completely break his spirit. "You think you're smart enough to pull this off? You're going right back to prison. And Candy, you stupid fucking–"

Noah tugs a rope, and it jerks Colton's neck back. He's tied like his brother, a tight knot right at his throat. It seems that the more he struggles, the tighter it gets.

I can't catch my breath. But I can't look away.

The rope grinds against the back of the chair. Colson's eyes bulge, and a gurgling sound bubbles in his throat.

My hands come up to my throat, gripping at an invisible rope that feels like it's tightening.

Noah is so still, just pulling the rope taut. He's not sweating or panting. It doesn't look like his heart is about to beat out of his chest like mine is. He's just watching as Colson's panic shifts, turning into surrender.

I should feel fear, but I don't. The only people in this room who would hurt me are dead and dying.

There is a voice in my head screaming: This is wrong.

But then there is another voice, a quiet whisper: he deserves this.

Both voices are mine.

FIFTY

"COME HERE, CANDACE." The rope hits the ground hard. The sound makes me jump. "Sit right here. You weren't supposed to see that part, baby. I'm sorry about that."

He pulls a lawn chair out of the boat, setting it up in front of me. I sit on it, running my fingers over the blue and white woven nylon straps that make up the seat and backing. "We had chairs like this when I was a little girl." In my mind, I can see my mom and grandma sitting on the back porch, smoking and gossiping.

That feels so far away from me right now. A different lifetime, maybe. Before I was broken and, in turn, broke everything around me.

My eyes sweep across the floor to Trent's body. It looks like he endured more than a body should be capable of.

Noah did that.

My Noah. The same man who gently washes my hair. Knowing that he hit Parker on purpose is different from what is sprawled out on the dirty floor of this boathouse. This is... darkness.

And I just sat and watched. I knew what was happening.

Across the room, he's washing his hands. Scrubbing them like a surgeon about to operate. For some reason, in the madness of this moment, it strikes me as funny. I know what he's doing–why. He wants to touch me.

The hands that just did this are going to touch my skin.

A pair of bloody bolt cutters is propped up against the wall. I don't have to work hard to imagine what he used those for. A shudder creeps down my spine.

"Hey." He kneels down in front of me, my knees pressing into his chest. "Look at me, Ace."

My chin wobbles as I meet his eyes.

"No one is ever going to hurt you, Ace." He presses a kiss to my thigh. "Do you believe that?"

"Yes." He won't let them. I know that.

He looks around the room; the wreckage laid bare beneath the single light bulb. Carnage. It almost looks fake. There is so much blood, it looks like an overdone slasher flick. But every drop of it is real, pulled out of them by force.

"Are you afraid of me?"

"No." I'm afraid. But not of him.

"You're trembling." He places his hands flat on my thighs.

"Are we going to prison?"

"No. They'll never find the bodies. And this boathouse will be demolished tomorrow morning, and the pieces burned. There won't be any evidence that points to any of us. With all the news about their criminal wrongdoings, everyone will believe that they went into hiding." He seems so sure that it will work.

His fingers graze my legs as he moves his hands up. It's slow, but it instantly catches my attention. Having his hands on me does something I can't explain.

"Do you trust me?"

"Yes."

"Good. I'll take care of everything." He leans forward, kissing my knees, then moving up to the top of one thigh.

He's inching forward so slowly I'm almost missing it.

"Noah..." My voice barely makes a sound.

"Come here."

He's up on his feet, lifting me up with him so quickly it makes me dizzy. He turns, taking my place on the seat with me in his lap.

In this position, I can feel him between my legs. A hard bulge in the front of his pants.

We're not really about to do this.

There's no...

His fingers slide up my thighs, disappearing beneath my skirt.

Everything suddenly seems amplified by ten.

"Noah, what—"

His fingers slip into my panties. "I want you to feel good. To remember this as the day you were set free. No more looking over your shoulder or worrying. Can I?"

I feel myself nodding.

"Fuck." His chest trembles.

His middle finger presses up into me until his palm is flat against my clit.

Whatever sound is trying to come out of my mouth chokes me.

"You're so wet. I knew you would be."

He has magic hands. With just a few quick motions, I'm transported out of here. I'm not in a murder shack in the middle of nowhere. I'm floating in a sky full of stars.

The blood, the gore, the bodies, they're gone. It's just us here, in the marshes, under the moon.

His finger curls, pressing against a place that makes my hips squirm, desperately looking for friction.

I press my palms into his chest, letting them slide down the sticky, blood-slicked skin, his muscles tensing beneath.

With his free hand, he pops the button on his jeans, never breaking the slow rhythm of his finger.

"Noah, please–" It's not enough.

"I just want to feel it around my fingers, baby. I'll fuck you." He sucks my neck. "I'll fuck you so hard that it will be the only thing you remember about tonight."

Slow and steady, he works his fingers until I'm delirious. Sweat drips down my neck, every muscle burning with fatigue. I'm so close, it's just not enough. It's too slow.

He moans and shifts his hips. "Seeing you like this–" he bites into my shoulder.

It's like I'm dangling, stuck. I can't reach the ground, but I can't climb higher either.

He slips another finger inside and flexes them wide.

"Stop teasing me!" I choke the words out.

His hand abruptly pulls away. I let out a whiny sob at the total loss of contact. It was too slow, but it was better than nothing.

I watch with wide eyes as he tugs his zipper down and pulls himself free. "Spit on it."

Too drunk with lust to be self-conscious, I spit down between our legs without hesitating.

"Good girl." His head falls back as he uses his hand to spread it out over the swollen head. His chest muscles twitch, and he hisses when he touches it.

Reaching out, I run my fingers over his face. There are droplets of blood splattered on his skin.

His eyes peek up from under his brows. He sucks my finger

into his mouth and bites it just hard enough to take my breath away. At the same time, the tip of his cock nudges against me.

His hands grip my hips tightly, shifting them enough to slip inside of me. Slow. One inch at a time.

He bites my finger harder, and I clench hard around him.

"Holy fuck." He pushes the rest in, holding me down on him.

As soon as he releases my finger, it's like the air in the room changes. He changes.

With the leverage of his hands on my hips, he moves me up at the same time he rolls his own hips. The sudden, quick burst of movement shocks me, and I scream. He pushes as deep into me as he can go, his jaw clenching. His eyes, his expression, it's pure determination. Where he is all focus–I am none. I can't form a coherent thought.

My head falls back, too heavy for my neck to hold it up. He uses the opportunity to lean forward and suck the column of my throat. His mouth is messy and desperate against my skin.

Sounds–not words or moans–just noises come from deep in my throat.

He fucks me like he hates me, but I've never felt so truly safe and loved.

My body jolts, clamping down on him. I'm helpless against it. It barrels through me, intent on taking me with it into oblivion.

I'm vaguely aware of the way he's grunting and moaning, the whispers of my name, the tightness in his body.

He releases my hips and wraps his arms around my waist, holding me tight as he rolls his hips frantically against mine.

For several minutes, we just sit, panting, with our bodies slumped against each other.

"What now?" I whisper when I'm finally able to speak.

"We need to get Clayton out here." He runs the tips of his fingers over my hips. "Let's go home, baby."

FIFTY-ONE

I SLIP into the bathroom and run into a stall. For the fifth time today, I check the news for updates.

Again, there isn't anything new. No breaking story about multiple homicides and the city's wealthiest family. No gruesome crime scene found. No mutilated bodies or evidence of any wrongdoing at all.

I'm coming apart at the seams.

It's been three weeks and I still can't catch my breath.

Noah is a rock in a storm. He's so steadfast it's actually pissing me off. At night, he sleeps. He eats and forces me to.

He keeps asking me to talk to him. And I don't know how. I can't find the words to say.

Aside from worrying that we're going to get caught, I feel so much guilt and shame. It's burying me alive.

Sometimes, I wake up in the middle of the night and look down to find my hands covered in blood. Then I really wake up—jolting upright, to find nothing there.

Something Colson said keeps playing over and over again in my head. He called Noah my watchdog. My watchdog. That

I unleashed on him and his family. I stood by and watched it happen. Colson wasn't innocent, but I don't get to decide who dies. Noah doesn't.

Or at least, he shouldn't.

My hands tremble as I slide the phone into my pocket.

Smoothing out my pants, I walk out of the bathroom and back to my desk.

I close my eyes and take a deep breath. I promised I would type and edit this press release before leaving. I would be done already if I just sat here and worked on it.

As soon as I pull open the document, my phone buzzes in my pocket.

Pulling it out, I stare at Noah's name on the screen.

Silencing the buzz, I set the phone screen side down on my desk. When I look up, something catches my attention, movement beyond my computer. Through the window on the door, I see him.

Fuck.

He beckons me with one finger–his tight-lipped expression not quite rage but definitely anger.

I'll do this first thing tomorrow.

I take my time packing my things. His eyes burn into me the whole time, but I don't look.

"See you tomorrow." I fake a smile at the aids sitting around the conference table.

They give an absent-minded wave, not even looking up to notice Noah holding the door open for me.

"Ace." He places his hand on the back of my neck, gently. We walk in total silence down the hall, through the lobby, and out the front doors.

If it weren't for this tension between us, everything would seem normal. He opens my door, buckles me in, and presses a quick kiss you my forehead.

The engine hums to life, and he drives in silence. It isn't until he makes a left turn when he should be making a right that I say something.

"Noah, where—"

"Talk to me, Ace. And I don't want to hear 'I'm fine' again. You're not fine. It's been three weeks. I haven't pushed or forced the issue, but now I need you to tell me what's wrong." His voice is steady, but there is something in it, something that makes my chest crack a little bit. It's vulnerability.

"I don't know what to say." I shrug and slump back in my seat.

"What are the nightmares about?"

My breath stutters in my throat. Of course, he knows about them. "Um, I keep being covered in blood. My hands. My hands are covered in blood."

"Ace," he pulls the car onto an old country road, one of the old highways that isn't used much anymore. "If I hadn't stopped him, do you think he would have stopped on his own?"

"No."

"What gives him the fucking right to rule over your life like that? You ended things, and he wouldn't let it go. He hurt you. He scared you. He got exactly what he deserved."

"But what kind of person does that make me?" I whisper.

"A fighter. Someone who doesn't let themselves be treated the way he treated you."

I sit with the words as he turns onto a gravel road. It hits me now where he's taking me.

"I feel guilty."

"Because you didn't stop me?" His lips tug up in the corners.

"Yeah. I didn't do or say anything."

He nods, letting me ramble through it.

"I just feel this weight in my chest." I fight the urge to sob.

A tight, painful ball lodges in my throat. "I didn't stop you. I didn't even try. Nothing. That must make me a bad person."

"You're not a bad person, Ace. I'm a bad person."

"You do bad things but..." The words get lost in my head. I don't know how to reason with it.

The gravel crunches beneath the tires, farther and farther into the middle of nowhere. We don't pass any cars, no homes or people. We're the last people left on Earth.

"You accept me." He reaches over, placing his hand on my knee. "You accept what I am. And I accept you too. You're free now, live. Do anything you want. You're safe to just exist in peace."

I chew my lip, thinking about that. I do accept him. Is that good enough?

"Is that everything that's bothering you?" He tightens his fingers.

"Um, no." My leg bounces. "Where are the bodies?"

He chuckles. "I don't know. Clayton took them. They're gone. No one will ever find them. Agent Dennis is already running down a few leads over in Morocco. Apparently, there have been a few sightings of them over there."

He makes another turn, leaving the gravel road for a trail through the grass.

"What about the–" the thought disintegrates. The boathouse.

It's gone.

He stops the truck, pulling the shifter into park in front of four cinderblock frame pieces. The only evidence that there was ever a building here.

"It was demolished, and the pieces were taken back to a scrapyard and burned. They're gone."

"Can I ask, how did you meet Clayton?" The memory of his long, spindly arms makes me shiver.

"Agent Dennis made that introduction." He unbuckles my seatbelt and slides me toward him.

"So, we're really going to be alright?" I still don't completely believe it.

"Yes. In that sense. But are we going to be alright?" He hooks my chin in his fingers, forcing my head up to look at him.

"Yes."

"Yes?"

"We will be. Because I love you. And you–"

"Are wholly devoted to you. Even death can't separate us."

EPILOGUE

THE BASS VIBRATES through my shoes, and the long stick heels feel unstable beneath my feet.

The violet lights flicker all around me.

The house is packed tonight. I run my fingers over the buttery soft material of my tight dress. It's too tight and too short. I feel dangerous, like a black widow luring men into a trap.

Spinning around, I lean against the bar to watch the band.

The lead singer has a raspy voice that makes my stomach clench. I imagine it playing in the background when Noah has his hands on me.

"Hey," a tall, handsome stranger slides into the small space between me and the next person.

"Hey."

"Can I buy you a drink?"

"Sure." My heart rate shoots up. "I'll take a vodka soda."

He smiles, a big, white smile that looks genuine. Maybe it is.

When he's distracted, I turn and search. I feel his eyes on

me, but I still can't see him. I can see his expression in my mind. The hard line of his mouth and the glint of rage in his eyes.

"Here you go." He slides the drink toward me. "I'm Devon."

"Candy." I shake his hand.

He chuckles. "That's quite a name."

I can't believe he's letting this continue. I expected him to step in immediately.

"Can I convince you to dance with me?"

"Oh." I take a sip of the liquid courage in my glass. "Sure."

This was not part of the conversation. Knowing that he's watching, and this is likely working him into a frenzy, makes me feel fluttery and wet. I wish I could see him.

He slips his hand in mine and leads me out into the middle of the floor. The fast-paced song blares around us as I let him spin me. I teeter in my heels, not drunk, but intoxicated by anticipation. I'm dizzy. My pulse is rushing.

If he isn't going to come get me, I'm going to keep playing.

I run my hands over my body. Normally, I would never feel confident enough to do this, but he's watching. I'm safe. When watching gets to be too much for him, he'll come get me.

One song ends, fading into another.

I feel loose. Knowing how worked up he must be is like fire in my veins.

"Are you here alone tonight?" He pulls me in close enough to yell into my ear.

I open my mouth to respond, but I'm cut off by a hand on my shoulder. "No, she's not." Noah slips in behind me, placing his other hand across my stomach. I can already feel him against my back.

"Oh," Devon looks surprised.

"Thanks for the drink. It was nice to meet you." I yell over the music as Noah drags me away.

The bouncer at the VIP rope opens it as we approach.

All the tables are taken but one—a single reserved table right in the center. The round booth-style seat is small, only enough for four people.

No one else in this section seems to notice us. They're busy with their bottles and friends.

"You let that go on a bit long, don't you think?" I slide into the seat.

"I wanted to see what you would do." His breath hits my ear. "If the next song had been a slow one, would you have kept dancing?"

"Maybe."

I yelp as he pulls me up into his lap. His arms snake around my waist and chest as he rests his chin on my shoulder. "Maybe?" He suctions his lips to my neck, sucking gently. "Stop wiggling your hips like that."

"I can't."

"Slip your panties off." He growls.

My eyes go wide. "What? Here?" I thought he would take me back to his office.

"Right here."

Shifting in his lap, I slip my panties down my legs and hand them to him. He tucks them into his boot, then slides his hand up my leg.

"I'm going to fuck you here, and you're not going to let anyone know what we're doing." He sweeps the tips of his fingers between my legs.

The rounded seat back of the booth offers a little bit of cover, but I don't see how we're going to do that without catching public indecency charges.

"Stand up and lift your dress so it will cover us." He urges me forward.

I move quickly, trying to sit before I draw any attention.

But when I try to sit, his hand stops me. I feel him move slightly before he guides me back down. Right onto his cock.

Clapping my hand over my mouth, I slide down. All the way until I'm fully seated, and he's inside of me.

A low rumbling 'fuck' is pressed against my neck.

"N-Noah!" I grab the table. "I can't do this."

He shifts his hips up, and I pinch my eyes closed.

Anyone who looks in this direction will know. He stops moving, but I still feel myself clenching and rippling around him.

"Wait," I beg. "I–"

He wraps around me again, pulling my back against him tightly. A bear hug that shields me slightly. I drop my head down, biting into his forearm as he fucks up into me.

"Did you want to dance with him, Ace?" He taunts me as his cock punches the air from my lungs. I shake my head. "I think you did. I think you wanted to feel his body pressed against yours."

"N-No!" I cry out.

"Why not?"

"Because I only want you!"

"That's right." He thrusts his hips, and my eyes roll back. "I want to spread you out on this table and eat your pussy while he watches. He thought he could touch you. He thought he could feel your body, but we're not the same, are we?"

"No." I feel myself shaking.

He grunts, his rhythm faltering. "Come. I want it dripping down your legs until we get home."

I have to bite him again to keep from screaming as a quick and violent orgasm hits me.

He grinds up, "Ready? Do you want mine?"

"Yes!" I force my eyes open, looking around the room at the people who are so close. It would only take a glance.

He groans and twitches, his head falling between my shoulder blades.

That was fast. No foreplay or teasing. But my body feels exhausted. The effort of staying quiet was draining.

"Now, let's go dance." He kisses me. "And after, I'm taking you to my office so I can really fuck you." He slips out of me, holding my dress down for me.

We slide out of the booth, and he leads me to the dance floor with my panties still tucked in his boot.

ENJOYED THIS STORY?

Visit myrandaraebooks.com for more than 40 other titles!

NOTE FROM THE AUTHOR

Dear Reader,

I wanted to take this opportunity to thank you. Writing books is my dream, and knowing that you've taken the time to read them means everything to me. I can't express enough how grateful I am for your support. If you enjoyed the story, it would mean the world if you left a review. Your thoughts help other readers discover the book. Even a few words make a huge difference! If you're not able to, that's okay—I'm just happy you're here. Thank you for being a part of this journey with me. I appreciate you more than you know.

With gratitude,
Myranda

ALSO BY MYRANDA RAE

SERIALS

🐺🧛 **fantasy/shifter**

Beyond the Ether

1 Blood of the Innocent

2 *Blood of A King

The Fairytales series

1 Captivated, Cursed

2 Love You Anyway

3 Finding Iris

4 Sucker for You

5 The Lost Girl

The Playlist series

1 Fix You

2 Beloved

3 Cherry

4 A Warrior's Heart

Sons of Sorsha (The Playlist) mini-series

1 Jack

2 Lucas

3 Samuel

4 Asher

👽🔍 scifi / aliens

Coiled Throne Series

1 The Coiled Throne pt. 1

2 The Queen Trials pt. 2

The Astrynian Warriors Series

1 The Destroyer's Little Pet

2 Havoc

An'eo Chronicles

1 Callisto

2 Proximus

3 Nyon

4 Kieran

5 Loide

Tribute to the Alphagods

1 Wrath

2 Pride

3 Envy

4 Lust

 contemporary

The Underworld duology

1 What's Done in the Dark

2 Will Come to Light

3 Zion (bonus mini-short)

STANDALONES

🐺👹 fantasy/shifter

- Alpha's, Kings & Play-things
- BEAST: Destined to the Hellhound
- Mark of the Damned
- Bound: Mates at War
- The Queen in Shadows
- Suck Me Slowly

👄🔥 contemporary

- Enemies Closer
- Unplanned: A One Night Stand
- PINK
- Lewd & Lascivious
- The Other Side
- When I Whisper His Name
- Just the Two of Us
- Going for Gold
- The Void He Fills
- Bound to Break

* Indicates Work in Progress